A RAKE'S KISS

Rivenhall's mouth broadened in a contagious grin as he observed Amanda's predicament. "A lady in distress, it seems." He stepped onto the first stone on his side, then the second, so that only two separated them, and extended his hand to her, leaning across the tumbling waters so her fingers could grasp his.

The contact left her breathless. With an effort, she recalled the precariousness of her position, clasped his hand firmly, and trusted in his strength as she jumped the unsteady stone and landed before him. His arm swept about her waist, and the next moment he stooped, his other catching her behind the knees and he swept her into his arms. She gasped, but whether in outrage or surprise, she honestly didn't know. A soft laugh sounded in her ear as he took one careful step, then reached the safety of the bank.

"I must make a habit of rescuing beautiful young ladies more often," he said, his tone provocative. He made no attempt to set her on her feet.

"Thank you, but I could have managed quite well without being carried."

"Ah, but I find it much more interesting this way. Do not you?"

"No," she lied. "I most certainly do not. Will you please set me down?"

He did, very slowly, holding her close against himself in a manner that she would have found shocking if she'd been able to think clearly. She tried to pull back, but discovered herself held securely. A slow, tantalizing smile played about his mouth.

"What?" he asked softly. "Would you leave without paying your forfeit?"

"Would you demand another of me?"

"I would."

Before she could protest, he caught her closer still, tight against his chest, and kissed her. . . .

—from "Seduction" by Janice Bennett

BOOK YOUR PLACE ON OUR WEBSITE AND MAKE THE READING CONNECTION!

We've created a customized website just for our very special readers, where you can get the inside scoop on everything that's going on with Zebra, Pinnacle and Kensington books.

When you come online, you'll have the exciting opportunity to:

- View covers of upcoming books
- Read sample chapters
- Learn about our future publishing schedule (listed by publication month *and author*)
- Find out when your favorite authors will be visiting a city near you
- Search for and order backlist books from our online catalog
- Check out author bios and background information
- Send e-mail to your favorite authors
- Meet the Kensington staff online
- Join us in weekly chats with authors, readers and other guests
- Get writing guidelines
- AND MUCH MORE!

**Visit our website at
http://www.zebrabooks.com**

NOTORIOUS
AND NOBLE

Janice Bennett

Judith A. Lansdowne

Jeanne Savery

Zebra Books
Kensington Publishing Corp.
http://www.zebrabooks.com

ZEBRA BOOKS are published by

Kensington Publishing Corp.
850 Third Avenue
New York, NY 10022

First Printing: July, 1999
10 9 8 7 6 5 4 3 2 1

Printed in the United States of America

CONTENTS

SEDUCTION

by

Janice Bennett

ONE

She felt his presence before ever she saw him. Something intangible changed in the drawing room, alerting her, setting her alight within. She looked up, straight at him where he stood in the doorway, a commanding figure in elegant evening dress, dark hair artfully tousled, the planes and angles of his face ruggedly superb rather than merely handsome. The glow of his dark eyes would have pierced her soul had their gaze fallen on her.

It didn't. Fair and slightly built, insignificant as always, Miss Amanda Grieves sat in the corner, withdrawn from her fellow houseguests. Her needle, so active only a moment before, stilled in her fingers, and she clutched her inevitable embroidery. At five-and-twenty, she knew herself to be beyond her last prayers. It came as a disturbing shock to discover that romantic dreams could still linger.

Her hostess, her godmother, the silvery-haired Lady Pelham, rose from the sofa with the stiffness of advancing years and bore down on this late arrival. The gentleman's eyebrows rose as he saw the elegant little lady, and he strolled forward with the confident air of one who expected an ecstatic welcome. Before she could speak, he swept her an elegant bow, capturing her hand with practiced grace and carrying her fingers to his lips.

"What are you doing here?" Lady Pelham demanded, glaring at him.

Amusement crinkled the corners of his eyes. "Why, I have come to play piquet, of course.

"Now, you listen to me, Rivenhall." Lady Pelham's voice lowered, becoming audible only to one sitting as closely and quietly as Amanda. "I'll not tolerate deep gaming—"

His eyebrows rose in exaggerated surprise. "What, not even with Pelham?"

"Especially not with Pelham. I'll not have him encouraged. I was at such pains not to invite any of his cronies, and now you appear." She regarded him with a kindling eye. "And I'll not tolerate any trifling, either. Is that understood?"

A slow, heart-stopping smile tugged the corners of his mouth upward. "What, not even if the lady is willing?"

"They are always willing, with you. I only wish I could count on you to know where to draw the line."

"Oh, I know where. But it is infinitely more enjoyable to choose not to draw the line, do you not think?"

"I think you are abominable," his hostess informed him.

"So you have said any time these last twenty years."

Fond exasperation replaced her ill humor. "Oh, be off with you. You know perfectly well where Pelham and the cards will be."

He laughed softly and kissed her cheek. "So I do, but I shall first inspect my fellow guests." And with that, he drifted away.

Amanda allowed her gaze to follow him, taking in the animal grace of his movements, the leashed power in his step. Dangerous. The thought flickered through her mind, then returned to unpack its bags and take up permanent residence. Definitely dangerous. On impulse, she set her needlework aside and moved to where her hostess still stood, a frown etching fine lines in her brow.

Lady Pelham turned to her with a long sigh. "What a

nuisance. Pelham must have invited him, of course. I'm dreadfully sorry. What your poor, dear late mama would say if she knew you were to have that man inflicted upon you, I know not." She shook her head.

"Who is he?" With care, Amanda kept her voice indifferent.

"You haven't met Lord Rivenhall? No, I suppose he was still in Jamaica when you were visiting London. You've lived so retired these past few years. I do wish you'd accept my invitations more often." She shook her head, then turned to the Reverend Mr. Somes, a retired clergyman whose favorite occupation was to doze over the sermons he some day intended to organize into a book.

Amanda returned to her chair, her curiosity fully roused. What had taken such a dynamic man to Jamaica? Restlessness? She scanned the room, spotting him almost at once, and any lingering uncertainty vanished. Not restlessness. His prudent family must have packed him off to prevent a scandal.

He seemed intent on creating a new one right now. He stood in a casual attitude, with one arm outstretched so he leaned against the wall, a crystal glass of Madeira in his other hand. Before him stood Diana Kingsford, a very pretty brunette, married the previous year to a serving officer who was now away with his regiment. She wasn't helping matters, either. She wore a very low-cut half robe of blond crepe over an underdress of peach silk that left little to the imagination. The man—Rivenhall, was that his name?—lowered his head to catch what she said, his expression one of a hunter who has cornered a very willing quarry.

Someone perched on the arm of her chair, and she looked up to see Bentley, her younger brother. The boredom that had marked his face earlier in the evening had vanished. Now he watched Mrs. Kingsford and her companion with a kindling light in his gray eyes.

"Lord, who'd have thought your godmama would invite him to her house party?" he breathed in her ear. "That should liven things up a bit."

Amanda blinked, surprised. "Do you know him?"

"Oh, as to that, everyone knows who Rivenhall is." He waved an airy hand. "Been setting the town on its ear since he came back from Jamaica last year. Inherited, you know. The barony, an estate in Sussex, and a pretty handsome income, by all accounts."

"Lady Pelham didn't introduce him," she pointed out.

A short laugh escaped Bentley. "Not surprising. The fellow's a hardened rake! No matron of any sense would present him to a green girl. Wouldn't have brought you to stay if I'd known he was here."

And that, as if he were three years the elder rather than the other way around. "Afraid he'd practice his wiles on me?" she asked sweetly. "How alarming. Should we leave upon the instant?"

"Oh, well, as to that, he looks far too busy to trouble himself with you, doesn't he?" Bentley said with irritating carelessness. "Besides, there seems to be considerable competition for his attentions. There are what, four other ladies present?"

Though only Mrs. Kingsford and herself were of an age to tempt Rivenhall. She let that pass, merely shaking her head. "If we left, you wouldn't be able to study his manner of tying his neckcloth."

Bentley grinned. "That's the ticket. Anyway, aside from being a bit of a rake, he's a capital fellow. Or so St. John says."

"And St. John is an authority?" She regarded her brother with a touch of unease. Young, eager, innocent, Bentley had inherited the baronetcy from their father a mere two years ago, and still thought worldly wisdom had come with it. Barely a year down from Oxford, he possessed every young cub's conviction that he was up to

snuff and a right knowing one. Amanda could have put
him straight on that point, of course, but knew better
than to try. And as for Bentley's friend, the Honorable
St. John Waddington, she'd as soon trust the judgment
of any schoolroom miss. At least then she'd be certain of
an opinion expressed without benefit of copious amounts
of claret.

Bentley's gaze narrowed on Rivenhall, and Amanda directed an appraising glance at that notorious gentleman.
She hoped it was his style of dress that her brother studied, and not his outrageous flirtations. He had Mrs.
Kingsford giggling in a manner quite shocking, under the
circumstances. Words trembled on the tip of her tongue
to inform her impressionable young brother that his
hero's behavior was less than desirable, but she stopped
herself from speaking. Young gentlemen never listened
to the advice of their elder sisters.

The portly figure of the Reverend Mr. Somes drew
abreast of them, and he beamed at Bentley with all the
benevolence of one who, being a close crony of their
grandfather, had dandled him upon his knee in infancy.
"There you are, my boy. Come keep an old man company. I feel like a comfortable tongue wag."

Bentley rose. "I should be delighted, sir."

"Have you been out to the woods, yet?" Mr. Somes
inquired. "No? The birds there are to observe here! I
saw a bullfinch this very afternoon. No, I assure you, my
dear boy, a bullfinch it was!"

Bentley cast a speaking grimace over his shoulder toward Amanda, but allowed himself to be led off. She
could only hope her brother would give the poor old
gentleman at least a quarter of an hour before making
his excuses. Surely he could feign interest in robins and
larks for at least that long.

Her gaze returned to the infamous Rivenhall. In truth,
it had seldom left him. What an infuriating man, to be

able to beguile one without speaking so much as a single word. Without even looking at her, for that matter. He had not the least notion she even existed. How could he, when he flirted so outrageously with another woman— and a married one, at that.

Lady Pelham approached the couple, directed a quelling glare at Rivenhall, and turned her attention to the blushing Mrs. Kingsford. With a soft word Amanda couldn't hear, she detached the young woman and led her away. Rivenhall watched their departure with amusement, then turned and made his way toward the door leading to Pelham's study, the room invariably set aside for cards during house parties. He vanished through it, and to Amanda it seemed as if a light had been extinguished in the room.

She stared at the door without really seeing it for a long moment, then shook her head and returned to her abandoned embroidery. There were some gentlemen who were simply too dangerous to so much as dream about. And for that matter, there was nothing more pointless than indulging in romantic dreams.

Before she had time to explore the depressing aspects of that thought, she was joined by Miss Abbott, a tall, plump spinster who had been a friend of her late mother's, a woman of lively disposition but no countenance and a regrettable tendency to recount lengthy tales to which she could never quite remember the endings. Amanda had merely to smile and make an occasional encouraging sound while she set her stitches, and as they both were well accustomed to this, neither minded in the least.

It had grown very late when she at last rose. Many of the guests had already said their good nights and made their way up the stairs to their various beds. As Amanda followed Miss Abbott into the hall, she became aware of Bentley coming toward her, his shoulders unnaturally stiff, his expression an unusual blank. A bleakness in his eyes caught in her stomach and tore at her. She hurried to him, caught his arm, and with a sickening dread recognized his expression as shock.

She drew him back into an empty salon across the hall, and he went with her, unprotesting. "What has happened?" she demanded as soon as the door closed behind them.

He stared at her, shaking his head, his eyes speaking far more eloquently than the incomprehensible noises that emerged from his mouth.

She planted both hands on his shoulders and gave him a gentle shake. "Bentley. Tell me. What happened?"

"I—I lost." His hands clutched his hair. "I never realized—how could I? To play for such stakes—"

"What stakes?" It took considerable effort to keep her voice calm.

"—at a house party," he went on, ignoring her interruption. "A friendly game. I had no idea." He pulled away and dropped onto the nearest chair, burying his face in his hands.

"You have lost a great deal of money, I gather?" she demanded, wanting to be sure of her facts.

A low groan escaped Bentley as he nodded.

"Were the stakes not made clear?" she pursued.

He made an indistinct noise, which she could take to mean anything she chose.

She chose to know for certain. "Bentley?" she said, inserting a commanding note.

Her brother swallowed and made a manful attempt to pull himself together. "He—he said five. I assumed he meant five-pound points, not five hundred."

Five hundred. Amanda sought refuge in a chair of her own. Bentley's fortune barely qualified as genteel, its yearly income covering the necessities of life rather than its luxuries. At five hundred pounds a point, it would take very few hands to beggar him. They'd have to sell up, leave their home, and all out of folly! She suspected he'd been vague about the size of the bet, and foolish beyond permission not to make certain of it. Fury welled within her, directed not at her brother, but at whoever would take such flagrant advantage of an obviously green boy. "With whom did you play?" she demanded.

"Rivenhall," came his choked response.

Rivenhall. That unconscionable rake. A gamester. Possibly even a Captain Sharp. She would like to tell him a thing or two, a few home truths that would, in the deplorable boxing cant employed by Bentley, give him a leveler. In fact, she could think of nothing she'd rather do. Still clutching her embroidery, she rose and strode from the room, leaving Bentley staring after her.

She made her way to Lord Pelham's study, where that notorious gamester had decreed three tables be kept at the ready for the use of his guests at all times. Amanda's godmother had confided her displeasure with the scheme and done her best to see that her husband did not invite any of his intimates who might be counted upon to turn a convivial week-long summer house party into a gambling frenzy. One of his reprehensible cronies, it seemed, had slipped through.

Amanda thrust the door open and strode into near darkness. The fire had burned low in the grate, and a tall figure stood beside the only lit candle, a snuffer in his hand. Amanda hesitated, realized this was not a footman but a gentleman, and the next instant recognized Rivenhall. Never one to run shy, she forged ahead. "I would like a word with you, my lord."

He turned and stared at her for a moment, then set the snuffer on the table. "Do you know," he said with amiable amusement, "never before have I heard quite so much contempt inserted into such innocuous words as 'my lord.' You really must tell me how you do it."

She curled her lip. "I would far rather tell you why I hold you in such contempt."

His eyebrows rose. "I foresee an entertaining few minutes."

"I fail to see how anyone could be entertained by such disgraceful conduct as yours!"

He offered her an apologetic smile. "I fear so much of my conduct is disgraceful, I cannot, at the moment, determine to which particular sin you are referring. Did I fail to keep a tryst with you? You must pardon my wretched memory."

Outrage swelled within her, intensified by the unexpected appeal of the notion of keeping a tryst with this dangerous gentleman. She suppressed it, and glared at him all the harder. "You have been gaming for outrageous stakes with the greenest of boys."

"Have I? Oh, you mean that young cub Grieves? Are you his nursemaid?"

"His sister. You ought to be utterly ashamed of yourself."

"Oh, no. I make it a point never to be." He crossed to the table and picked up a glass half full of a deep ruby liquid, which he drained.

"Your behavior was despicable," she informed him.

He inclined his head. "We've established that, I believe." He reached for the bottle and poured its dregs into his glass.

He was three-parts disguised, she realized, and somehow that made his behavior all the worse. Her voice dripping disgust, she said, "You are in a disgraceful state."

He grinned, a very disarming expression, and raised the glass to her. "I know. Believe me, my dear, it's the best possible way to pass a house party."

"A house party," she repeated, getting back on track, "which makes it all the more outrageous for you to take advantage of a callow youth. You are no better than a Captain Sharp."

A deep, rich chuckle broke from him. "My dear girl, what, in heaven's name, could you possibly know of such things?"

Her jaw clenched, but with an effort, she said, "You can have no idea how delighted I am to afford you so much amusement. But in all fairness, you must admit your behavior is shameful in one who is supposedly a gentleman."

For a long moment he eyed her, dangling the glass between his fingers. His attention concentrated now on her, and his face, already reddened by drink, took on a deeper hue. He seated himself once more at the table and reached for another bottle—his fourth, it seemed, from the empty ones lying about. He refilled his glass, tossed off the contents, then studied her from head to toe through an obvious haze of wine. A slow, deliberate smile tugged at the corners of his mouth. "So you think me less than a gentleman."

She allowed her expression of disdain to stand as her answer.

"Very well, then," he enunciated with care. "I will give you the opportunity to redeem your brother's vowels." His gaze lingered on her a moment longer, then dropped to the deck of cards that lay in an untidy heap before him, and he fingered them, squaring them as of long habit.

She regarded him in uncertainty. "And how may I do that, my lord?"

"A game." He looked up, directly into her eyes. "One hand. If you win, you may have his scrawls." He gestured toward the few scribbled vowels.

"And if I lose?" she asked steadily. "I have nothing more than pin money, hardly a wager to compare with my brother's debt."

The drunken glint in his eyes brightened, blurred, then gleamed. "Your stake," he said, his speech slurred, "will be your virtue."

Shock stiffened her, robbing her of speech. The audacity to suggest anything so repugnant—and so reprehensibly intriguing . . . An odd sensation stirred within her, but firmly she banished it. She fixed him with a look that should have reduced him to rubble. "I do not find you amusing, my lord."

"Neither do I." He frowned as if considering his words, then amended them. "At least, I don't at the moment. I am quite serious this once. That is the only stake I shall accept from you. If you lose, you will spend the night with me."

Her lip curled. "Is it always your habit to play for the highest possible stakes against opponents who are not in the least up to your weight? How proud it must make you."

His eyebrows rose. "What, do you lack courage?"

She glared at him. She was no gamester, not even more than tolerably good at piquet. Without unusual luck, she hadn't a hope of winning. "Your terms," she said through clenched teeth, "are ludicrous and insulting."

He inclined his head, his tantalizing smile lingering, his gaze resting about a foot below the level of her chin. "My terms," he mimicked her outraged tone, "are the only ones you will get. How important is it to you to redeem that young fool's vowels?"

"If I lose, will you still return them?"

"If you lose, I will still return them. In the morning," he added with a deliberate, devilish smile.

She hesitated only a moment. Then, with a trembling hand, she grasped a chair, pulled it out, and sat down, depositing her embroidery on the table with considerable force. If she thought about her wager, the enormity of her stake, she wouldn't be able to go through with it. But she couldn't let this man destroy Bentley, rob them of their home, whatever the cost to herself.

And would the cost truly be so terrible?

"Your cards?" His deep voice recalled her attention.

She looked down to see them lying before her, covering a stray strand of green silk that escaped from her needlework. With fingers still shaking, she picked up her hand, arranged it, then discarded two and replaced them. Rivenhall exchanged only one, they made their declarations, and the play began.

It ended all too soon.

For a long moment, she sat in silence. She'd known, of course. The outcome had been obvious from the start. Yet—

"Mine, I believe," he said.

And she knew, from where his gaze lingered, that he did not speak of the game.

TWO

Amanda stared at the cards, at Rivenhall's powerful, tanned hands as he swept the fateful pieces of pasteboard together. What had she done . . . ? The reality of it began to penetrate, the realization that she had, indeed, traded her virtue for her brother's financial well-being, and to a man—she couldn't call him a gentleman—who would not scruple to collect his bet. The hollowness in her chest, the sinking sensation in her stomach, must be fear. The rapidity of her pulse left her dizzy, and heat surged through her. Those powerful hands would soon—

Well, she didn't know exactly what they would do, but he would know. He undoubtedly had vast experience in such matters, unprincipled rake that he was. The certainty of that brought even more warmth to her cheeks. To be handled by him, indoctrinated into the mysteries of his bed—

Why wasn't she swooning with the horror of it? Why, in fact, did the thought fascinate her, intrigue her, set her tingling with anticipation? Where were her own principles?

She wasn't about to let him glimpse the upheaval, the conflicting and incomprehensible nature of her emotions. She straightened, her back rigid with pride, and looked down her nose at him in a manner, copied from a ferocious aunt, designed to put him firmly in his place.

"I suppose," she said in a tone that wavered perilously between sarcasm and sincerity, "you believe we both have a rare treat in store for us."

The corners of his bleary eyes crinkled in sudden amusement. He poured more wine into his glass, drained half of it, then regarded her over the crystal rim. "What, no maidenly blushes? No missish alarm?"

"As you see, I am deplorably prosaic." Yet it took considerable effort to keep her voice steady.

He leaned back in his chair, regarding her with an appreciation aided by the amount of claret he had consumed. After a moment, his gaze fell to the table, where her hand rested on the linen cloth she embroidered. He reached for it, held it up, and examined it with a frowning intensity. "A meek little spinster who sits in corners and embroiders," he said, "yet who faces a ravening—or do I mean ravishing?—wolf with no qualms."

She inclined her head.

"Or are there qualms?" He left it a question, dangling between them.

Indeed there were, but whether they were for or against their looming encounter, she couldn't be certain. But even if she must surrender her virtue to him, he would not claim her pride as well. Her chin rose. "Would it matter to you if there were?"

A short laugh escaped him. "No," he admitted. He toyed with the needlework. "Clever with your fingers, aren't you? I'll tell you what. I will give you one chance to redeem your virtue."

Hope, somewhat diluted by regret, surged through her. "And to what do I owe this undoubtedly uncharacteristic display of generosity?"

He frowned. "I don't know." His words blurred. "Wine, I suppose. I seem to be a bit fuddled. But you will excuse that, I feel certain."

"And what is my chance?" she asked, before he might forget.

"Chance? Ah, yes. I have a fancy to carry a copy of a certain painting with me. On"—he broke off, considering for a minute—"on a handkerchief. If you can render the picture in your neat stitches by the end of the week, I will accept that in lieu of—more tangible payment, shall we say?"

"You will accept my stitchery in place of my—my virtue?" she demanded. Relief struggled against insult, and lost. To have her needlework valued over her person she found lowering in the extreme.

"Before we leave this house party, you will have your brother's vowels. And I shall have either your embroidery or"—and his slow, devilish smile transformed his expression—"you."

"Very well." She rose. "Do you have a handkerchief with you?"

He held out a generous square of fine lawn to her, but when she took it, he retained his hold. "There is one condition. You must not decline any activity or social engagement to complete your work. We don't want to give rise to any gossip, do we?"

"We most assuredly do not." She considered, gauging the time requirements to fill so vast a square, knew it to be considerable, but nodded. She had, after all, no choice. "Very well. What is this picture you desire?"

A glint of unholy glee lit his eyes. He rose, came around the table, and placed his hands on her shoulders. The touch sent a thrill through her, alarming yet delightful, and for a moment she couldn't catch her breath. Then he was turning her away from him, around to face the wall behind her, and disappointment seeped through her.

"There," he said softly.

His breath tickled her ear, stirring the tendrils of hair that clustered there. His hands remained on her shoulders, his fingers touching her skin. Very gently, absently, his thumbs caressed her neck.

With an effort, she focused her attention on the painting that hung before her, and her eyes widened. She should have known, of course, that he'd want a risqué subject. This rendering of Leda and the Swan was certainly that. Its sheer sensuousness washed over her; coupled with the broad-shouldered presence pressed close behind her, it left her weak.

"A bit complicated," he pronounced, his tone thoughtful.

"The feathers will take a very long time to depict," she agreed, but they were far from the worst of her problems. Leda's ample charms were on full display, without so much as a wisp of drapery to preserve her modesty. "Allow me to compliment you upon your execrable taste, my Lord Rivenhall."

His deep chuckle sounded, and his hands smoothed over the bare skin of her throat and shoulders. "I shall solace my lonely nights with thoughts that she—or you—will soon be mine."

Amanda pulled away from him, her face burning. "I will wish you good night, then," she said with ice dripping from her voice. Without another glance at him, she stalked from the room with as much dignity as she could muster.

To her relief, none of the other houseguests lingered in the hall. No sounds drifted down from the upper floors, either; the others must have sought their beds some time ago. She mounted the stairs by the weak glow of the gas lamps which the servants had turned down for the night, and made her way to the spacious chamber she occupied on every visit to her godmother.

She opened her door, and drew up short at the sight of a figure hunched in the wing-back chair before the fire. It rose, resolving itself into Bentley. He took a shaky step toward her, his face haggard, his eyes beseeching.

"What happened?" His words came out more as a cry for reassurance than anything else.

Anger welled within her, for his careless gaming, for exposing her to Rivenhall's insulting wager. But sisterly compassion won out. "Be easy," she said, as lightly as possible. "He is allowing me to redeem your vowels."

"He— *How?*" he demanded, incredulous. "What do you have that could possibly equal such a sum?"

The truth never entered his mind. Brothers never held flattering images of their sisters, of course, but the implied if unintended insult still stung. "It is possible he has an ounce of proper feeling, though I doubt it. If he had not been disgustingly foxed, he should never have made such a suggestion." And she told him about the embroidery, omitting any mention of their true wager.

He took the giant square of lawn she held out and eyed it in dismay. "Cover the entire thing? By the end of the week? Get stitching! You haven't a moment to lose!"

"I had intended to begin at once," she said pointedly.

"Then do so." But rather than departing, he set about pacing the chamber, pausing at every turn to stare over her shoulder until she forcibly evicted him from the room.

Bentley's absence, though, brought her little relief. Her abigail, Jennings, who had been hovering at the door, bustled in, muttering dark words about the lateness of the hour. Knowing from long experience the uselessness of protest, Amanda allowed herself to be tucked between sheets, then bade her woman good night and pretended to compose herself for sleep. Jennings hung the evening gown in the cupboard, straightened the hair brush, comb and lotion pot on the dresser, satisfied her-

self that everything else seemed in good order and finally left.

Amanda waited while she counted to one hundred to
assure herself her maid would not return, then threw
back the covers and turned up the oil lamp that burned
beside her bed. Every candle the room boasted she lit,
gathering them on the worktable that stood by the chair
before the hearth. She wanted to stitch the outline of
that reprehensible painting before it faded from her
mind.

Sitting before her fire, her needle working quickly, she
allowed her mind to review the dreadful evening. She
could think of nothing that could compare with the out-
rageousness of Rivenhall's behavior. The infamy of the
man! Her needle stabbed at the stretched cloth, sketching
the spread of the swan's massive wing. She was no bit o'
muslin, but a lady of quality. The man must be wholly
without morals, without honor, without decent feeling
ever to have made such a wager with her.

Her needle slowed. He must have been aware of it, too,
to have allowed her a chance to escape. She despised him
utterly, of course—that went without saying—yet she
couldn't get his gleaming dark eyes or his devilish smile
out of her mind. Irritated both with him and herself, she
doubled her efforts on her stitchery, laboring long into
the night until her tired eyes could no longer focus on
her delicate work.

She rose again early, dressed without the aid of Jennings, and made her way to Lord Pelham's study. For a
long while she stood before the picture, studying the patterns of color, the details of line and form. She'd made
a couple of errors in her outlining, but could fix them
without too much trouble. She would need to go into
Brighton, though, to purchase silks in a variety of flesh
tones. Indiscreet flesh tones, in particular. Why on earth
hadn't Leda the modesty to drape something—any-

thing—over her voluptuous form? But she supposed Lord Rivenhall wouldn't have found the painting nearly so fascinating if she had.

Breakfast would not be laid out yet for another hour. She settled in a chair, repaired the previous evening's inaccuracies, and set to work depicting the innumerable feathers. She'd need to acquire more white silk, as well, not to mention the silvery gray with which the artist had highlighted each quill.

The unmistakable scent of sausages and cinnamon buns roused her at last. By then, she had completed the base work for one extended wing and begun on the breast. A break to assuage her hunger would only make her work all the faster afterward, she decided, and tucked the cloth into her workbag.

It was still early by house-party standards; the time lacked a quarter of an hour before nine. Yet as soon as she opened the door into the sunny parlor, she sensed another's presence, knew even before she saw him that she was not alone. A flurry of nerves danced in her stomach, and her hand clenched the door handle.

Rivenhall, of course. No one else could create such a riotous reaction within her. He sat at the table, a plate heaped with eggs, ham, sausages and rolls before him, a tankard of ale at his side. His riding coat fit his broad shoulders to perfection, and a single lock of his waving dark hair curled artlessly over his forehead. When he looked up, she could see no traces of his previous night's indulgences marring his piercing green eyes.

Faint lines creased his brow as he regarded her, then they cleared, and that slow, intriguing smile tugged at the corners of his mouth. "Miss . . . Grieves, is it not? Forgive me, but I do not believe we were properly introduced."

"We were not," came her short response. She turned her back on him and concentrated her attention on the numerous chafing dishes that filled the sideboard. There had been nothing proper whatsoever about their meeting last night.

His chair creaked and scraped as he shoved it back to rise. "I believe, though, unless my memory is much mistaken, that we enjoyed a game of cards."

"Enjoyed?" She spun about to fix him with an indignant glare. "What, may I ask, was the least bit enjoyable about that game?"

"The stakes. The anticipation of winning and enjoying the outcome. And it would be very enjoyable. Of that I assure you."

She managed a falsely sweet smile. "Yes, I do like to embroider. Fortunate, is it not? And only see what progress I have made." She drew out the handkerchief and displayed it.

"You have completed that much all ready?" His eyebrows rose, and he directed a thoughtful, appraising glance at her. "A lady of determination, it would seem."

"A *lady*"—and she stressed the word—"of honor."

"And enterprise." His bright eyes gleamed. "It is not too late to change your mind and pay your debt in the manner I originally suggested. I assure you, it would be far more agreeable than pushing a needle in and out of a piece of cloth."

Her lip curled. "Far more agreeable for whom?"

The gleam intensified. "For us both."

She gave him her most disdainful, dismissive stare, then pointedly turned back to the selection of her breakfast. Footsteps sounded on the thick carpet, stopping just behind her. She tensed, and the erratic sensation that tingled along her skin warned her he stood very close. She picked up a lid at random, found she had no appetite for the eggs coddled in cream sauce that lay within, and reached for the next.

His hand extended over her shoulder, and he grasped

the ornate knob of the lid before she could. Quickly, barely avoiding contact, she snatched her own hand back. The wide lapel of his coat brushed against her shoulder blade; if she were so imprudent as to lean back—just a very little—she would find herself pressed against him. Instead, she leaned forward.

A soft, tantalizing chuckle escaped him as he lifted the lid, allowing the steaming aroma of sausages and onions to fill the room. "Always a good choice," he said softly in her ear. "May I serve you with some?"

"No." The word came out through clenched teeth. It amazed her how he could insert such a note of intimacy into so commonplace a question.

"Ah, I see I have a challenge on my hands to find just the right delicacy to please you. And I assure you, I never retreat from a challenge."

That, she reflected bitterly, she could well believe.

Warm breath brushed along her neck, moving from her shoulder to her right ear, then played through her fair, curling hair to her temple. Why must her muscles betray her, her knees trembling and her arms limp at her sides? She should push him away, inform him in no uncertain terms she found his attentions repugnant.

Only she didn't, and that was the maddening part.

"Now, that is a heavenly aroma, is it not?" he murmured against her ear. His lips teased along her skin, nuzzling, as he leaned forward to sniff in an exaggerated manner.

"Do you think so?" She eyed the plate of cinnamon buns a touch wistfully, but forced herself to ignore the tempting scent that enveloped her. It took every ounce of her resolve to maintain her composure when she spoke. "I find it rather common. Certainly nothing to intrigue one."

He chuckled, a sound of pure appreciation. "I see I

must educate your palate." He selected a bun and held it just before her mouth.

Instinctively, she drew back from it—a mistake, as that pressed her against his chest. Sensuous possibilities flooded her mind, of sinking her teeth into the delectable pastry, of relaxing into the circle of his arm, of drowning in the huskiness of his voice. Of abandoning her embroidery and paying her gaming debt with the fullness of her being.

Instead, she leaned forward, snatched up the closest lid, and found herself face to face with a rather revolting selection of kippered herrings. On impulse, she scooped some up on the serving fork and presented them to him over her shoulder, directly into his face, saying, "Nothing more down to earth than fish first thing in the morning, is there?" And certainly nothing more perfectly suited to shatter the alluring mood he'd created.

Apparently, he shared that opinion. He drew back, eying her offering with distaste. Then amusement flickered once more in his eyes. "A resourceful lady," he murmured.

"And one who *will* complete her embroidery, my lord."

A light, rambling voice sounded in the corridor, and the door to the breakfast parlor opened. Mrs. Easham, a sprightly, round woman approaching middle age, entered, followed by Mr. Somes, and Rivenhall retired a tactful step.

Mr. Somes brightened as he saw Amanda. "An owl, my dear. Right outside my window, I promise you! I was just telling Mrs. Easham what a delight it was, to bear me company through the long night."

"I'd prefer something—or rather, someone—other than an owl," Rivenhall murmured, for Amanda's ears alone. "This hand goes to you, it seems, but the game is far from over." Still holding his cinnamon bun, he returned to his place at the table.

Amanda deposited her kippers on a plate, dismayed at the prospect of having to actually eat them. But that would be a small price to pay for having so neatly repelled her tormentor. She resumed her browsing of the dishes, making selections at random just to give her hands something to do. Her thoughts strayed far from the meal, far from the inconsequential chatter of her fellow houseguests as they began to fill the room.

Lord Rivenhall called it a game, but he had declared outright war against her. That he fought to win, she hadn't a doubt. That he might succeed, she admitted as a distinct possibility.

And however much she might regret his tactics, she had to admire them as well. If his intention were to seduce her, he was going about it in exactly the right way.

THREE

He was a cad, of course. Rivenhall knew it perfectly well. In fact, he long had prided himself on that fact. Never yet had he failed to seduce any woman—whether fashionably impure or lady of quality—who caught his fancy.

And Miss Amanda Grieves, drab little spinster that she might appear, had certainly caught his fancy.

What made him so particularly a cad this time was his pursuit of an *unmarried* lady of quality.

He knew just how much society would accept and forgive. Ladies protected by wedlock could take what lovers they chose, as long as they conducted their affairs with discretion. Ladies without the protection of a husband could not.

And thinking of that particular lady . . . She really wasn't drab in the least, despite first impressions. She might sit in corners, hiding behind her embroidery, but her sparkling gray eyes observed everything and her quick mind missed little. And just thinking of those bright eyes and quick mind sent through him a wave of pleasurable anticipation to match wits against her once more, and at the earliest opportunity.

He found her in Pelham's study. The card tables had vanished, he noticed; Lady Pelham had won her way—but not soon enough for Miss Grieves. His quarry stood before Leda and the Swan, holding a variety of embroidery silks in her hand. For the first time he really looked at the painting, at Leda's voluptuous immodesty, at the swan's lecherous leer. What had ever possessed him to request an embroidered copy of that monstrosity? A desire to shock Miss Grieves, of course. Lord, when he was in his cups, he showed such little discretion.

Except in his choice of a playing partner. Since breakfast, she had altered her appearance; donning her armor against him, he supposed. She now wore a severe morning gown of dove-gray muslin, made high at the throat and with long sleeves. Her mass of fair hair she had drawn back into a chignon, but despite her best efforts, tantalizing tendrils escaped to play about her cheeks.

He strolled forward, considering with relish the most disconcerting thing to say to her. She blushed so very delightfully.

Some sound, perhaps a brush of boot on the carpet, must have betrayed him, for she spun about. An unreadable expression flickered across her countenance, to be replaced almost at once with disdain. "Oh," she said. "It is only you."

That slight emphasis on the "only" was a good touch, he reflected with amused approval. He hadn't expected her to be quite so accomplished in the art of giving a set-down. She was proving herself a worthy opponent. Which reminded him, it was time for his next gambit. He fixed her with a benign smile and said, "It is far too beautiful a day to remain indoors. You really ought to be outside, enjoying the morning."

Her smile held unparalleled sweetness. "I quite prefer it in here. And as I have not a single social obligation at the moment that requires me to be elsewhere, here I shall remain."

He shook his head. "A walk in the gardens would be

much more pleasant. Will you do me the honor of accompanying me?"

The look she directed at him, he noted in delight, could freeze a hearth fire. She opened her mouth for what would undoubtedly be a scathing retort, but before she could speak, he added, pointedly, "This is an invitation," then watched with enjoyment as she struggled to master her indignation.

She had very speaking eyes, he decided. And what they were saying to him now should reduce him to a pulp. She was too much of a lady, though, to put her sentiments into words.

Instead, she confined herself to stuffing her embroidery back into her workbag, tossing it onto a chair, and stalking to the door. "You are an unconscionable—" She broke off, obviously searching for a word of sufficient severity to convey her disgust of him as they navigated the corridor.

"Out-and-outer?" he suggested. "Buck of the first head?"

"Scapegrace, you mean. Or rakeshame!"

He regarded her in mock horror. "Never did I think to hear such words from your lips."

She stopped just before the dining room, turning to fix him with an annihilating glare from her remarkably fine eyes. The angry jut of her chin pleased him, as did the faint curl of her lip. No simpering miss, this, but a lady of pride and courage. He was going to enjoy himself immensely. And to think he'd expected to be bored at the Pelhams' little gathering.

He held the door for her. "Yes?" he prodded, all encouragement.

She opened her mouth, then closed it again with a snap and marched forward.

He caught up to her in only two strides. "Behaving like

the lady you are will put you at a deplorable disadvantage with me, I fear."

"Being the lady I am should have been sufficient to protect me from your odious machinations."

"Oh, I try not to let matters like that prejudice me."

"Prejudice?" she cried. "If you had the least sense of shame, or finer feelings—"

"Ah, but I do not, you see." He unlatched the French windows that gave onto the terrace. "It makes life so much more entertaining, do you not agree?"

"I most assuredly do not!" She swept past him, head high, eyes blazing.

A chuckle welled inside him, but he fought it back. Together they descended the steps leading to the formal rose garden with its gravel paths and fountain. Beyond he glimpsed Mr. Somes and Lady Pelham just approaching the shrubbery. The other members of the house party had vanished, some into Brighton for the day, others to ride or drive about the countryside. Perhaps Miss Grieves would honor him with her company on such an expedition. He'd have to find the perfect moment to invite her. Preferably when she was about to begin embroidering.

"The rose is an admirable flower, do you not think?" she inquired with exaggerated politeness as they reached the first of the showy shrubs.

"But its beauty can hardly be compared with yours," came his prompt response.

"Nor its thorns." She accompanied this with a spuriously flirtatious smile.

It caught him in mid-stride, staggering him. Lord, who would have thought the chit had it in her? A lady of many parts, it seemed, and every one of them became more desirable to him by the minute. He caught up to her, offering his arm. She hesitated a moment, then just rested her fingers on his sleeve.

He'd made a better wager last night than he'd realized.

He still didn't know what had prompted that bet. Sheer audacity, perhaps. Or hoping to amuse himself by scandalizing a spinster. He'd certainly been bored, with a dull, depressed ache that had haunted him since his return from Jamaica. He had a title, an estate, a sizable income, a string of expensive little birds of paradise, everything he wanted just for the asking.

Was that the problem? Had life become too easy? Did he miss the heart-pounding joy of a challenge?

His gaze fell on Miss Grieves, who strolled at his side, ignoring him. She challenged him. Teasing her, he came alive. And he enjoyed that sensation. He did not enjoy being ignored by her.

He covered her fingers with his hand, pressing them. She tried to snatch them away, but he caught a firm hold, grasping her hand in his. His thumb caressed her palm, and she struggled, then submitted, her stony gaze fixed before her. "Thorns add a certain spice to beauty," he said.

She made no response.

"This afternoon," he went on as they paused before a large bush filled with particularly fine white blossoms, "you must come riding with me."

"No," came her calm reply. "I must not."

Disappointment flickered in him, for the denial of her companionship, but mostly for her going back on her word. "Our agreement—" he began, somewhat stiffly.

"Our agreement," she interrupted, "was that I should not refuse any social engagement, not that I must break them in order to gratify your vanity."

"I was not gratifying my vanity," he was stung into retorting.

"As you wish." Her tone implied she didn't believe him for a moment.

He ground his teeth. "I perceive you have a previous engagement?"

"I do."

"And may I ask what it is you do?"

"You may, but I shall not answer. It is enough for you to know it is of a social nature, embarked upon with other members of the house party. Does that not fulfill your requirements?"

It did, of course, but perversely, he wanted to know exactly in what activity—and in what company—she would pass the afternoon. His thoughts ran the other gentlemen of the party in review, dismissing them one by one as inconsequential, and finally he hazarded, "Are you going to observe the birds with Mr. Somes?"

"No," came her maddening response, and she walked on.

"Your brother, perhaps?" he pursued.

She cast him a pitying glance. "My brother has not the least interest in birds."

"I meant," he forged on, keeping his temper in check, "do you spend the afternoon with him?"

She came to an abrupt halt, turning to face him squarely. "It is no part of our agreement, my lord, that I must give you a detailed account of how or with whom I spend my time."

"I merely wish to assure myself," he declared, not the least bit truthfully, "that you are indeed involved in a social engagement and not simply hiding from me in order to embroider."

Her eyebrows rose sharply, and when she spoke, her words dripped hauteur. "Do you have the audacity to doubt my word? Of course, I cannot expect a man of your reputation to understand the concept of honor, but—"

"I understand it perfectly well," he snapped, and resumed walking.

She fell into step beside him. "To be sure, understanding a concept and partaking in it are two completely different matters."

His teeth clenched, and he strode on, fuming. It was not until they reached the end of the formal rose beds that it dawned on him that he had abandoned his teasing seduction of her. Abandoned it, in fact, because of her masterly handling of him. Reluctant humor dispelled his ill temper, and he directed an assessing gaze at her. "My dear Miss Grieves, I believe I shall award the second hand to you, as well."

She inclined her head in acknowledgement.

"But I shall not make the mistake of underestimating my opponent in the future." He took her hand, carried it to his lips, then deliberately turned it over and pressed a kiss into her palm.

Something that might have been alarm—or revulsion—flickered in her eyes, but before she could speak, he said: "I shall see you at nuncheon." He bowed, then strode away. Beating a strategic—if hasty—retreat.

Miss Amanda Grieves presented certain problems to him. Her conduct was unquestionably that of a well-bred lady, and her poise impressed him, as did the neatness with which she parried and diverted his advances. He fully intended to give her a fair chance to win free of his dishonorable wager—as a gentleman, he could do no less—yet perversely, he began plotting his next ploy to divert her from her task.

He did indeed see her at nuncheon, but nothing more. She sat between Miss Abbott and Mr. Somes, and never so much as cast a glance in his direction. It dawned on him halfway through the meal that his gaze seldom left her. Annoyed with himself, he changed his seat on the pretext of obtaining more ham from the chafing dishes, and settled beside the radiant Mrs. Kingsford. That Miss Amanda Grieves appeared oblivious to this move didn't bother him in the least, he assured himself. He frequently carried on multiple flirtations, and only the ladies minded.

As the meal drew to its close, Miss Abbott sprang to her feet. "I so look forward to our expedition to Brighton, my dear Amanda. Let me but fetch my bonnet, and I shall be with you in a trice."

As the two ladies started from the room, Rivenhall rose, effectively blocking their way. "Brighton? Do you know, that sounds a most excellent plan. I shall be only too happy to drive you in my curricle. You won't mind sitting close together."

Miss Grieves directed a pitying smile at him. "We are already three, I fear. Mrs. Easham has expressed a desire to accompany us, and we are to go in Lady Pelham's barouche. And as we do not need an escort to ride at our side for so short a journey, you need not trouble yourself."

"Oh, dear me, no," Miss Abbott agreed, eying him with patent disapproval. "We shouldn't dream of imposing on you, Lord Rivenhall. And a gentleman would be most dreadfully bored, because we intend only to visit a shop where I might purchase some wool and where Miss Grieves might purchase more embroidery silk."

"What?" He turned his gaze fully on Miss Grieves. "Do you run low? I should have thought a lady so addicted to the pastime would have brought sufficient silk with her."

"It just goes to prove that even you can be mistaken, my lord. But as it chances, my work progresses so quickly, I find I need different colors sooner than I had anticipated. If you will excuse us?"

He had to give her full marks for that one, as well. She could certainly be aggravating, but he could not deny the pleasure of crossing swords with so valiant an opponent. She began to mount the steps, and his gaze narrowed on the graceful movement of her retreating figure. Definitely, an enjoyable opponent.

Miss Abbott returned first to find him still standing in the hall, lost in thought. She looked him over, sniffed, and went into the Gold Salon where she perched on the edge of a chair to await the rest of her party. She didn't enjoy his company, Rivenhall guessed. It didn't surprise him. Few truly respectable ladies did.

Fifteen minutes later, he watched with an irritated sense of loss as the barouche departed, then made his way back to the house. The afternoon lay before him. Perhaps he would ride; that might vent the energy that welled inside him, the restlessness that he'd prefer to expend in teasing Miss Grieves. But she wasn't the only female present at the house party. There were others, and some not averse to a spot of dalliance.

In fact, had it been Mrs. Diana Kingsford with whom he'd embarked on that memorable wager, the suggestion of paying in any other manner would never have come up. That lady would have accompanied him back to his room right then and there. Complimentary, of course, but at the moment the thought of so easy a conquest didn't please him in the least.

Still, he set off in search of her. He found her, after a rapid tour of the lower floor, in the music room, by the simple expedient of following the uncertain notes of the pianoforte. She sat at the instrument, studying a sheet of music, and with a sense of surprise he recognized the mangled chords of "Scarborough Fair."

She looked up as he approached and stopped torturing the instrument, a welcoming smile on her undeniably pretty face. "My lord," she said, accompanying it with a throaty laugh. "You catch me at my practice. Perhaps you have some suggestions?"

The invitation in her voice was unmistakable. He joined her on the bench as she obviously expected, and indulged her in a light flirtation until it dawned on him that his heart wasn't in it. He played the role of rake rather like an automaton, going through the motions without any intent or real enjoyment. That puzzled him, until, while outwardly continuing his flirtation, he reached the conclusion that it was because his attention remained focused on a more challenging seduction. The difficulty of his intended conquest of Miss Grieves made such an easy one as this seem dull by comparison.

He was lying in wait for her when the barouche at last returned from Brighton. As it pulled around the circular gravel drive and came to a halt before the front door, he left his post at the window of the Gold Salon, timing it so that he emerged from the room just as the party of ladies entered the main hall. He greeted them with a beaming smile—and was rewarded by a sniff from the elderly Miss Abbott and a reproving stare from Mrs. Easham. Miss Grieves simply ignored him and headed for the stairs.

How could he resist? "Miss Grieves," he called after her. "Might I have a word with you?"

"Can it not wait?" she inquired. "I have but this moment returned. As you quite clearly saw."

But it couldn't. Now that she was here, he found himself more impatient than ever to have her alone once more. "Just a quick consultation," he assured her.

With an elaborate sigh, she returned to his side. "What is it you wish now, my lord?"

The other two ladies lingered, watching them. Rivenhall solved the problem by taking Miss Grieves by the arm and leading her toward Pelham's study. "I desire to see these silks you have purchased."

"See the— What in heaven's name for?" she demanded. "I assure you, I am quite capable of selecting the materials I need to complete my embroidery."

"But I have such a very great stake in the outcome of your handiwork."

She glared at him, but once they had entered the study, she rummaged in the package she carried and drew out a handful of neatly wrapped silken threads.

He took them, holding them up, separating them with all the air of one who had never encountered anything so fascinating in his entire life. After a moment he carried them to the picture and began to match them to their counterparts in paint. The third color he tried was a pale beige pink, and he shook his head. "I wouldn't have thought this was right for a flesh tone, but it matches fairly well. How did you ever come to select it? Did you use your own—er, self for a sample?"

Soft color tinged her cheeks, and a chuckle escaped him. He was right; she did have the most delightful blush. He liked it excessively. In fact, he would have to see to it that she blushed far more often.

He next selected a rosier shade, its purpose in Leda's voluptuous contours obvious. He considered making a lewd remark, but suddenly it didn't seem amusing, only coarse and vulgar. That gave him pause. There was something about Miss Grieves that brought out the worst in him. Apparently, she also brought out the best.

He found that disturbing.

FOUR

Lord Rivenhall, Amanda fumed, did an excellent job of making it difficult for her to work on her embroidery. At his instigation, she had spent a lively morning engaged in a tournament of battledore and shuttlecock. True, she had managed to set a few stitches between her turns, but it had not been easy. Nor had she accomplished much.

She returned from this outing on the back lawn tired and heated from the exercise, and went straight to her room to amend her appearance—and to steal the half hour or so before nuncheon would be laid out with the tasteless Leda and her swan. Surely Rivenhall wouldn't pursue her there, of all places.

She was right; he did not. But before she had done more than cover one half of a square inch of the hand-kerchief, a knock sounded on her door and Bentley strode in.

"There you are!" he exclaimed. His tense expression eased a trifle. "At work at last, I see." He paced with his long, restless strides to the window, then turned to face her. "Can't think why you've been gadding about so. Almost as if you don't want to finish that piece."

She set her work in her lap and eyed him, a scathing comment on the tip of her tongue. But he had no idea of the true nature of her bet, and she had no intention of telling him. As far as he knew, the consequences of her failure to complete her stitchery fell on no one but himself. His ill temper stemmed merely from the fact he had been a fool, and knew it. And worse, he had to be rescued from the consequences by his sister.

"Do you want every member of the house party to know what you have done?" she inquired, keeping her voice mild.

He started. "Why on earth should they?"

"If I am seen to work on this every moment, someone would undoubtedly ask questions. Particularly as the subject becomes obvious."

"Lord," he breathed. "I hadn't thought of that."

He hadn't thought of a great many things, but she let that pass. "I shall work on it when I am alone. In fact, I was alone until you arrived."

"Well, I'm not stopping you, am I?"

"It is easier to concentrate when I am not talking," she snapped, her temper fraying.

He hunched a shoulder. "I only came to see how you went on."

"Very well, thank you. And what shall you do after nuncheon?"

He brightened. "Oh, a few of us are going out to practice shooting. Should be capital fun." Then his brow furrowed once more. "And you'll come back here to work some more on that?"

"It is certainly my intention," she assured him.

But it was not Rivenhall's plan.

She'd slipped quietly into the breakfast parlor, where the servants had laid out the nuncheon, filled a plate, and was about to beat a strategic retreat back to her room when he hailed her. She turned slowly, forcing a smile to her lips as he bore down on her. It froze as she caught sight of the wicked gleam that burned in his eyes.

He drew her to the table, to the end at which Miss Abbott and Margaret Easham already sat. He pressed her into a chair and, with impudent laughter lighting his countenance asked, "Do you sketch, Miss Grieves?"

"Indeed she does," cried Miss Abbott. "Dear Amanda, I am so glad you came in just now. Mrs. Easham and I are planning a sketching expedition this afternoon. Just some little way into the woods, where there is the most delightful pond, and somewhere nearby there is even a shallow waterfall cascading over the rocks, and an old footbridge. Do say you will join us."

"Yes," Rivenhall said, making no attempt to hide his evil grin. "Do say you will."

For one moment she allowed the full venom of her glare to rest on him; then she turned to her mother's old friend with a warm smile. "Indeed, I shall like it of all things."

"Well done," murmured Rivenhall.

His words sounded so softly—and so unexpectedly sincere—that Amanda thought she must have misheard. She shot him a quick glance and surprised an expression of admiration on his features as his gaze rested on her. She looked away at once, her heart beating in an oddly capricious manner.

"There, then." Miss Abbott rose. "I shall gather my sketching box and be with you shortly."

They set forth just over a quarter of an hour later, Mrs. Easham and Miss Abbott talking in a lively manner, Amanda trailing them, silent. Rivenhall's opinion of her didn't matter one whit, she assured herself. The only thing that mattered would be to defeat him—and in the face of the insurmountable odds he stacked against her. She *would* defeat him, and take the greatest of pleasures in doing so.

Only it might mean she would have no sleep whatsoever for the remainder of the week. She'd had little enough, already.

The walk to the pond took longer than Amanda had

anticipated. The other two ladies settled upon the grass, took out their pads and pencils, and set to work with enthusiasm. Amanda sketched as one bound by honor, but every pattern of shadow and light, of rock and ripple, took on the outline of Leda and her swan. At last, her conscience satisfied that she had done her best, she set aside her sketchbook and picked up her embroidery.

The warmth of the afternoon flowed over her, slowing her needle. Yet when Miss Abbott and Mrs. Easham rose at last, she found herself reluctant to return to the house. After assuring them she would follow within the hour, she watched them depart, then leaned back against the tree, allowing the peace of the idyllic setting to ease the tension she had suffered since first laying eyes on Rivenhall.

She awoke with a start to a sensation of chill in the air. She rubbed her bleary eyes; then recollection of the afternoon, of her neglected embroidery, flooded back. Still groggy, she cast an uneasy glance at the darkening sky, and it confirmed her fears. She must have wasted hours.

Twilight hadn't crept up on her, she reflected ruefully; it had leapt like a lion on its unsuspecting prey. It must be terribly late; the sun had long since sunk beneath the line of trees. She collected her sketchbook and embroidery, shoved them both into her workbag, and set forth for the house.

Within a few hundred yards, the last vestiges of her path vanished in the gathering dusk. Root and rock lurked in the deep shadows, forming traps for her uncertain feet. For that matter, weeds and vines had overgrown this trail. With a sinking heart, she realized she had strayed onto some disused walkway; she must have lost the correct one some distance back. At this rate, she would be hopelessly late for dinner, and her dear godmama would have every right to be vexed with her.

As she stood there, pondering her predicament, she

became aware of the splashing of water. The cascade, and the footbridge. If she found it, she could cross to the other side of the stream. Then, instead of taking the circuitous route through the woods by which she had come, she only had to traverse a small copse to find herself at the edge of the open fields of the home farm. A short walk across these would bring her to the north lawn and an easy—and unannounced—entrance to the house by way of the conservatory.

Heartened, she hurried forward, moving as swiftly as possible over the uneven terrain. At last she emerged from the tangled vines and underbrush to find herself facing the stream. And there, indeed, stood the footbridge—or at least the long-abandoned remains of one.

She eyed the splintered rails without enthusiasm, then transferred her gaze to the brook itself. About seven feet across, she decided, far too great a distance for her to jump. But possibly not an insurmountable barrier. Large stones emerged from the water, flat, evenly spaced and steady looking. Someone, it seemed, had provided an alternative mode of crossing. If she were careful, she might still return before anyone became seriously alarmed for her.

She hung her workbag over her arm, lifted the hem of her skirts, and touched the first stone with the toe of her jean half-boot. Not a single wobble. Encouraged, she put her weight on it, her free arm extended to give her balance, and stepped forward, reaching for the next step.

The fourth nearly proved her undoing. It listed beneath her foot, and she wavered, fighting for her balance.

"Here." A deep, masculine voice, holding no little amusement, hailed her from some distance in front of her.

She looked up, but she had already recognized Rivenhall's voice. "What are you doing here?" she demanded.

Yet pleasure warmed her—at being rescued, not at seeing him.

"I have come to find you. Miss Abbott and Mrs. Easham assured me they expected you back hours ago, and they were becoming most concerned." His wide mouth broadened in a contagious grin as he observed her predicament. "A lady in distress, it seems." He stepped onto the first stone on his side, then the second, so that only two separated them, and extended his hand to her, leaning across the tumbling waters so her fingers could grasp his.

The contact left her breathless. With an effort, she recalled the precariousness of her position, clasped his hand firmly, and trusted in his strength as she jumped the unsteady stone and landed before him. His arm swept about her waist, and the next moment he stooped, his other catching her behind the knees, and he swept her into his arms. She gasped, but whether in outrage or surprise, she honestly didn't know. A soft laugh sounded in her ear as he took one careful step, then reached the safety of the bank.

"I must make a habit of rescuing beautiful young ladies more often," he said, his tone provocative. He made no attempt to set her on her feet.

She considered trying to free herself, but that would hardly be dignified. And more to the point, she greatly feared he might enjoy her struggles. She settled for saying, with a hint of coldness: "Thank you, but I could have managed quite well without being carried."

"Ah, but I find it much more intriguing this way. Do not you?"

"No," she lied. "I most certainly do not. Will you please set me down?"

He did—very slowly, holding her close against himself in a manner that she would have found shocking if she'd been able to think clearly. She tried to pull back, but discovered herself held securely. A slow, tantalizing smile played about his mouth.

"What?" he asked softly. "Would you leave without paying your forfeit?"

"Would you demand another of me?"

"I would."

Before she could protest, he caught her closer still, tight against his chest, and kissed her. For a moment she froze, shocked and outraged, then a wave of chaotic sensations swept through her. Longing for she knew not what overcame common sense, and she returned the caress with an ardency she'd thought alien to her nature. A stolen kiss, she thought with hazy indignation, should be brutal, or tentative. So why must she find this wholly and alarmingly wonderful?

As abruptly as he'd seized her, she found herself free. She faced him, too stunned—and too confused—to react, to give him the blistering set-down he so richly deserved. He, too, stared at her, his dark eyes glinting, his expression unreadable.

He stepped back and swept her a mocking bow. "It has been a pleasure to be of service."

The gleam in his eyes disturbed her, but more so did the proprietary air with which he seemed to regard her, as if he counted her already his own. That, she couldn't allow. She opened her eyes to their widest, and adopted her most blistering, sarcastic tone. "What a delightful experience for us both, to be sure," she drawled. "Why, now that I know what I have to look forward to, I shall abandon any pretense at embroidery completely."

Without awaiting his response, she pushed past him and marched toward the copse. She would, in fact, redouble her efforts at her stitchery. No matter how glorious his touch might be, she would not—*could* not—succumb to a man who treated romance like a game of conquest.

His deep, appreciative laugh drifted after her, sending

her pulse racing in a manner that should have been foreign to one of her staid disposition. Until she had the misfortune of meeting Lord Rivenhall, she had always considered herself to be a practical young woman, level-headed and with her feet firmly planted on the ground. Yet every time she encountered him, she found herself teetering, and not just on unsteady rocks in the middle of streams.

A short walk brought her out of the trees and into the fields of the home farm. These she crossed, then hurried across the neatly scythed lawn. She'd bypass the conservatory door, she decided, and then circle around to the music room and let herself in by the French windows.

For the moment, no one sat at the pianoforte or the harp, which allowed her to pause a moment to compose herself. But only a moment. A glance at the ormolu clock on the mantel warned her she was unconscionably late; Jennings would have despaired of her this half hour and more. Feeling somewhat like an errant schoolroom miss, she slipped along the corridor and up the stairs without encountering anyone.

Her abigail awaited her in her chamber, her narrow features set in lines of disapproval. Not until she had helped Amanda out of her soiled walking dress did she speak.

"I would never stoop to criticize, Miss," she said, as she tossed a dinner gown of peach crepe over Amanda's head, "but how I am to turn you out with any degree of credit, I cannot say."

"I use you shamefully," Amanda agreed, and was rewarded with a sniff and a silence that lasted until Jennings was arranging her long hair into a vastly becoming style.

A knock sounded on the door, and a vexed exclamation escaped the sorely tried abigail. Amanda called for the intruder to enter, and Bentley stuck his head into the room.

"What, not ready yet?" He sprawled in a chair, one leg swinging idly. "I must say, that Rivenhall is really a Trojan."

She spun about to stare at him, eliciting a cry of protest from Jennings. "How can you say that!" she demanded.

"Oh, as to that wretched evening of piquet, he must have been badly foxed. You have to admit, he found a graceful way out of making me pay."

Amanda would admit no such thing, but she bit back the words. Bentley, she reminded herself once more, had no notion of his idol's despicable "way out."

Jennings put the finishing touches on her hair, then turned to the jewelry box. "The pearls, Miss?"

Amanda considered for only a moment. "The topazes."

"You cannot mean it, Miss!" Jennings shook her head. "What your dear mama would say."

A half-laugh escaped Amanda. "For heaven's sake, I am no green girl in my first Season."

"Nor your second, for that matter," stuck in her ever-helpful brother.

"Thank you, dear Bentley. As my brother has so kindly pointed out, I am an ape leader."

Jennings gasped. "You are no such thing, Miss."

"Well, I am five-and-twenty, and have no inclination to be wed. What else would you call me?"

"Nothing so vulgar," her abigail sniffed.

"The topazes," Amanda repeated, and studied her reflection while Jennings retrieved the necklace and earrings from the meager contents of the box. The jewels would set off the simplicity of the peach crepe, lending her a sophistication that pearls could never equal.

And she wanted to appear sophisticated tonight. She wanted to appear cool and collected, to make it abundantly clear to a certain gentleman that his behavior had been too contemptible for comment—or at least beneath her notice. If only she'd been blessed with glowing dark curls like Diana Kingsford instead of her pale mass of yellow hair. Dark coloring always made one appear so strong.

Bentley eyed the result. "Elegant," he pronounced with a grin. "Are you trying to impress anyone in particular?"

"Yes, that most exacting of all critics. Myself."

"The hardest of all," Bentley agreed. He waited while Jennings draped a shawl of Norwich silk over Amanda's elbows, then escorted her down the stairs.

The meal dragged its way through course after course, and Amanda's impatience grew with each new presentation. At last it drew to a close, and she escaped to the drawing room with the other ladies. She took the precaution of sitting beside Miss Abbott before beginning work on her embroidery. Now Rivenhall could not object to her stitching on the grounds that she shunned any social obligations; she could pursue both occupations at once. Listening with only half her attention to a lengthy anecdote, she began filling in the background of stormy sky.

The expression of vexation on Rivenhall's face when the gentlemen joined the ladies delighted her. It wasn't easy besting him, and she took her meager victories where she could find them. She directed a sweet smile at him, responded to Miss Abbott's most recent comment, and redoubled her efforts on the handkerchief.

A minute later, though, he stood before her, his devilish smile dancing in his eyes. "Miss Grieves, will you not honor us by playing upon the pianoforte?"

She opened her eyes to their widest. "But I cannot desert Miss Abbott."

"My love, of course you must!" cried the vexing Miss Abbott. "Oh, dear, it will be of all things the most delightful to hear you play again. It has been this age! And will you not sing, as well? How I remember that delightful tune your dear mama used to love so. Would you play that ballad for me?"

Amanda managed to maintain a polite expression of acquiescence, but it taxed her considerably. She made her way to the instrument, followed by her mocking tormentor, and took her seat. Rather than leaving her, he adopted a position at her side, sorting through music, presenting her with the lengthy requested ballad, promising to assist her in any manner possible.

Each time he turned a page—quite unnecessarily, for she knew the music perfectly well—his arm brushed hers—also quite unnecessarily. It played havoc with her concentration, evoking sensations of his cradling her against his chest, of his mouth claiming hers in a kiss that still burned on her lips. It didn't mean anything to him, she reminded herself with a ferocity that left her aching for denial. He made a very effective game of seducing her, nothing more. Her reaction to it appalled her.

As soon as she could, she excused herself on the pretext of seeking her bed, but in fact to have several undisturbed hours with her embroidery. She settled once again in the chair before her fireplace with a branch of working candles at her side, but instead of concentrating on her stitching, her thoughts wandered back to the evening when she first saw Rivenhall. Perversely, she recalled every encounter since then, every word, every touch, every sensation, until the settling of a log on the grate recalled her with a start to a sense of the present.

She looked at the handkerchief clutched in her hand, started to set a stitch, then frowned. Lord Rivenhall's lingering presence in her mind—or had he taken up residence in her being?—had driven the images of Leda and her feathery companion from her completely. Vexed, she wrapped herself in her dressing gown, picked up her candle, and made her way down the stairs to Lord Pelham's study.

Standing before the painting, she held her candle aloft, trying to engrave the varying shades into her memory.

Yet even as she concentrated on her task, her flesh seemed to tingle, as if Rivenhall touched her. He might almost be at her side, so vividly did she feel his presence.

"What brought you here?" his deep voice asked, little more than a whisper from the midst of the darkness behind her. "A desire to see Leda—or me?"

She didn't answer, merely allowed his rich tones to roll over her, through her. Some part of her had known he was there, sensed him, wanted him. He moved then, his footsteps the merest brushing on the softness of the carpet, until he halted behind her, so close her shoulder brushed against his chest.

"The color of that rock in the foreground should be difficult for you to match in silk," he said, his voice still hushed.

"I can blend something quite similar," she managed. His breath warmed her cheek; he must be looking down at her. If she had any sense, she would move away from him. Apparently, she didn't have any sense. She caught herself, barely stopping from swaying back against him. Why couldn't he be a decent man instead of an unconscionable rake?

Because, a little voice warned her, she wouldn't be attracted to him if he weren't dangerous, if there weren't an aura of intense masculinity about him.

With an effort of will, she pulled away from him. "There. I have studied what I needed. I shall return to my room now." She started for the door.

Before she had taken two steps, he caught her by the shoulders, spun her about, and dragged her into his arms. His hands, rather than pressing her close, slid illicitly and tantalizingly over her back, her waist, her shoulders. His mouth demanded her very soul. She burned, returning his caresses with a passion she couldn't control. Nothing mattered but him, the wild sensations he created in her, the certainty that she belonged in his arms.

At last he drew back, and his lips brushed hers in a last, tender kiss. She caught at it, stealing one more before relinquishing her joy, then stood gazing at him, helpless, unable to break the spell of his weaving.

His lips pressed gently on her forehead. "I wish you a good night, my dear." And with that, he strode from the room.

She sank onto the nearest chair, shaken. How could any contact between two people be so earth-shattering, so perfect, so all-enveloping? If this were a sample of the unknown pleasures that awaited her in his bed, those ladies who cried out for the preservation of their virtue at all costs were sadly misled.

And would it be so very dreadful, the thought pushed its way into her mind, for a spinster without any hope of marriage to indulge herself in just one night of such wondrous, glorious passion?

FIVE

So, Miss Amanda Grieves had succumbed to his practiced seduction. Rivenhall possessed far too much experience not to recognize the signs. Had he remained in his host's study so much as another two minutes, she would have lost her precious control. He could have led her upstairs to his chamber and into his bed, and she would have come willingly, helplessly.

Damn it all, had he remained there another two minutes, he would have lost his own precious control, and taken her with the passion that burned, hot and terrible, throughout him.

He paced to the window of his room and glared out through the darkness, across the lawn toward the copse of trees. He'd succeeded, and rage filled him rather than the anticipated satisfaction.

She was no *fille de joi,* to be taken in casual conquest to fulfill a drunken wager. Nor was she one of any score of young ladies without a thought in their heads beyond gratifying their matrimonial ambitions. Had she been, he could have taken her and known not a moment's qualm. Or better, why could she not have been a bored young matron like Diana Kingsford with a weather eye cocked for an entertaining lover? Instead, he had preyed upon a lady of character and charm, who deserved better than a rakehell.

He shunned his large and empty bed, instead settling himself in a wing-back chair. For a long while he brooded on the perversity of fate; then at last drifted off, still disgusted with himself.

He went late on purpose to the breakfast table, then couldn't decide whether he was pleased or disappointed that she wasn't there. Pleased, he assured himself. That was the reason he'd come late; he knew she habitually breakfasted at an early hour. He didn't want to see her.

He repeated this thought while he consumed a rare beefsteak and tankard of ale. He would go riding this morning, he decided, a long, reckless dash across country to release this pent-up energy that made him so restless. Having reached this decision, he promptly abandoned it, for the simple reason that if he rode, he would not see Miss Amanda Grieves for the several hours he'd intended to be gone.

Which reminded him; he hadn't seen her yet this morning. He abandoned his half-eaten breakfast and went in search of her.

He made a quick tour of the salons and gardens, encountering every other member of the house party except the one he sought. He responded to all greetings with a tolerable civility that grew more and more curt as he failed to unearth her. Then her obvious location struck him, and he set forth for Pelham's study.

And there she stood, before the picture of Leda and the Swan, bending slightly to examine the swirl of water in the lower right hand corner. Satisfaction flooded through him, and for long minutes he leaned against the doorjamb, studying her every bit as intently as she studied the painted patterns of color. Why had he never noticed how slender she was, how softly rounded her curves? She straightened, and he marveled at the grace of so simple a movement.

She started for the sofa, where the handkerchief and

silks awaited her return, only to stop short, her eyes widening, then clouding, as her gaze fell on him. Uncertainty—or was it fear?—flickered across her expressive countenance, and she looked away. "Good morning," she said with only a trace of a quaver in her voice, and resumed her seat.

"You stayed up late," he declared, annoyed. He could see the strain in her eyes. She'd undoubtedly sat up half the night, if not longer, sewing desperately to save her virtue.

"I had the best of all possible motives." She didn't look up. Instead, she concentrated on setting her stitches, as if she were afraid at any moment to be dragged away from her task.

He turned on his heel and strode from the room. Let her work, poor child. The devil take it, he wished—savagely so—that he had never made that infamous wager with her. To have treated her with so little respect, subjected her to so coarse an insult, was unpardonable, the trick of a vulgar makebait. It dawned on him that he would coolly put a bullet through any man who treated her in so damnable a manner.

Yet he had done so.

What had possessed him to behave like the merest shabster, a curst rum touch? He cast his mind back to that first night, when his head had been bleary from too much wine. She'd faced him with contempt, he remembered that much. Her attitude had amused him, yet it had irritated him as well. It had made him want to shock her out of her self-righteous wrath, to scandalize her. Yet she hadn't responded with missish simperings or a fit of the vapors, as he'd expected. She'd shown pluck, courage, honor—every admirable quality he had lacked.

He couldn't cancel the wager. But he would see to it that she had every opportunity to complete that embroidery, even if it meant keeping all the other members of the house party away from her. He would begin with himself. Yet he could think of nothing he wanted to do that did not involve Miss Amanda Grieves.

Six other guests, along with their host and hostess, graced Pelham Court. Surely he could entertain himself without her. He could go bird watching with Mr. Somes. Or angling with Mr. Easham. Or he could escort Diana Kingsford on a riding expedition. Or go shooting with Sir Bentley Grieves.

Sir Bentley. Miss Grieves's brother, the cause of her concern. That young cub could use a bear leader, someone to try to insert some sense, or at least some worldly wisdom, into his empty head. Struck by a sudden—and highly unprecedented— fit of nobility, he decided to undertake that role.

He found him in the billiards room, moodily taking odd and unsuccessful shots from difficult angles. Rivenhall watched for a few moments, then asked, "Would you care to go into Brighton this morning?"

Bentley, who had just started a shot, sent the ball skittering wildly around the table. He watched it until it rolled at last to a shaky stop, then said simply, but with considerable feeling, "Yes."

A quarter of an hour later, Rivenhall stood in the main hall, drawing on his driving gloves, waiting for his curricle to be brought round. Behind him he heard Bentley's excited voice, then the softer, more melodic answer of Miss Grieves. He spun about to see them emerging from the Gold Salon and was struck by the contrast between the quiet elegance of the lady and the gangly, dashing style of the young gentleman. Definitely, the lad needed taking in hand.

Miss Grieves paused, eying him with undisguised suspicion. "I hear you have invited my brother to accompany you into Brighton." *What mischief,* her tone implied, *are you brewing?*

"I felt like a breath of sea air, and wanted company. If you like," he added to Bentley, somewhat rashly, "I shall teach you to handle the ribbons."

"I—" Bentley broke off, flushing with pleasure. "By Jove, do you really mean it? Will you? That would be capital, my lord. I told you he was a regular Trojan," he added to his sister.

Had he indeed? The words took Rivenhall aback. What had he ever done to earn the boy's good opinion? He'd only succeeded in winning an enormous sum from him at cards—and at what should have been the sanctuary of a house party, at that—which should have had the opposite effect.

They left a few minutes later, with Bentley taking uncertain control of the pair and Rivenhall's tiger perched grimly behind. The lad proved to be an apt pupil, showing distinct promise and an innate skill, and Rivenhall ceased to worry for his much-loved blacks. In fact, as the hours slid by, he found himself well pleased with his companion, a state of affairs he could not have imagined when they set forth.

Upon reflection, he could discover only one flaw in the day: Miss Amanda Grieves did not share it with him. He made do with her brother, introducing him to a select club, listening to his confidences, advising him on the best way of identifying and avoiding cardsharps, even nipping in the bud a desire by his young charge to commit the sartorial atrocity of purchasing an unsuitably spotted neckcloth. The boy wasn't a complete fool, merely inexperienced and a shade too eager to appear all the crack. A steadying hand on his rein was all he needed.

They returned to Pelham Court late that afternoon, both in surprisingly good humor. Rivenhall left Bentley in the care of his own groom, to be talked out of purchasing one of Pelham's horses. As he strode off in search of Miss Grieves, he could hear the lad's voice extolling

the virtues of the animal, and the groom's more nasal
assertions that the dratted screw was touched in the wind.

Altruism sat oddly on his shoulders, Rivenhall reflected. His day-long effort left him absurdly pleased with
himself, yet in all honesty, bear-leading that young cub
hadn't proved nearly as dull as he'd assumed it would
be. In fact, he'd quite enjoyed the whelp's flattering
hero-worship.

He went first to Pelham's study, but Miss Grieves wasn't
there. He then made a methodical search of every salon
and drawing room, and his impatience to see her grew
with every blank he drew. At last he set forth around the
grounds, and finally ran her to earth in the rose garden.
She sat on a stone bench near its center, stitching indus-
triously, the westering sun gleaming on her flaxen hair.
He had to fight the urge to run his fingers through it,
to feel its silky softness.

As he crunched along the gravel path to join her, she
looked up, and an air of apprehension settled over her.
He cursed himself for causing her additional distress.
"Your brother came to no harm at my hands," he assured
her at once.

"Indeed?" Her eyebrows rose in patent disbelief.

Her reaction irritated him. But then, she hadn't a single reason to assume he had an ounce of either consid-
eration or kindness in him. That thought he found deeply
disturbing.

"Indeed," he confirmed. He reached for her embroidery, spreading out the handkerchief he no longer recognized as his own. "You've accomplished a great deal."

She still had a long way to go, though. Considering the
quality of her work, it amazed him that she had completed as much as she had. Another lady might have done
the job quickly, carelessly, contemptuously, as it undoubtedly deserved. But not Miss Amanda Grieves. She had
lavished loving care with every stitch, blending her colors

to exquisite shades, honoring every detail of that appalling canvas.

Except for Leda. So far, she had done no more than mark the outline of that provocative female form. He couldn't help but wonder in what detail his well-bred Miss Grieves would portray that lady's unclothed voluptuousness.

He seated himself on the bench at her side, looking forward to giving her an account of his day with her brother. But rather than allowing this, she retrieved the handkerchief from him and rose, stuffing her silks into their bag as she did so. With a polite nod of her head, she started for the house.

He caught up with her in three long strides. "You are in quite a hurry."

"It is time to dress for dinner."

And that was all he got out of her. She walked quickly, as if finding his presence distasteful—as well she might. He contented himself with walking at her side, though he was compelled to leave her in the hall when she was claimed by Miss Abbott. He watched the two ladies mount the stairs together, and felt oddly bereft.

Once in his own room, he dressed quickly, impatient at his man's slowness. Much sooner than his valet could like, he pronounced himself ready and hurried down to the salon where the party gathered before dinner. Only Mr. Somes was before him, and he found himself watching the door, waiting for Miss Grieves to enter at last.

One by one, the others put in their appearances. Rivenhall joined in the small talk, though it seemed even more fatuous than usual. The elderly Mr. Somes cornered him, droning on about the regrettable lack of proper feeling among the wealthy, the neglect of their duty toward the poor, and the only thing that kept Rivenhall polite was his respect for the man's age and cloth.

Then Miss Grieves entered the room, and suddenly the

evening brightened for him, as if myriad candles had all burst into flame. She moved with such grace, she had dressed with such quiet elegance, his heart swelled with pride in her. He followed her with his gaze, oblivious to anyone else.

"Rivenhall?" Mr. Somes tugged at his sleeve. "Are you all right?"

Rivenhall turned back to him, still bemused. "What? Oh, yes. Let me write you a draft on my bank. Will a thousand pounds help, do you think?" Absently, he drew out his notebook, scrawled the necessary information, tore out the sheet and handed it over.

Mr. Somes opened his mouth, closed it again, and stared at the paper in his hand, for once bereft of speech.

Rivenhall crossed the room to where Miss Grieves stood with Lady Pelham, smiling at something her hostess said. She glanced toward him, and a wary expression crept into her beautiful eyes. Yet he would have sworn a touch of wistfulness lingered there as well.

Neatly, he detached her from Lady Pelham. "You were long in coming down. Have you been embroidering?"

"I assure you," she informed him coldly, "I did not neglect any social duties by doing so. I also assure you I will have it completed on time."

"By Saturday night at eleven? That leaves you very little time."

Her chin rose. "Do you doubt me?"

"No," he admitted with devastating honesty. "I admire you."

Her eyebrows rose. "Indeed," was all she said.

Somehow, this wasn't going as well as he'd hoped. He tried again. "May I see what you have added?"

"As you wish. I have left my workbag in the drawing room, though. Why not wait until after dinner?"

Lord Pelham claimed his attention then, asking about his visit to Brighton, and Miss Grieves slipped away. His gaze followed her, and he caught the backward glance she cast at him. Satisfaction mingled with uncertainty— and left him hopelessly confused.

Throughout the ensuing dinner, his attention wandered from his food, all the way down the table to where Miss Grieves sat in conversation with Mr. Somes. Yet almost every time he looked at her, she also glanced up, then quickly away. Either she sensed his scrutiny with unerring accuracy, or she watched him in the same manner—no, with the same intensity—with which he watched her.

Diana Kingsford, who sat on his right, gave his arm a coy rap. "You are quite distracted this night. I must suppose I am boring you."

"Impossible," he announced at once, but in truth she did bore him. Her opulent charms seemed coarse, her flirtatious manner vulgar. And as for her willingness to cuckold her husband, he found it blatant and no longer in the least tempting.

Nor, he realized, did he experience even the faintest desire to flirt with any female whatsoever—with one notable exception.

Lady Pelham rose at last, signaling the ladies to withdraw. Rivenhall found himself left to the decanters of port and brandy, and the society of men. This state of affairs didn't please him, either, and he brooded on this unaccountable change in his attitude.

An invitation to play piquet with his host—for stakes outlandish enough to appeal to him under normal circumstances—he refused without a thought. Bentley looked up, obviously intrigued and appalled by the sum named, a wine-borne recklessness glittering in his eyes. Rivenhall rose. "A game of billiards, my boy?" That would at least keep the young scapegrace from the gaming tables.

Bentley agreed with delight. Mr. Somes announced his

intention to join them, and the threesome made their way to the billiards room.

Normally, Rivenhall enjoyed holding a cue and took keen interest in devising the precise angles required for his shots. Tonight, he derived little pleasure in the pastime. With increasing frequency, his thoughts wandered to the ladies. Miss Grieves would be embroidering, of course. He wondered if he might ask her to perform upon the pianoforte once more. Her voice, with its rich, musical quality, was made for singing; he would take great pleasure in hearing her again. But that would take much-needed time from her work, just to satisfy a whim of his.

"Rivenhall?" Mr. Somes's amused voice recalled him.

Rivenhall took his turn. The sooner the game ended, the happier he would be.

Bentley cleared his throat. "I've been thinking about that horse, my lord. I just can't believe he's such a gasper. I'd rather like to try him. Would you care to ride with me in the morning? Not for long, of course," he added quickly. "And not if you shouldn't like it. But I should value your opinion."

"An excellent plan," Rivenhall declared, yet the prospect left him cold. *Why?* he wondered. He loved to ride, loved the freedom of racing cross-country, loved the sense of unity with his mount. So why didn't he want to go?

Because Miss Grieves would not be with him. If she were to ride, it would be a very different matter.

It dawned on him, with a jolt that sent reverberations throughout his entire being, that he no longer found pleasure in any pastime that did not intimately involve Miss Grieves. Piquet, billiards, riding—it was all the same. If she were not at his side, nothing appealed to him.

Almost, he might have fallen in love with her.

But that, of course, was preposterous. If he ever succumbed to love, it would be for a lady who sparkled with spirit, who rose to any challenge, who could parry any verbal sword thrust, who could give as good as she received.

A lady, in fact, exactly like Miss Amanda Grieves.

Good lord, he *had* fallen in love with her.

The realization appalled him, leaving him at a loss to know what to do about it.

SIX

Amanda eyed her handiwork with a frown, set another stitch, and said absently, "How true."

Miss Abbott smiled brightly at her. "Indeed, it is, my love," she declared, and resumed her rambling tale.

Amanda embroidered her way along an outflung wing. She had no idea what Miss Abbott talked about; her thoughts remained fixed on her task at hand. Or rather, on why she dawdled so over plying her needle.

She should be stitching furiously in order to finish this odious handkerchief by the next night. Yet she labored over every detail, taking her time, even revisiting Pelham's study to doublecheck her accuracy. The only explanation could be that she didn't want to finish this wretched work on time.

She stabbed the needle through the fine cloth, jabbed her finger, and pulled it away with an exasperated exclamation.

"I do say so indeed, my love," said Miss Abbott, nodding, and continued her story.

I am being foolish beyond permission, Amanda told herself in silent wrath. No lady of quality could consider, for so much as a moment, *deliberately* laying down her virtue. Evocative memories of Rivenhall's teasing touch, of his dancing eyes, of the scent of bay rum that clung to him, filled her mind, haunting her. Ruthlessly, she thrust them to the back, tamped them down, refused to luxuriate in them. She would finish the lecherous swan and depict all of Leda and her scandalous charms with just the sketchiest of stitching.

After all, Rivenhall probably wouldn't mind. He'd given her the entire day to work on it, leaving the estate in the company of her brother, of all people. That, surely, had not been an expedition of pleasure for him. The more she thought about it, the more she became convinced only one explanation could exist for this abrupt change of tactics on his part. He now wanted her to finish. He'd lost interest in her. He'd rather have her embroidered rendition of the risqué artwork on his handkerchief than her person.

She found the idea lowering.

On impulse, she jumped to her feet, called a vague excuse over her shoulder, and went to confront Leda in person. For a long while she stood before the canvas, candle in hand, studying the lady's flagrantly displayed charms. The term "opulent" came to mind. Amanda mentally compared her own physical attributes with those of the statuesque Leda, and found herself sadly lacking.

Apparently, Rivenhall did, too.

Well, if Leda was what he wanted, she'd see to it he got her in every exacting, deplorable detail.

The door opened behind her, and she spun about, embarrassed by her turbulent emotions, and stared straight into the glowering face of Rivenhall himself. He stopped just over the threshold, excused himself, and started to withdraw.

"I am so sorry," Amanda said before she could stop herself. "Have you come to visit Leda? Never fear, you may have her to yourself. I was just leaving."

He hesitated, then came into the room, closing the door behind himself. His gaze rested on Amanda, studying her with an odd, perturbed expression in his eyes.

Slowly, almost reluctantly, he moved forward until he stood only a few feet from her.

Her chin rose. She was no fool to be bewitched by his rugged good looks, the aura of power that emanated from him. She *didn't* want to smooth an errant lock of hair from his forehead or feel the strength of his arms about her once more. She especially didn't want her knees to go weak, as they did now, just from his being so near.

"How do you go on?" His voice came out harsh from too much drink, rasping from the repression of some strong emotion.

"Perfectly well, my lord." In defiance—but whether of him or her own errant longings, she couldn't be sure— she held up her handiwork. "I shall finish easily."

He took a corner of the fine lawn and examined it, spreading it over his hand to clearly display the multitude of stitches, the blending of colors, the exquisite details so painstakingly rendered. "You are doing a remarkable job," he said.

The sincerity of his tone took her aback. Teasing and taunting—these she knew from him. Sincerity seemed alien to his character. It confused her. She pulled the handkerchief away from him. "The rewards of honest labor," she said. "You should try it some time. Or do you only take pride in the reprehensible?"

As soon as the last words escaped her mouth, she regretted them. A sudden gleam lit his eyes, her only warning. Before she could beat a prudent retreat, he dragged her into his arms. His kiss silenced her protest, burning her mouth, leaving her weak and clinging to him, oblivious to all but the tangy, spicy scent of his skin and the mulled-brandy taste of his mouth. Her hands caught at the back of his neck as she melted against him, savoring every aspect of his touch and the wild, riotous sensations that ran unrestrained through her.

Caution, rational thought, prudence had no chance. All that mattered she found here, in his arms. And here was the only place she wanted to be.

Abruptly he released her, then pushed her away. For a long moment he stared down into her face, fury rampant on his own. Then he turned on his heel and stormed from the room.

Amanda moved on unsteady legs to a chair, where she collapsed. What had happened? Why had everything changed? What had been teasing, tantalizing, fun for him, suddenly had become bitter and angry. She blinked rapidly, refusing to allow the tears that brimmed in her eyes to fall. Somehow, she had given him a disgust of her.

And try as she might, she could not convince herself this was all for the good.

Rivenhall strode into the hall, then stopped, not sure where to go. His natural instincts would be to seek out the study, a peaceful room since Lady Pelham permanently had exiled the cardplayers, but he'd just left there. And not for anything would he return to Miss Grieves.

Miss Grieves. Amanda. He started back, to allow his gaze to dwell upon her, then firmly resisted the desire. What right had a disgraceful libertine like himself to torment the most delightful—and eminently respectable—lady he had ever known?

He strode along the corridor until he reached the dining room, but the efficient butler had long since removed the decanters. And a decanter was what he wanted. Thwarted, he continued his search, going next to the salon where they had gathered before the meal. He'd prefer brandy, but he'd accept Madeira.

Here, luck favored him, and he poured a glass full of the ruby liquid. He drained it, poured another, and sprawled in a chair, glowering into space, his eyes seeing not the upholstered furnishings, cherry-wood tables with their knickknacks and gewgaws, the Aubusson carpet, but Amanda's sweet face. Every angle, every expression, every flash of her huge gray eyes, he knew by heart.

He went to pour himself another glass, and this time brought the decanter back with him.

Only a cad would have kissed her just then. For the first time in memory, he took no pride in being a cad. It only filled him with fury at himself.

He'd done nothing to earn the sweetness of her response. He'd done nothing but insult her, treat her like some casual bit o' muslin. He'd behaved in the foulest manner possible.

Yet she'd clung to him, gazed at him as if he were in some manner admirable instead of the creature he was, wholly devoid of virtue.

He disgusted himself.

He'd set out to seduce her, and he hovered on the verge of success. If he returned to the study, right now, and kissed her one more time . . . Heat raged through him, desire for her, to feel her in his arms, to savor her kiss. He wanted nothing more than that.

Or did he? For once, the satisfaction of physical desire trailed some other, indecipherable need. He set to work deciphering it.

This involved the draining of the decanter, which he completed all too soon. A return to the tray revealed that only ratafia and cooled negus remained to lubricate his thinking process—not a difficult choice—and he settled once more in his chair with the former at his side. He took a healthy swallow from his newly filled glass, and the scent of almonds brought Amanda vividly to mind.

Amanda. He could have his night with her. Desire coursed through him. In less than twenty-fours, he could claim her. She would honor her bet, come to his bed, do all he required of her. He could see to it that she found intense delight in it as well.

But she would never forgive him.

He brooded on that, making considerable inroads on the ratafia. He wanted her—more intensely and achingly than he'd ever wanted any woman—yet somehow, everything had changed. He'd planned a simple seduction. He'd cared only for the gratification of his own libidinous desire, not a whit for the cost to Amanda. Yet that cost to himself, now, would be just as great.

If she never forgave him, if she never spoke to him again, he couldn't bear it.

When he took Amanda—*if* he were so fortunate as to be able to possess her—he didn't want it to be a sordid, disgraceful affair. Not for one night, he realized. Not even for a liaison of a few weeks or even months. If he took her, he wanted it to be for the rest of their lives. Nothing else would satisfy him.

But what were the odds a lady of her character would be willing to wed a ramshackle libertine like him? He was a gambling man, but these were odds on which he would not care to wager.

Yet he intended to do just that.

He would drive up to London, leaving at first light—only a very few hours from now, in fact. If he had a fresh pair harnessed for the return journey, and if he wasted not a moment on his errands, he could procure a special license, buy a ring, and still be back before eleven o'clock. And then, if Amanda had not yet completed her embroidery, he would ask her to be his wife.

What she would say to that was another matter. She might accept him to sustain her honor. Or she might reject him, preferring a spot of tarnished honor to a lifetime tied to a man she might well despise.

Or she might take the dilemma out of his hands before he returned. With another whole day to embroider without interruption, she might well finish the handkerchief. Then he had only to accept it as her payment in full and watch her walk away.

The door to the salon opened, and Rivenhall hunched down in his chair, not wanting to see anyone. Unless it was Amanda. The intensity of his desire to gaze upon her tore at him, warning him he could never just let her walk away. Whether or not she finished that damnable bit of embroidery, he had to try for her hand. Without her, he could never be happy.

He peered carefully around the shielding upholstered chair back, but only a footman, bearing a snuffer, came into view; the man withdrew at sight of an occupant. It must be time and past that Rivenhall sought his bed. He rose and made his way to the main hall, where three chambersticks remained on the table at the foot of the great oak staircase. Might one of them be Amanda's? He climbed the first eight steps, paused, then marched back down and made his way to the study.

She sat in a chair she had drawn up before the painting, with a multi-branched candelabrum at her side. She worked feverishly, stitching in a silvery gray color, outlining and highlighting each feather. His heart swelled with pride, in her conscientiousness, in her determination, in her spirit that would not give up.

Neither would he. He would fight for her.

She had turned when he'd opened the door, but had resumed her work. He watched her for a few moments, noted the tensing of her slender shoulders beneath the light covering of her Norwich silk shawl, the straightening of her back, the lifting of her head. She might give the appearance of ignoring him, but her posture betrayed her. Yet whether her awareness of him lay in attraction or anger, he couldn't be certain.

At last, she said without looking at him: "Did you wish

to speak to me, or am I interrupting your tryst with Leda?"

He did wish to speak to her, but now was not the time. He stared at the elegant curve of her neck, at the curling mound of fair hair pinned into artless curls about her head. No suitable words came to him to express the longing to touch her, the desire to call her his own, to share his life with her. Not yet. Not until this detestable bet was over with, finished, and could be put behind them. Then he could speak.

"I must assume I am *de trop*," she said, her gaze still on her work. "But my need for Leda is greater than yours, so tonight you must share her." She turned then, her arched eyebrows raised, a look of pure contempt on her features.

He would prefer her smile. Assuming an air of nonchalance, he said, "I came to tell you I will be away tomorrow."

She opened her eyes wide. "What a tragedy," she declared in a voice of complete indifference. "However shall we manage to get along?"

"How, indeed?" He went to her, claimed one hand, and carried her fingers to his lips. "Will you convey my apologies to your brother for me? We were to ride in the morning." He tightened his hold on her. "I shall not see you before I go."

"I shall try not to fall into a decline."

She wouldn't, he reflected as he made his way up the stairs to his chamber. Unlike himself, she was the master of her own emotions. He might have come close to seducing her, but in the end, her head would rule her, not her heart.

And her head had no reason to love him.

SEVEN

An entire day, all to herself, without any threat of interruption from Lord Rivenhall. It didn't seem possible to Amanda. It also didn't seem to offer any joy, such as welled within her each time she saw him.

More fool, she.

Yet she wasn't fool enough to let her opportunities slip. As soon as she had breakfasted, she retired to the study and set diligently to work. Her fingers might ache from the long hours of clasping the needle, her eyes might blur with strain and exhaustion, but she would finish. And she would fling the completed piece at Rivenhall with all the contempt it—and he—deserved.

And then— Well, she didn't know what would happen then. One thing of which she was certain—she would not hide behind excuses, either contrived or real. If she went to his bed, it would be of her own free choice, because she wished it, and *not* pretending it was because she had lost the wager.

She *must* finish before eleven o'clock.

She stitched steadily, breaking only for a light nuncheon, needing those few minutes to rest her eyes and hands. As soon as she had consumed a few mouthfuls, she slipped away once more and returned to her labors in the study.

She *would* finish, even if it meant she could never see or stitch again.

Her tension increased as the minutes sped past. With every tick of the mantel clock, her precious few remaining hours slipped away. Her fingers cramped, and still she worked on. Yet despite the efforts of the day, she had not yet completed Leda's upper portions when Jennings came in search of her, informing her she had been waiting that half hour and more to dress her charge for dinner. Amanda went with reluctance, taking the handkerchief with her to set stitches even while her abigail arranged her hair in a smooth, elegant style, drawn back from her face. Approved by Jennings at last, she hurried down to the salon to find she was the last to arrive but one.

As soon as she entered, the butler followed her through the door and announced dinner. Amanda, vividly aware of the identity of the absentee, turned to her hostess. "Will not Lord Rivenhall be joining us?"

"He said he might be quite late, and not to wait for him. Oh, dear, Miss Abbott has her shawl entangled. Excuse me, my love." And Lady Pelham hurried to the aid of her guest.

So Rivenhall would not be present. A lack of that gentleman could only improve the meal, she assured herself, but the thought carried no conviction. Whatever occupied him, whatever kept him away, she resented. The house party would end on the morrow; she and Rivenhall would go their separate ways, probably never to meet again. These few days out of time, out of the everyday world, were all they would ever share. What had happened here with him—the shocking wager, the outrageous flirtation, her own passionate response—she would always remember, though it held no reality or relevance to her life.

The meal proceeded from course to delectable course, but Amanda had no very clear idea what she ate. She

possessed little appetite this night. She wanted only to
finish, to return to her embroidery, to complete her task
before Rivenhall returned.

The door to the dining room opened, but this time it
admitted no footmen laden with steaming trays. Rivenhall
himself stood there, his gaze scanning the diners until it
rested on Amanda. It burned into her, probing, questioning. For a long moment she returned it, trying very hard
to convey defiance with the upward tilt of her chin and
a disdainful stare that threatened to turn into a smile of
welcome. But that would never do. She returned her attention to her plate, and Rivenhall made his way to the
foot of the table to make his apologies to his hostess.

She hadn't actually completed the embroidery yet.
That knowledge filled her, sending a tingling thrill of
nerves, of longing, through her. He could still ensure that
she did not fulfill her wager, simply by remaining at her
side this evening. Then once the others had retired to
their beds . . .

Remembered sensations—of his touch, of his kiss, of
the strength of his arms as he swept her off her feet—
flooded her mind. She took a sip of wine, but that did
nothing to cool the heat that flushed through her. It
would be easy not to finish—in fact, there was every likelihood she could not, no matter how hard she tried. Then
there would be no terrible decision to make; she would
have no choice but to go to him.

But that was the coward's way. The choice must be hers.
The guilt if she chose to stay with him—or the regret, if
she did not.

He watched her. She could feel his gaze, steady, demanding she look at him, demanding so much more of
her. She studied the collop of veal on her plate, and
found it wholly unappetizing.

The ladies retired to the drawing room, and Amanda
set feverishly to work, protected as usual by the verbose

Miss Abbott. Minutes sped by, then half an hour, then an hour, and still the gentlemen did not appear. Amanda completed one of Leda's hands, then concentrated on her face. *Where was Rivenhall?* Why didn't he interrupt her? She didn't know whether to feel gratitude or offense.

The butler carried in the tea tray, and the gentlemen— with the exception of Lord Pelham and Rivenhall—at last made their appearance. Amanda drank her cup, then said her good nights and slipped away to her room. Apparently, he intended to give her every chance. She had begun to suspect he possessed any number of excellent qualities—a fact he kept closely guarded for the sake of his rakish reputation.

She settled in a comfortable chair, arranged her working candles, and resumed her work. Leda's face appeared in delicate silk. Her eyes stared back at Amanda, one half-closed in a knowing wink. As the hands on the clock swept past ten-thirty, Leda's mouth took shape, then the dimple in her chin. At five minutes before eleven, Amanda set the final stitch.

She had done it. Triumph filled her, wavered, and faded beneath a touch of regret, which she firmly banished. Triumph alone she would allow. As for her decision—well, that must wait until after she had presented her payment to Rivenhall.

Thought of him sent a thrill of nerves dancing along her flesh. She glanced in her mirror, straightened her hair, braced her nerve, and set off to keep her appointment.

His room, she knew, stood four doors down the corridor, next to Bentley's. If she were seen, it might be thought she searched for her brother. That at least would preserve her reputation. She knocked, a tentative, nervous gesture, then entered without awaiting a response.

* * *

Rivenhall sat before the hearth, his booted feet extended to the small fire that crackled with a comforting warmth. On an occasional table at his side stood a decanter of wine and two glasses. The clock on the mantel struck the hour, then ticked on. And still she didn't come.

Then a scratch sounded on the door, and it opened. He tensed, listening to the hushed brush of her slippers as she entered the room, the soft thud and click as the latch closed them into the privacy of his chamber. Her footsteps approached, then stopped.

He shifted in his chair so he could see her, standing hesitantly behind him, a roll of colorfully stitched fabric clutched in her hand. Her face, even in this wavering light, looked unnaturally pale. Nervous. Though why she should be, he failed to understand. It was he who staked his future happiness on the outcome of this night. After a few moments, just to break the silence that stretched between them, he said, "You are two minutes late."

"Your clock is fast." The words came out choked, as if her voice refused to cooperate. She advanced several steps toward him, then stopped three feet away and held out the embroidered handkerchief.

He had to lean forward to reach it; she kept a prudent distance between them. Without a word, he unrolled the fine lawn and examined her exquisite work. She had done Leda full justice, he admitted ruefully. He honored her for not shirking a task that must have brought a blush to her maiden cheeks and would have sent a lesser lady into a fit of the vapors.

At last he set it aside. "You have kept your part of our agreement, Miss Grieves. I shall now keep mine." And with that he rose, went to his dresser, and returned to hand her several slips of paper.

"Bentley's vowels?" Her voice quavered. "All of them?"

"All of them," he confirmed.

She looked at them, one at a time, and her jaw tightened. Then, still one at a time, she fed them into the flames, watching until the fire reduced each one to ash before adding the next. "It is finished," she said at last, and her voice held an odd, undecipherable note.

He could make nothing of her expression either, not the relief he had anticipated, not the contempt for him that might so easily rule her now. She simply stood there, staring at the grate, unmoving. Then abruptly, she turned on her heel and started for the door. She had paid her debt, and now she would leave.

If he were such a fool as to let her go.

"Miss Grieves." An unfamiliar tightness in his throat made it difficult to speak her name.

She stopped, but didn't turn around.

"Will you play one more hand of piquet with me?" One more hand, that could mean the world to him.

She remained frozen for one long moment, then looked over her shoulder at him. "For what stakes this time, my lord? I have not the time to embroider another picture before the house party breaks up in the morning."

He drew a deep breath. "If I lose, I will undertake your brother's education in matters of gaming."

Her lip curled. "I can well believe that."

"What I mean," he said through teeth that tended to clench, "is that I will take him to London, introduce him to the gaming establishments, and teach him how to protect himself against Captain Sharps and ivory-turners. Within a month, I pledge to you he will no longer be a pigeon ripe for anyone's plucking."

Her mobile eyebrows rose. "That is value, indeed." She sounded surprised. The next moment, the haughty, skeptical look returned to her face. "And what stake would you dare to demand of me?"

"There is only one thing I want from you." His gaze met and held hers, and he forced from his mind the knowledge of how much he might stand to lose in the next few moments. In a voice as steady as he could manage, he said, "Your hand in marriage."

"My—" She broke off, her mouth open, her eyes incredulous. *"Marriage?* A—a hardened rake like you wants a *wife*? But would that not interfere with your flirting?"

He regarded her with unaccustomed solemnity. "I have discovered there is only one lady with whom I wish to flirt."

She looked away, at the door, as if she longed to escape through it. Yet she made no move to do so. The moments ticked by on the small mantel clock. At last, she asked, in a very small voice, "What would you have done if I had not finished the embroidery?" She turned then, facing him fully. "Would you still have made this second wager with me? Or would you merely have had me pay that first debt?"

There could be only one answer. He drew a folded sheet of paper from the inner pocket of his coat and handed it to her.

She opened it, frowned as she looked it over, then shook her head. A variety of emotions flickered across her face. "A special license," she breathed, as if not quite believing it.

"It is why I went to London."

That drew no response from her. She stood staring at the paper, remote, withdrawn. Hardly the response which a gentleman hoped to his proposal of marriage.

Did she doubt his sincerity? Suddenly, it became urgent for her to know he did not make an empty promise. "I spoke to Mr. Somes after dinner. He is waiting in the library to perform our marriage. If you agree, that is."

"You mean if I lose." She said it absently, as if the words themselves held little meaning for her. She continued to stare at the paper, not at him.

"You might win." Then his tension, his fears of her

refusal, surfaced with a rush. Harshly, he demanded, "And if you did lose, is being tied to me too great a price to pay for your brother's protection and worldly education?"

Finally, she looked up at him, and one corner of her mouth tugged upward. "Do you know, I must be the most absurd creature, but I find I desire to marry for love, or not at all."

The supreme confidence that had carried him through any number of delightful associations deserted him utterly. He gazed at her, memorizing the lines of her face, the elegant carriage of her head. "Can you not come to love me?" he asked. "I have certainly come to love you."

Her eyes widened. For a long, silent moment she stared at him; then she looked down at the special license she still held. Slowly—very slowly—she shook her head. "No, my lord. I cannot *come* to do something that I already *have* done."

"You—" He worked that out, then bore down on her, catching her by the shoulders, holding her both to support himself and to keep her from escaping. "You love me?" he demanded, not quite able to believe it.

Humor sprang to life in her eyes, as if she recognized and appreciated this alteration in their circumstances, that she, rather than he, now held the upper hand. She could torture him, pay him back for the torment he had inflicted upon her. She could tear his heart from him, if she chose.

Instead, she cupped his face between her hands. "I have loved you from the first moment I saw you, though I have only just now allowed myself to admit it."

Relief rushed through him. Gently, tenderly, he gathered her close. His mouth found hers in a kiss that began tentatively, then gained in confidence with the passion of her response. For a very long while he held her, relishing the feel of her in his arms, the sweet scent of violets that clung to her hair, the tantalizing tickle of her fingers as they ventured around the back of his neck.

Too tantalizing, in fact. With an effort of will, he set her from him. "My dearest love, if we stay here even a moment longer, poor Mr. Somes will be left waiting until morning."

Laughter lit her eyes. "What, are we not to play our hand of piquet?"

"I dare not," he said. "You might win."

She slipped her arms about his waist. "My dearest love," she breathed. "I already have."

FASCINATION

by

Judith A. Lansdowne

ONE

He entered the ballroom with a clacking of bootheels and a jangling of spurs. From beneath the low-crowned hat pushed far back upon his head, sodden black curls dangled limply down over his brow. His surtout and boots and pantaloons were mud-spattered, his starkly drawn countenance frowned, and his eyes—his telltale blue-green eyes—smoldered. As he made his way through the gathered revelers, conversations ceased. The music sputtered to a halt and the dancers came to an apprehensive standstill. While beyond the long windows the wind roared and thunder rumbled as lightning split the skies, inside the ballroom all sound dwindled to a decided hush.

He acknowledged no one. The irate turquoise of his eyes saw nothing they did not wish to see. His measured strides carried him, unfaltering, across the polished dance floor and directly up before a tall blond gentleman who stood with a lady in pale blue velvet upon his arm and a look of pure horror upon his face.

"Did you think that I would not take an interest in it, Tolly? Or did you truly believe it would never reach my ears?"

Before any sort of reply could be made, a fist encased in wet black doeskin gloves connected with Lord Tolliver's handsomely waistcoated stomach, doubling him over and causing the young lady upon his arm to step hurriedly aside. A second fist, much like the first, cracked against Tolliver's jaw and spun him backward, his head bouncing hard against the wall. Lord Tolliver sank slowly and silently to the floor.

Without a glance to left or right, Tolliver's assailant spun about and stalked back across the dance floor and out through the doorway by which he had entered, leaving behind him a considerable hubbub. The Hawk had returned to Hawkworth Aerie, and his stepmama's house party was about to take a most interesting turn.

It did occur to Priscilla that perhaps she ought to do something about Lord Tolliver, who lay groaning practically at her feet, but she had not the least idea what. She did not have her reticule, so she could not offer him a sniff of vinaigrette. And she had not the least intention of kneeling down beside the man and cradling his head in her lap. The best she could think to do was to step farther away so that someone else might offer him aid. Certainly everyone must have seen what happened.

With a whisper of velvet and the merest scuffle of her white kid slippers upon the floor, Priscilla shuffled quietly to her right. And then she noted her sister Sarah virtually flying across the ballroom floor. In mere seconds Sarah was on her knees beside the unconscious Lord Tolliver, wailing, tears staining her reddening cheeks—the only patches of color upon a countenance gone chalk white.

"Priscilla," declared Lady Cecily Wight, coming up beside Miss Pritkin, "cease staring. Let us go to the parlor and order up tea. We are merely in the way here."

"But I do want to know that Lord Tolliver will recover, Cecily."

"Of course he will recover. He has not been shot, for goodness sake."

"No, merely levelled by two of the most beautifully accurate blows. Did you see it? Do you know who it was felled Lord Tolliver? He is not one of the guests, I think. At least, I have not been introduced to him."

"Come away, Priscilla," Lady Cecily insisted again. "Sarah is making quite enough ruckus over Tolly as it is. And Tolly's mama will add to it in a moment, I will lay you odds. We may as well adjourn for tea and then traipse off to bed, because the dancing is over for tonight. Sometimes I could wring his neck."

"Whose neck? Lord Tolliver's?"

"No, you gudgeon, Hawk's."

"That was The Hawk?" gasped Priscilla. "Oh, my goodness! I never thought— But he was not to be here. Lady Hawkworth assured Mama that The Hawk would not be in residence."

"Apparently, Lady Hawkworth was mistaken. I expect Teal did not bother to inform her of his intended arrival. He seldom thinks to inform anyone of anything."

The merest flicker of a smile lit Priscilla's lovely brown eyes and twitched at the corners of her mouth. The Hawk. Why, even as far away as Newcastle, the Earl of Hawkworth was legendary. He was a scoundrel, a rogue, the blackest of all the black sheep ever born. So very black, in fact, that by the time Priscilla had reached the age of fourteen, she had taken to listening at doorways whenever her papa chanced to mutter Hawkworth's name, in the hope that she might hear the very latest of The Hawk's adventures.

Once, she recalled, the tale had consisted of The Hawk shooting a pickpocket and leaving the corpse to molder in New Bridge Street without so much as notifying the Watch, because his lordship had been late for an assignation with his mistress.

Another time The Hawk had won a hundred thousand pounds on one turn of the cards at Watier's. Of course, the gentleman who had lost the money had gone straight out and killed himself, but that had only added to the interest of the tale. And only a year ago, she recalled, her papa and mama had been discussing in hushed voices the likelihood that the Earl of Hawkworth had been the man who had seduced and then abandoned Lady Caroline Hadley, who had, in her grief at being rejected, pierced her heart with a dagger. They and everyone else had supposed it to be The Hawk who had jilted her, because Lady Caroline had bequeathed to him all of her jewels with her very last breath. Oh, the Earl of Hawkworth was a dastard and a villain and a gentleman to be feared. And Priscilla had seen him at last, this very evening, practically face-to-face!

What an adventure the remainder of this house party is like to be, Priscilla thought. Only if he remains, of course. I do so hope that he remains. "Oh, my," she murmured as she and Lady Cecily reached the opposite side of the ballroom, "what is all *this* commotion?"

"Keep back. Keep back," ordered an elderly lady in a pink turban, brushing the girls aside. "We must have air. Lady Hawkworth has fainted dead away."

"Well, and I knew how it would be," mumbled Strange, tugging Hawkworth out of his thoroughly soaked clothing. "You could not wait one moment. Not one. You had to leap from your horse, barge into the house, stroll right into that ballroom and clobber poor Lord Tolliver."

"Yes, I did," declared Hawkworth angrily.

"You could not wait one more hour, by which time the dancing would have ended and her ladyship's guests would have gone to their chambers for the night?"

"No, I could not."

"Just so," sighed Strange. *"That* is why you are a social pariah, my lord."

"I am not a pariah."

"Ho, no," replied the elderly valet with a shake of his greying head.

"Well, and I do not give a fig if I am, Strange. Be deviled if I will allow Tolly to strike Jane and then waltz off to a house party as pretty as you please. You do not mean to tell me that you think I ought to have ignored the whole thing?"

"No, my lord. I mean to tell you that you ought to have waited for a private moment with Lord Tolliver."

"Yes," mumbled The Hawk, sinking gratefully into the steaming water of his bath. "And then I would have been accused of attacking the dastard from the rear in the rose garden or some such. You know I would have been accused of that. I cannot win."

"No, my lord," agreed Strange, collecting Hawkworth's sodden clothes, "you never can."

"No, I never can," muttered Hawkworth, leaning back in the great brass tub and letting the water slosh over him. "No matter what I do, I am wrong to do it. I was wrong to be born and I have been wrong ever since."

"Such self-pity," Strange observed, attempting to sort Hawkworth's clothes into a manageable bundle. The Hawk had neglected to divest himself of his surtout and hat before he came upstairs and those two things alone were fairly dripping rainwater and mud onto the carpet as Strange juggled his load. "If I did not hear the self-pity with my own ears, I should never have believed it of you, my lord."

"Yes," grinned Hawkworth boyishly from his bath. "I should never have believed it of me either, Strange. Leave the boots and spurs for Joseph, eh? Or is he asleep? Damnation, of course he is asleep. It is past midnight. Well, leave them anyway. He shall come and fetch them in the morning. The mud will come off all the easier once it has caked."

"Indeed, my lord."

"Yes, and leave my hat, too."

"Your hat, my lord?"

"Uh-huh. I have a fancy to wear it."

"Now, my lord? In your bath?"

"In my bath," Hawkworth replied, seizing the hat from Strange's grip and plopping it atop his sodden curls. "I pay taxes upon the thing, Strange. I had best wear it as often as possible. What a government we have, to tax a man's hat and his windows. I am thinking of boarding up half the windows in The Aerie, Strange. At least half of them. Save myself a deal of money that way."

"And were you thinking of selling half of the horses, as well, my lord?" Strange asked, smiling. "The tax upon horses is astounding, I hear."

"Oh, at least half of them. Possibly the whole lot. Except Turnabout, of course. I cannot think of one person who would consent to purchase Turnabout."

"Not once they attempt to ride the beast, my lord. The government ought to pay you monies for keeping him."

"Just so," laughed Hawkworth, in much better spirits than he had been upon his arrival. "Just so. Reverse taxes for keeping Turnabout off the market. A likely sounding bargain. Strange?"

"Yes, my lord."

"You will check upon Tolly for me, will you not? I mean to say, you will see that he is not dead or anything."

"I shall look into Lord Tolliver's condition as soon as I have taken your things belowstairs, my lord."

"Thank you, Strange. I should hate for Tolly to be dead. So many witnesses, you know, to swear that I had done the thing. He had a young lady upon his arm when I walked in. I have never seen her before. Blue velvet, she wore, and a necklace of sapphires."

"I shall ask Mr. Butler for her name, my lord," nodded Strange and bustled out of the chamber.

The Hawk settled back in the tub, resting his head

upon the edge of it, which forced his hat, of course, to
slip down over his eyes. But that was no bother; he simply
closed them.

Priscilla told herself that she ought not to do the thing.
But she had never listened to her own good advice before
and she certainly had no intention of doing so now. Truly,
she could not resist. Hawkworth Aerie was such a fascinating house. It roamed up and down over an entire hillside and was stuffed with history. Paintings, tapestries,
furniture from centuries ago, even armor and weapons
from the very days of King Arthur. With a glint of mischief
in her warm brown eyes and a tiny nod of her head that
set her short golden curls to bouncing, Priscilla pushed
aside the pocket doors that stood partly open and stepped
down four steps into a long, ill-lit corridor.

"Most likely there is no one quartered here," she murmured to herself. "There are merely two candles to light
the way. I expect this corridor is used only by the servants
to get quickly from one section of the house to another.
I will simply take a quick peek and be back in my own
bedchamber well before Sarah comes to bid me good
night. It will take her forever to come. She is likely still
crying over Lord Tolliver."

Her blue velvet skirt whispering around her, Priscilla
took the nearest of the candles into her hand and made
her way down the dim corridor, pausing to gaze at the
ornate woodwork, the carefully carved cornices, the wonderful brass door latches, and the most beautiful paintings she had so far seen upon the premises.

Why do they hide these away in this empty wing? she
asked herself silently, studying one after another of the
absolutely gorgeous landscapes. I should hang them in
the drawing rooms and the dining rooms and the parlors.
And this one, she thought, gazing at a scene of the valley

below the house in summer, this one I would put in my own bedchamber if I lived here. I most certainly would.

Mindful, however, that she had little time in which to satisfy her curiosity, Priscilla tugged herself away from that particular landscape and continued on down the corridor. She had hoped to discover one or another of the doors to the chambers standing open, but they were all closed. Her fingers itched to open just one and peer inside. There was no telling, after all, for how long this particular section of the house had stood empty. Why, the chambers might be furnished with trappings three or four centuries old.

"Or they may simply be empty," she murmured. "Still, the corridor is carpeted and apparently clean. Perhaps the chambers are kept in readiness should more guests be invited than the other sections of the house can accommodate."

It can do no harm, she thought, as she reached the far end of the corridor, to look into just one of the chambers. I will just open this one door and look about and then hurry back to my own room. With a tiny shiver of anticipation and a gleefully mischievous dimple appearing in her left cheek, Priscilla reached for the latch, pressed it down, and swung the polished oak door inward. And then she gave the most unladylike squeal.

"What the devil!" Hawkworth exclaimed, startled from his lethargy. He pushed his hat back on his head, stood straight up in his bath, and spun around toward the sound. Then he promptly sat back down, his incredible turquoise eyes staring in disbelief at Priscilla, who stood frozen in the doorway holding her candle with one hand, the other hand pressed tightly to her lips.

And then Hawkworth's lips twitched madly upward, and his eyes sparkled with glee. "Lost, are you?" he queried, attempting to suppress the most outrageous urge to burst into laughter.

"Oh!" Priscilla managed from behind her hand, her cheeks flaming, her eyes wide and fastened upon him. "Oh!"

"Your hand, sweetling, would be put to better use over your eyes rather than lingering over your lips as it does," Hawkworth pointed out helpfully.

"I—I know," Priscilla mumbled, her hand remaining where it was. "I—I—d-do apologize for—for—"

"For continuing to stare at me in my bath instead of fainting dead away or running off down the corridor screaming at the top of your lungs as any proper young lady ought?" asked Hawkworth, amiably.

"N-no," giggled Priscilla, lowering her hand to reveal a most impish grin. "F-for entering without kn-knocking. D-do you always wear your hat when you b-bathe?" she managed, striving to keep from bursting into laughter. He must think me a raving lunatic, she thought. But she could not help herself. He looked so very outlandish, naked in his tub with his hat upon his head.

"Always," Hawkworth replied. "Never know when a lady will enter and a gentleman will be obliged to tip something." Whereupon he tipped his hat to her with considerable aplomb. "I am Hawkworth. I would bow, sweetling, but that would require my standing and I do not think I ought to do *that* again. I suspect *that* would send you off into whoops, would it not?"

"Yes," giggled Priscilla. "I am so very s-sorry to have come barging in upon you. I thought the room to be unoccupied. I am Miss Priscilla Pritkin."

"Miss Pritkin who is not easily overset, eh?"

"I am obliged to confess it," Priscilla nodded. "But I have helped to bathe my little brothers many times, my lord, and in my own defense, I really feel that I must point out that you, though older than Harry and Robert, possess nothing that I have not seen in a tub innumerable times."

"Yes, I do, Miss Pritkin."

"You do?" gurgled Priscilla. "What?"

"A hat, sweetling. A most disreputable and soggy hat."

TWO

"We ought to go home at once," sighed Sarah, settling down upon the little settee before the fire in the sitting room that she and Priscilla shared and playing uneasily with the cherry riband upon the front of her flannel robe.

"Go home? Oh no," Priscilla protested, tying her night-cap securely beneath her chin. "We cannot go home, Sarah. We have just arrived."

"Two days ago."

"Yes, but the party is to continue until next Tuesday. Mama and Papa will not expect us home before Friday."

"No, I realize that they will not, Priscilla. But Mama and Papa are under the impression that Lord Hawkworth is not in residence. They will not wish us to remain now that he is here. They will be most upset, in fact, to discover that we have so much as laid eyes upon *that man.*"

Priscilla grinned impishly, remembering how much of *that man* she *had* set eyes upon, but she could certainly not mention *that* to her sister.

"And when they hear what the villain did to poor Arlin!" Sarah continued, taking no note at all of her sister's wicked grin. "Well, if it should reach their ears before we reach home, Papa will set out to fetch us straight away."

"Certainly word of it will not reach Newcastle until someone who is at this party leaves this party," Priscilla protested. "Gossip cannot float out into the air by itself."

"That is not the point."

"No," declared Priscilla. "The point is that you are exceedingly fond of Lord Tolliver and he of you, and we have come here to discover whether you truly wish to marry the gentleman or not. That is the point, and I mean to keep you to it."

"Yes, I know that is what Mama and Papa intended when they allowed us to come—that I should make up my mind about Lord Tolliver—but the Earl of Hawkworth is in this very house, Priscilla!"

"Pooh! His presence is not important. What *is* important is Lord Tolliver, Sarah. He makes no secret of his preference for you. Papa expects the gentleman to request your hand in marriage at any time. Perhaps Lord Tolliver will even accompany our coach to Newcastle when the party ends for that precise purpose. But he will not do so unless he is quite certain that you will accept his proposal. You must stay and make certain of your heart, Sarah."

Sarah lowered her gaze to stare into the fire and sighed again. "Do you think so? But we truly cannot remain, Priscilla. Not with Lord Hawkworth in residence."

"I do not see why not."

"Because Lord Hawkworth is a rogue and a scoundrel and no one of any consequence will have the least thing to do with him, that is why not. Papa would have an apoplexy to think that we happened to be in the same room with him for an instant. He would never condone our spending near a week in the same household with that villain. Even Lord Hawkworth's own stepmama does not wish to be seen with him. And Lord Tolliver—Oh, poor Arlin, I do hope he is fully recovered. To be attacked so, right in the midst of the dancing! Lord Tolliver does all he can to avoid meetings with Lord Hawkworth in public places. He has told me so."

The tiniest smile played about Priscilla's countenance.

"Did you notice how handsome Lord Hawkworth is, Sarah? Quite as handsome in his way as is Lord Tolliver."

"Yes," muttered Sarah. "One an angel of light and the other an angel of darkness."

"And he has the devil of a right cross, too."

"Priscilla, do not say devil."

"Yes, well, but Lord Hawkworth does have the devil of a right cross, Sarah. And he has—"

"What?" asked Sarah, turning to face her sister and taking immediate note of the dimple flashing in Priscilla's cheek and the glint of mischief in her eyes. "What has he, Priscilla?"

"A most remarkable hat," giggled Priscilla.

"A what? Priscilla, you are being totally nonsensical."

"Yes, I am. But so are you. If you marry Lord Tolliver, Sarah, then Lord Hawkworth will become your step-brother-in-law and so a member of our family. Have you not thought of that?"

Miss Sarah Pritkin scowled. "Yes," she murmured, "I have thought of that. But there is nothing to be done about it. It is not Lord Tolliver's fault that his mama married Lord Hawkworth's papa. Arlin has already admitted to me that he does not wish to cut the relationship completely—"

"Well then, it cannot make the least difference whether we come to know Lord Hawkworth now or later, can it? For know him we must if you and Lord Tolliver make a match of it. Even Mama and Papa must make Lord Hawkworth's acquaintance at the wedding."

"Oh, do not go speaking of weddings," Sarah demured prettily. "Things have not gone so very far as that."

"No, but they have gone far enough that you call Lord Tolliver Arlin."

Sarah blushed. She had only just begun to take the liberty of using Lord Tolliver's given name and the intimacy of it still thrilled her. "Well, perhaps we will not go home just yet," she said on a tiny whisper. "Perhaps Lord Hawkworth does not intend to remain at Hawkworth Aerie."

"Fiddle!" declared Priscilla, "even if he does, there is not one reason for us to leave and every reason for us to stay."

"And perhaps he is not such a rogue as the gabblemongers say," Sarah murmured hopefully. "Perhaps he will not do anything else untoward while he is here."

Priscilla thought that to be a rather useless longing. A gentleman who thought nothing of interrupting a dance in order to punch his stepbrother senseless, and who held lengthy conversations with perfectly unknown young ladies while he was naked in his bath, gave little hope of proving to be a perfect gentleman for any lengthy period of time. But she did not tell Sarah this. She had not, in fact, so much as mentioned to Sarah that she had actually made Lord Hawkworth's acquaintance. She simply smiled gaily and gave her sister a most supportive hug, kissed her cheek and then took herself off to bed.

It did occur to Hawkworth, as he tied a black silk scarf rakishly around his neck the following morning and shrugged into his black velvet riding coat with the double row of brass buttons, that Miss Pritkin might well have brought the entire household down upon them both the night before. He was prodigiously grateful that she had not.

Be asking her father for her hand, had she screamed a bit, he thought, or had she brought a witness or two running to catch us. Probably honor bound to propose marriage anyway, but I will not. I would be honor bound to tell her about Sidney at the same time, and then she would not have me anyway. Bedamned if any woman will have me once word of Sidney spreads through the *ton*.

Still, I should like to get to know Miss Pritkin better. *You possess nothing I have not already seen.* Of all the things to say. What a splendid look upon her face when she said it, too. Yes, I should like to know Miss Pritkin a good deal better, I think.

"I shall need to discover her whereabouts," he murmured, brushing at his dark curls.

"*Her* whereabouts, my lord?" Strange halted in his disposal of Hawkworth's nightshirt and turned a questioning eye upon the gentleman. "Oh!" he exclaimed then. "Miss Priscilla Pritkin."

Hawkworth spun around and stared at the man. "Miss Priscilla Pritkin? What do you know of Miss Priscilla Pritkin, Strange?"

"Well, that is to whom you refer, is it not, my lord? The young woman upon Lord Tolliver's arm last evening when you—when you made your feelings concerning a certain matter quite clear to that particular gentleman? She wore blue velvet, you told me, and a necklace of sapphires. Miss Priscilla Pritkin, Mr. Butler informed me, of the Newcastle Pritkins."

"Yes, right," Hawkworth nodded. "Stupid of me to forget I had requested her name from you. You do not happen to know—"

"Riding to Swarthsford Abbey, my lord, with Lord Tolliver and your stepmama and others of the party."

"With Tolly? Have they left already, Strange?"

"Indeed, my lord. Over an hour ago. Went by way of the high road because her ladyship would ride in the cabriolet, my lord. She was never one for sitting upon the backs of horses, your stepmama. They intend to take nuncheon at the Bear and Bell upon their return. Another group of guests break their fasts in the yellow morning room, my lord."

"I do not give a fig what they break, Strange."

"No, sir. But I did think, my lord, that perhaps you

would care to eat something with them before you dashed off in pursuit of Lord Tolliver and Miss Pritkin. You do intend to dash off in pursuit of them. I can see it in your eyes."

"I am not hungry in the least. Toss me my spurs, will you, Strange? And send out to the stables for Turnabout. Tell them to bring him 'round to my door, eh?"

"Ahem."

"What, Strange?"

"Mr. Butler, my lord, did impress upon me to impress upon you, my lord, that Miss Priscilla Pritkin is one of the daughters of Viscount Pritkin and not a young woman of uncertain parentage. She is not a one to be dallied with. He wishes you to understand that precisely, my lord."

Hawkworth grinned. "Ho! Did Butler say that?"

"Just so, my lord."

"Such disrespect. Has the man no fear in his heart to send such a message to his employer?"

"None," declared Strange.

"That is what comes of having servants who have known you since you were in leading strings," sighed Hawkworth. "Tell him that he need not worry, Strange. I do not intend to dally with the girl at all. I do intend to have words with Tolly, however."

"I shall pass on the message, my lord. What were you intending to do with the girl, if I may ask?"

"You mayn't ask, Strange. It is none of it your business, nor Butler's either. Just go and send for Turnabout, will you? I shall need to ride like the devil if I am to catch them up."

The remains of Swarthsford Abbey stretched and yawned lethargically beneath a high February sun that glinted upon broken stones and sagging rooftops. Weak rays of sunlight probed long-abandoned crevices and flickered amidst moldy paving blocks. Where once a colony of monks had pursued their daily activities cloistered and free from strife, silent echoes of their activities lingered only in the minds of those who came to view the skeletal remains of the once bustling residence.

Elms and oaks, blackberry and bayberry, had long since overrun the abbey, and some of the saplings had had the sheer audacity to sprout within the hallowed halls and chambers that struggled to remain upright. A number of ivy plants had even taken root in what remained of the many chimneys and beneath the cracked and potted and tilted floors.

"I am quite relieved that the sun is shining," Lady Cecily declared as Mr. Crosby helped her from the saddle. "I should genuinely hate to be in such a place as this when the light is dim or thunder rumbling overhead."

"Do you think it is haunted?" asked Priscilla, gazing eagerly about. "It does look as though it ought to be haunted."

"Oh, quite," nodded Lord Tolliver.

"Indubitably," added Mr. Crosby.

"Roundheads rode down out of the forest and beheaded every monk in the place," Lord Dugan assured the ladies over his shoulder as he helped the dowager Lady Hawkworth to step from the cabriolet. "Blood everywhere. Howling and screaming. Not a man of them survived. Monks, I mean. Roundheads never got so much as a scratch, they say."

"Peter, of all things," admonished the dowager. "You will terrify the young ladies. It is nothing but a tale, at any rate, told by firelight to frighten the children and keep them away from this place."

"Yes," Tolliver nodded. "But it never did work."

"It did not?" asked Sarah, taking the arm Lord Tolliver offered her.

"No, never. There is not one child in the countryside who has not gone tramping through this place at one time or another."

"You, Lord Tolliver?" asked Priscilla, smiling.

"Indeed," harrumphed his mama. "Came near to breaking his leg in the doing of it, too."

"It is not worth speaking of," Lord Tolliver demurred with an odd wrinkling of his nose. "Come, let us look the place over, shall we? No ghosts this morning, I assure you, and no broken legs either. We shall be most circumspect in our wanderings."

Lord Dugan, with the dowager Lady Hawkworth upon his arm, led the way. "It was the Roundheads," he muttered to himself rather loudly, for he was growing old and deaf and must mutter loudly in order to hear himself. "And a Hawkworth who sent them flying, Althea. But not in time. Not in time. The Falcon, I believe. Yes, he would be the one. Always think of him when I see The Hawk. Looks a good bit like his great-grandfather, that one."

"I wish you will not call Teal that dreadful name, Peter. He adores to be called by it and it brings out the very worst in him whenever it reaches his ears."

"Which is not hard to do," commented Mr. Crosby, behind them. "Bring out the worst in The Hawk."

Lady Cecily giggled, but Sarah gazed with worried eyes at Priscilla, who held to Tolliver's other arm, and then she looked up at Lord Tolliver's handsome profile. "You were not injured terribly last evening, were you, Arlin?" she asked breathlessly. "I was so very worried about you, but no one would say how you did. And this morning down you came, thinking nothing of yourself but only intent upon keeping your promise to lead us through these ruins."

Lord Tolliver stopped in his tracks to stare down at her. "I suffered only a blow to my sense of righteousness, dearest Sarah. I assure you, I am otherwise without the least pain. If I had not slipped upon the floor and hit my head, I should not have gone down at all."

"Balderdash," murmured Priscilla under her breath. "He had you stumbling on the first punch and that right cross knocked you flat."

"What did you say, Miss Priscilla?" asked Tolliver, never taking his gaze from Sarah.

"Nothing, my lord. I was simply commenting upon the intricacies of the building. You must not mind me. I shall go ahead and walk with Lady Cecily and Mr. Crosby, shall I?"

"If you wish, Miss Priscilla," nodded Tolliver. "Did Hawkworth frighten you, Sarah?"

"He nearly frightened her into running off to New-castle the very first thing this morning," Priscilla de-clared, releasing Lord Tolliver's arm and strolling off to catch up Mr. Crosby and Lady Cecily. "I should attempt to draw a more likely picture of Lord Hawkworth for her, if I were you," she called over her shoulder. "We shall be gone the next time he does something the least bit unseemly else."

"No, will you, Sarah?" asked Tolliver, taking both her hands into his own. "But you cannot let my stepbrother frighten you away. I—I—love you, Sarah," he whispered. "Do not let that rogue drive you from me."

Sarah could not believe her ears. She blinked up at him amidst the dappled sunlight, trembling. "You *love* me, Arlin?"

"Forgive me, my dear. I ought not to have been so bold to proclaim it as yet. It is too soon, I know, and offends your sensibilities. But my heart is filled so by the mere sight of you— Sarah, please, do not say that I am to be forever without hope of gaining your affections be-cause I am quite accidentally related to Hawkworth."

"N-no," managed Sarah. "No, I shall not say such a thing as that. I shall never say such a thing as that."

"Then I may breathe easier," smiled Tolliver, bringing one of Sarah's hands after the other to his lips and kissing each tenderly. "And Hawkworth will not remain, my dear. I cannot think he will remain at Hawkworth Aerie more than two nights at the most. He is on his way to meet his cronies at some hunting lodge, I expect, and merely broke his journey at home because it proved convenient. It is quite likely that he will be gone even before we return home this afternoon." And Tolliver once again offered Sarah his arm and led her off in the wake of the others, pointing out this and that about the ruins and setting her heart to trembling with each little attention he paid her.

THREE

The Hawk strolled into the Bear and Bell intending to meet the little party when they halted for nuncheon on their return from the abbey. He would take Tolliver aside and say what must be said and then, perhaps, allow himself to indulge in a bit more of Miss Priscilla Pritkin's company. He took up a stance before the long mahogany bar and grinned. "Afternoon, Archie," he greeted the proprietor. "You have not had sight of Tolliver and his friends as yet, have you?"

Archie Langford shook his head. "Ladies with 'em?" he asked disinterestedly.

"Yes, and my stepmama. Taken them off to view the ruins. Stopping here for nuncheon, or so I am told."

"He'll be wishin' fer a private parlor then. Here, Molly, run an' see that all is at the ready in the back parlor," Langford called to his daughter as she set tankards of ale before two of the public room loungers. "Got high an' mighty company acomin', we does."

Hawkworth snickered, which caused Langford to gaze down his perfectly aristocratic nose at him.

"What?" asked Hawkworth.

"Nothin', yer lor'ship," Langford sighed.

"Tell me," urged Hawkworth.

" 'Tis merely I be thinkin' o' what high-sticklers Lor' Tolliver an' Lady Hawkworth be, an' I be contemplatin' that rag what ye have wrapped about yer neck. Willn't like it, they won't. Still not learned the intricacies of tyin' a neckcloth, eh? Ye be well onto twenty-eight or nine by now, ain't ye, Hawk? An' still ye cannot dress yerself proper?"

"Looking for a facer, are you, Archie?" Hawkworth responded with a gleeful smile.

"Indeed, but ye ain't the gent ta give it me."

"Step outside into the yard, Archie, and we will see about that," declared The Hawk.

"Oh! I am shakin' in me boots, I am," proclaimed the proprietor, pretending to tremble violently. "Look at me, lads. His bloody lor'ship 'as offered ta give me a facer an' I am quakin' like a mouse with me tail in the cat's mouth."

Since Archie Langford stood six feet and five inches tall and had a neck like a bull, shoulders wide enough to use as a bridge across a stream, and a chest as broad as all southern England, his referral to himself as a mouse set the men seated in the public room to laughing uproariously.

"Obviously, you are in great need of a settler, Archie," Hawkworth drawled lazily. "Come with me, sir, and I will be pleased to bestow one upon you. Let us just stroll out the door, good host, and down the steps to the stable yard."

"Ho! And wouldn't I jist love ta take ye up on it!"

"I beseech you, Archie. Do take me up on it."

"Well, an' I cannot ignore no lord who be beseechin' me."

"No, you cannot. Quite improper."

"Best do it then," Archie replied with a nodding head as he untied the apron from around his waist and stepped out from behind the bar. "After you, m'lord," he insisted, bowing.

Hawkworth spun on his heel and strolled back across

the pine floor, out the front door and down the steps
into a yard that still held mud puddles from the rain the
night before. Behind him he heard the steady clumping
of Langford's enormous feet. Ten men of various and
sundry occupations, and therefore various and sundry
states of dress, piled out of the Bear and Bell after the
two, talking excitedly.

"I got a pound what says The Hawk takes 'im this
time," shouted Mel Farmer, who was, in fact, a farmer.

"Yer on," called David Noble, who made a living for
himself by tending Squire Niven's garden.

The other eight onlookers allowed as they would bet
on one or the other of the men as well and pound notes
flew from pockets and pouches and settled into the hand
of the Reverend Jason Market, who had just then stepped
down from his horse in search of warm cider to drive the
chill of a particularly long and early ride from his bones.
"Not again," Reverend Market laughed.

"Again," The Hawk nodded, doffing his hat and hand-
ing it into Farmer's care. He shrugged out of his velvet
jacket and left Hal Jonson holding that.

"We ain't holdin' ta none o' those fancy rules what
they got in Lunnon, ye ken," Langford advised Hawkworth, grinning. "This ain't about ta be none o' them
polite little mills ye be accustomed ta."

"I know, Archie. I know. Same rules as always. None."

"Aye, none," agreed Langford gleefully, and tapped
Hawkworth's cheek tenderly with one bearlike paw. "Ye'll
be sorry, lad. I promise ye that."

Hawkworth knew that he would. He had been sorry
countless times before. Truth to tell, the Earl of Hawkworth had been rising to Langford's teasing challenges
ever since the innkeeper had offered the first of them
upon The Hawk's eighteenth birthday. But Hawkworth
could not resist rising to the bait any more than Langford
could resist tossing the bait out before him.

It is because I like Archie, Hawkworth thought to himself, staring into Langford's smiling, eager eyes. And I think he has been dreadfully ill-used. And as long as I allow him to pummel me senseless every now and then, it provides him some consolation and makes me feel less responsible. But I am not responsible for it in the first place. I was not even alive then. Still, I am the only one of the aristocracy who will let him take out his frustrations, it seems, and that is the point of it.

Archie Langford had never once lost a battle with The Hawk. Likely, he never would. The Hawk always threw his heart into the fight, however, despite past confrontations, because it made Archie hugely happy to best a nobleman who was trying his damnedest not to be bested and provided Archie with great solace for the accident of his birth.

It was in the midst of providing Archie with this solace—while he was being twirled about above Archie's head, in fact—that the particular reason he had come to the Bear and Bell entered Hawkworth's mind and the stable yard as well. The earl landed with an *ooph!* and a splash in one of the mud puddles, levered himself up upon his elbows and stared soggily upward into Miss Priscilla Pritkin's amazed and enormously appealing eyes. Beside her, another young lady sat upon one of Hawkworth's own bays and glared. Tolliver stared down his nose at The Hawk and sniffed disdainfully.

"Playing about in the mud, are you, Hawkworth?" laughed Mr. Crosby, riding up beside Tolliver. "I should cease to do it directly if I were you. Your stepmama's carriage will be turning into the yard any moment."

"She will be most put out with you, my lord," offered Lady Cecily, bringing her mount to a halt beside Crosby's. "You know how she feels about mills. She has expounded upon them often enough from the time we were all children."

"The Hawk do not quiver in 'is boots over his step-mama's sensibilities," growled Archie Langford, stepping forward and offering the earl a hand up. "Good af'er-noon, my lady," he added, once Hawkworth had gained his feet. " 'Tis a pleasure ta see ye."

"You had best say so, Mr. Langford, or I would not think you worthy of my patronage," declared Lady Cecily. "And I should tell my papa that you were rude to me, too."

"Hush, Cecily, do not threaten the man," Hawkworth grumbled. "Archie Langford does not quiver in his boots for fear of you any more than I quiver for fear of my stepmama. You are come to enjoy a nuncheon. Take your friends and do it and be grateful that Archie lowers him-self to serve you."

Priscilla, who had come to think Lady Cecily a most forthright and authoritative young woman in the past few days, was most amazed to see that young lady close her mouth promptly, without the least argument, and allow Mr. Crosby to assist her from the saddle.

"Come, Sarah, Priscilla," Tolliver murmured, taking his cue from Crosby. "We shall have our nuncheon as planned and ignore these barbarians." He helped Sarah from the saddle, but was not quick enough to help Pris-cilla for Hawkworth, in muddied shirtsleeves and wet pan-taloons, was there before him.

"Do not you touch her. You will cover her in mud, Teal. You are filthy with it."

"It is merely the back of him is filthy with it," Priscilla replied blithely, resting her hands upon Hawkworth's broad shoulders as he swung her to the ground. "Thank you, my lord," she added softly. "Were you winning?"

"Winning? Against Archie? I should think not," Hawk-worth replied as his stepmama's cabriolet drew to a halt in the yard.

* * *

The small party of sightseers lounged about the private parlor of the Bear and Bell awaiting their meal, all of them attempting to avoid any conversation whatsoever that involved the Earl of Hawkworth, for it was quite evident that the dowager Lady Hawkworth had no wish to so much as acknowledge her stepson's presence at the inn. They spoke of the abbey and the weather and the approaching Season in London. Lord Dugan then thought to expound upon the price of corn and had just begun to do so when the door to the parlor opened and Hawkworth, his face scrubbed and his black velvet jacket hiding most of his muddied shirt, stepped into the room. "You will not mind if I join you," he drawled lazily, taking up a stand beside the hearth, one elbow resting upon the mantelpiece and his soggy backside turned strategically toward the fire.

"Sir, you cannot possibly intend to sit down at table in all your dirt," protested Lady Hawkworth.

"I do, ma'am," Hawkworth replied. "I have not eaten since last evening and I am famished."

"But you are—it is—you cannot—"

"I rather think I can, madam. It is a long ride back to the Aerie. You will not like to think of me fainting from lack of nourishment along the way."

"No, of course not. Can you not eat in the public room with your—friends, Teal?"

"Well, I could," drawled Hawkworth, his eyes searching about the room and coming to rest upon Priscilla. "But I think I will not. Come, madam, there are none of you precisely clean either. You have all been out rutting about that wretched abbey for an entire half-day."

"But not flailing about in mud puddles like some species of swine," grumbled Tolliver.

"No," Hawkworth replied solemnly, his eyes still upon Priscilla. "But some species of swine, Tolly, flail about in filth much worse than mud. Though I need not remind you of that. You know all too well what sorts of filth I speak of, do you not? Just so," he nodded when no answer was forthcoming. "We shall cease discussing swine, then, for the moment. Though you and I, brother dear, will resume certain elements of that discussion at a later time."

Their nuncheon arrived before any more could be said, Molly Langford entering with a large tray filled with veal pies fresh from the oven and hot cider and tea and coffee and an enormous platter upon which a banana pudding and three different kinds of pastries had been charmingly arranged.

"No, no, take the head, Tolly," The Hawk urged as the party gathered around the table. "It is your expedition after all. You ought to sit at the head, no? You always do when I am in London. I shall be perfectly satisfied to sit between these two lovely young women," he grinned, taking up a stance between Sarah and Priscilla. "Close your mouth, Tolly, do, and introduce me to them, eh? Cecily I have known since we were children and Dugan and Crosby for years on end. Pleased to see you again, Crosby, by the way. But these two flowers of the English countryside I have yet to meet."

Lord Tolliver's jaw dropped.

Lady Hawkworth glared at her stepson with undisguised loathing.

"My lord, may I present Miss Pritkin and Miss Priscilla Pritkin," Lady Cecily provided prettily, "of the Newcastle Pritkins."

"Of course," nodded Hawkworth, his oddly colored eyes dancing with good humor. "The Newcastle Pritkins. Your servant, ladies." And he took Sarah's hand into his own and kissed the back of it. Then he took Priscilla's hand, and turning it over, kissed her tenderly upon the inside of her wrist. "I am delighted to make your acquaintances. Shall we not be seated?" And releasing Priscilla's hand, he drew her chair back for her in the most gentlemanly fashion.

"You are utterly audacious," Priscilla declared as she rode beside Hawkworth toward the Aerie.

"Why do you say so?"

"To go scuffling about in the mud with an innkeeper and then to force yourself upon us in all your dirt!"

"Scuffling? Scuffling? I will have you know, Miss Priscilla Pritkin, that I do not scuffle."

"Oh?" asked Priscilla, perfectly delighted with the false sense of outrage he assumed. "What *were* you doing then?"

"I was being flattened by a giant. Beaten to a pulp. Quite possibly out-and-out murdered."

"No!" Priscilla could barely keep from laughing.

"Anyone can see that you are not from around here at all. You would know what danger I was in else, when you came upon me. Archie Langford is a regular devil with his fists."

"Then why did you fight him?"

"Because I always fight Archie. Whenever he asks. Well, he does not ask exactly. He taunts me and then I invite him out into the yard. And then he pounds me into oblivion."

"He always pounds you into oblivion?" asked Priscilla, her eyes open wide.

"Yes, well, whenever I am at home. He does not do it in London. Only because Archie does never go to London."

"Lucky you," giggled Priscilla. "You ought to take up permanent residence in town, I think."

"Never," Hawkworth declared, his eyes sparkling. "If I did not come home at least four times a year, poor Archie would go stark raving mad. Who would he have to lay

waste to? Not Tolly. Tolly would never think to fight him.
And Crosby is not titled, you know, and so fighting Crosby
would prove useless. And Dugan is much too old."

"Why must he lay waste to anyone?"

"Well, because Archie Langford ought to be the Duke
of Keyesborough. Yes," nodded Hawkworth noticing the
disbelief in Priscilla's eyes. "He ought to be a duke. But
he was born upon the wrong side of the blanket, so he
is merely a poorly educated innkeeper instead. And it
does give him great solace to beat the daylights out of
one of the nobility every now and then in retribution for
all that was forbidden him. Of course, it would give him
greater solace to pummel old Keyesborough, but that
gentleman will not set foot in the Bear and Bell, so Archie
must make do with me."

Priscilla did not quite know what to respond. "You are
perfectly mad," she declared after a long pause.

"Indubitably."

"And you are a considerable rogue besides."

"And you are perfectly splendid, Miss Priscilla Pritkin,"
grinned Hawkworth, his remarkable turquoise eyes alight
with laughter.

Feeling herself begin to blush, Priscilla gave her mount
a nudge with the heel of her boot and sent the animal
into a gallop. In an instant Hawkworth's great hulk of a
horse was galloping beside her. She spurred her mount
onward into a run, and the Earl of Hawkworth laughed
and did likewise. "You will not be rid of me so easily,"
he called across to her. "In fact, so long as you are within
my sight, you will not be rid of me at all."

"He is a devil," muttered Lord Tolliver, watching the
two riders disappear around a bend while keeping his
own mount to a slower pace beside Sarah.

"Who?"

"The Hawk. See, he has taunted your sister into a race.
He is a devil born and has no sense of decorum besides."

Sarah was quite certain that Lord Tolliver's words, though generally true, were unjust at the moment. She knew that Priscilla would have needed no taunting to spring her mount into such a wild run, and she might well have told Lord Tolliver so if something else had not just then entered her mind.

"Why did his lordship hit you last evening, Arlin?" she asked instead.

"How should I know? He just does things. Look how he fought with Langford in the stable yard. And think how he sat down to dine with us in all his mud. He is mad, Sarah. But you must not let that bother you," Tolliver added instantly. "We do not share a drop of the same blood, Hawkworth and I. We are merely thrown together because my mama married his papa. I attempted to thwart the marriage, but I failed. I was merely ten at the time. I doubt I shall ever truly forgive her for marrying Hawkworth and forcing me to be civil to Teal, but still, there is little enough I can do about him even now."

"Teal?" asked Sarah. "His given name is Teal?"

"Yes. Teal Hawkyns Harte. Stupid name, no? Mama thinks they named him that for the color of his eyes, but I do not."

"You do not?"

"No, I think they named him for the wild ducks who come to the pond in Hawkyns. They are called teals. Yes, I am quite certain of it. His mama and papa named that devil after ducks."

FOUR

"Why do you not return to London at once, Teal? There is nothing for you here. You detest the country," grumbled Tolliver.

"And I am ruining your party, am I not?" Hawkworth, his muddied clothes exchanged for fresh, stood with shoulders propped against the bookshelves in the library and watched his stepbrother pace the room.

"Yes, you are. Ruining it completely. Everyone thinks of departing early because you have come."

"Why? What have I done? Nothing. I have been most circumspect. I have not called anyone out or kissed any of the young ladies, or fallen down drunk in the middle of the drawing room. No, nor have I set fire to the stables or added poison to the tea."

"You have been here a night and a day merely. Give yourself time, Teal."

"Whoa! I was not expecting that particular jab!" Hawkworth's incredible eyes lit with humor.

"What were you expecting?" Tolliver frowned, coming to a halt directly across the room from Hawkworth and planting his hands upon his hips.

"To hear some sniveling and a plea for understanding and perhaps even to see a tear or two because I assaulted you in the midst of your little dance last evening."

"As to that, you ought to have selected a more opportune time and place to do the thing, but I cannot fault you, Teal, for the punches."

"You cannot? Tolly, I am flabbergasted! No denials? No excuses? No self-righteous indignation? Not even a bit of outrage? What the devil has come over you?" Hawkworth's voice remained low and quiet, but his eyes flashed. "Wait! I know! It is all play-acting on your part to make me less cautious. Once I have swallowed the thing whole and admit to myself that you are a changed man, you intend to take advantage of my stupidity and shoot me in the back."

"I do not shoot people in the back!" bellowed Tolliver.

"Merely because you cannot shoot straight enough to hit them, m'dear," murmured Hawkworth. "Striking young women in the mouth and breaking their teeth, that is more in your line."

Tolliver opened his mouth and closed it again without responding. He stuffed his hands deep into his pockets and lowered his head to stare silently at the bright colors of the Aubusson carpet.

"I meant to have this out with you upstairs at the inn, Tolly, where no one would chance to walk in upon us, but you would not join me there when I asked. I will say it here and now, and you had best listen closely," Hawkworth whispered, his eyes losing their sparkle and becoming hard and gemlike. "And you had best take my words to heart, for I mean them, every one. If Jane Dudley ever comes to me again with so much as a bruise upon her arm and claims it was put there by you, I will call you out, Tolly, stepbrother or no. I will call you out upon the killing ground and I will aim true. I care not what the law says you may or may not do. I say that you may not hit your mistress or any other woman and if you do so again, you will not live beyond the following sunset."

Tolliver made the oddest sound deep in his throat. Then he raised his head and looked directly into Hawk-

worth's cold, hard eyes. "It will never happen again, Teal.
I will never raise my hand to Jane or any other woman
again regardless of the provocation. You have my word
on it."

"I do? So easily as that? Without the least excuse or
protestation or the merest bit of sniveling?"

"I acknowledge that I was wrong to treat Jane in such
a manner, is that not enough for you? You have made
your point. Now you may take yourself back to London
and play with your scurvy friends and think no more
about it."

Hawkworth raised his quizzing glass and studied his
stepbrother intently from head to foot and back up again.

"What? Why are you staring at me? You doubt my
word?"

"I have cause to doubt it," Hawkworth replied, letting
the glass fall upon its riband. "But we were merely
halflings then. I will forget the past, Tolly, since we are
both a good deal older, but you had best not go back
upon your word this time."

"No, I shall not. In fact, I am intent upon bidding Jane
farewell. I shall pop around to Rundell and Bridges next
time I am in Town and buy her a parting gift. One that
will make her smile and forget our—little confrontation."

"Why?"

"Because I have discovered the woman of my dreams,
Teal, and her father is an old Puritan and would never
allow me to approach her if he discovered that I was keeping a mistress in Town."

"The woman of your dreams? There never was any particular woman of your dreams, Tolly, that I recall. Unless
you mean one of those innocent heiresses you were accustomed to go on and on about when you turned
twenty—a rich, romantical little fool who will give over
all her funds to finance the rebuilding of that ramshackle

estate of yours and ask nothing in return but to be duped into thinking herself loved by you."

"Gad, but you are a cold, cynical fish, Teal. I cringe to hear you speak. I tell you that I have grown and changed and come to believe in the prospect of love and happiness. But you—you never change and you believe in nothing."

Hawkworth straightened and stuffed his hands into the pockets of his pantaloons. "I believe in nothing that you tell me at any rate," he mumbled, "except, perhaps, that you will never strike a woman again, now that you know what it will get you. Who is this fortunate wench you long to wed, or is it a secret?"

"No, it is not a secret. Not at all. It is Miss Pritkin."

"Miss Pritkin?" The Hawk's eyes flashed. "Miss Pritkin of the Newcastle Pritkins? May I ask, Tolly, is Miss Pritkin likely to have you?"

"Rather," declared Tolliver in a tone of distinct triumph.

Priscilla knew beyond a doubt that she ought never venture beyond the pocket doors that led into the section of the house inhabited by the Earl of Hawkworth again, but she could not seem to help herself. Sarah had gone up to take a nap and Cecily had gone out to stroll about the grounds with Mr. Crosby, Miss Donovan and Mr. Trimble, and the other young ladies and gentlemen had gathered in the parlor of the west wing to take tea and play at Joints and Jumbles. And since she wished to do neither, she had begun to wander about the house again, studying this cornice and that figurine and noting this tapestry and that suit of armor, until at last she found herself, at this very moment, standing just outside those very pocket doors.

"I ought not," she told herself. "I know it now to be

the place where his chambers lie and it would be most
brazen of me to stroll into that corridor alone and unat-
tended as though I had every right to be there. But I do
so wish to see that painting again, and in more than can-
dlelight."

The painting, like a thing bewitched, drew her onward
despite her best intentions. That oil of the valley below
Hawkworth Aerie on a fine summer's day rose in her
mind like a thing alive and beckoned to her. Treading
softly, Priscilla stepped beyond the pocket doors and
down the corridor to the place where it hung. Quietly
she opened the door directly opposite it and a flood of
sunlight flowed through a veritable wall of windows,
across the chamber and out into the corridor to light the
painting. Priscilla smiled and turned to study the intriguing oil. Really, it was the most remarkable thing. An un-
seen sun glistened off the ripples of a little stream that
meandered over rocks and gravel through the tall grass
of the valley meadow. And the grass, filled with clover
and pinks and jezebels, rippled in a soft breeze.

If I inhale deeply enough, she thought, staring at the
landscape, I ought to be able to smell those flowers. Oh,
I do so wish it were mine. Perhaps his lordship will sell
it to me. No, I could not possibly ask him to do that.
People do not go about offering to purchase other people's paintings when they are not for sale in the first
place. But it is the loveliest thing I have ever seen. Tranquility virtually flows from it. That is what I should have
titled it, had I been the artist—Tranquility.

Deeply involved in enjoyment of the painting and the
wanderings of her own mind, Priscilla did not so much
as hear the angry jangling of The Hawk's spurs as he
stomped into the corridor. She did not notice him at all,
in fact, until he seized her by the shoulder and spun her
around to face him.

"Oh!" she exclaimed, rudely jolted from the peace of the valley into the very real present.

Before she could so much as say *oh!* again, the Earl of Hawkworth seized her other shoulder and leaned down and placed his lips determinedly, roughly, and without the least regard for propriety, upon her own.

Priscilla did think to push him away. In fact, her hands balled themselves into fists and her elbows bent and her fists went up against his broad chest, but then they simply rested there, doing nothing to free her from his grasp.

His hands, however, left her shoulders and began to wander down her back, forcing her closer to him, fastening her more tightly within the forbidden circle of his arms. "If you will appear before me like an enchantress outside my own chambers, I will have this at the very least. I will have this," he murmured as his lips left hers and roamed to cheek and chin and throat. "It is the very least, the very least." And then his lips were upon hers again and his kiss grew soft and sweet and most delicious. The very taste of him set Priscilla's toes to tingling inside her slippers and her heart to singing and her ears to ringing with warning bells of excitement.

"There," he growled at last, pushing her away as suddenly as he had snatched her up. "I shall not be without a memory at least. Now go and marry Tolly." And without waiting for a word of reply, he stomped off down the corridor toward the chambers Priscilla knew to be his own.

"M-marry T-Tolly?" she stuttered, attempting to catch her breath and stop her mind from reeling and her heart from lunging against her ribs and her ears from ringing. "Marry Tolly? What on earth does that mean?" she called, and lifting the bronze skirts of her afternoon dress, she dashed down the corridor in his wake. "Why the deuce would I marry Lord Tolliver? You stop right there and answer me, you—you—Hawk!"

"Cease your pretensions, Miss Pritkin," Hawkworth fairly roared, stopping on the instant and spinning back to face her with such quickness that Priscilla could not stop and ran smack-bang into him and sent him crashing back against the door to his chambers. He said nothing at all for a very long moment; then he merely mumbled, "Ow."

"What pretensions?" exclaimed Priscilla without the least curiosity to know why his roar had diminished to the mumbled *Ow,* nor any sympathy for his having crashed directly into his own door. She wobbled the merest bit, then regained her equilibrium and placing her fists upon her hips, drew herself up to her full four-foot-nine and stared straight up into his eyes.

"Ow," mumbled Hawkworth again.

"Ow, what, for goodness sake? I could not possibly have hurt you. Why, I am a mere moth and you a regular piece of granite."

"Yes, well, this piece of granite, my dear moth, has just had a china doorknob thrust full-force into his back. Ow," he said again.

"Pooh, as if such a tiny thing would bother *you.* What did you mean that I should go and marry Tolly?"

"Just what I said. You are Miss Pritkin, are you not? You are in love with my stepbrother, are you not? You do intend to marry Tolliver?"

"Me?" squeaked Priscilla. "Me?"

"Yes, you. Do not pretend to me that you have not the least idea that he intends to propose marriage to you. Tolly has already told me it is as good as a done thing between the two of you. And I do not give a damn!" he added after a moment's thought. "I only wondered what it would be like to kiss you, and now I know and now you may spend the rest of your life kissing Tolly and I shall not care a fig."

"Well, of all the dunderheads," Priscilla replied, her

hands unfisting and dropping to play among the folds of her skirt. "For your information, my dear Lord Hawkworth, it is my sister Sarah who is in love with Lord Tolliver. You *do* remember Sarah? She sat beside you at nuncheon a mere two hours ago."

"Sarah? Your sister, Sarah?" Hawkworth pushed himself upright, away from the door and the knob.

"Indeed. Sarah and Lord Tolliver met last Season in London, and they have been in communication ever since. He has even been to Newcastle twice to visit her."

"Oh. Well, confound it, how was I to know?" Hawkworth grumbled. "When Tolly said Miss Pritkin, the only Miss Pritkin who entered my mind was you. I thought he meant to marry you. And then I came upstairs and there you were as if by magic, and I—I expect I ought to apologize for—"

"Attacking me in the corridor? Forcing yourself upon me? Kissing me in that most—most—"

"Most what?" asked Hawkworth, brushing back a dark curl which had fallen low above his right eye.

"Most vulgar fashion!" exclaimed Priscilla.

"Vulgar? What was vulgar about it?" Hawkworth queried, his eyes beginning to glow. "Do you mean that the way I kissed you was vulgar or just the fact that I kissed you at all?"

"All of it," declared Priscilla. "All of it was vulgar. At least—a young lady does not wish to be attacked in a corridor, seized by the shoulders and forced into a kiss."

"Oh?" Hawkworth's right eyebrow cocked the slightest bit and his lips twitched upward at the corners.

"Do not act the dunce, sir," Priscilla scolded, her eyes sparking with the oddest mixture of passion and mischief. "A young lady wishes to be lured into a kiss with pretty words and whispers and gentle persuasions. She wants a gentleman to put his arms tenderly around her, just so."

Priscilla took the earl's hands and placed them at her back.

"She wishes the gentleman to stare with awe down into her eyes, into the very depths of her soul." Priscilla placed her own arms about Hawkworth and stared up into his eyes so that he could not avoid staring downward into hers.

"She wants the gentleman's lips to press softly, tenderly, against her own with a certain hesitance, a particular timidity that is born of a mixture of longing and need and respect." And so saying, Priscilla stood upon her toes and drew Hawkworth down to her and brushed his lips with her own.

It was the merest whisper of a kiss, but it set The Hawk's heart to pounding as no other kiss had ever done. And when she released him, he was caught in a place between wonder and laughter. "Miss Priscilla Pritkin, you are disgraceful," he murmured as she released him from her embrace and then released herself from his.

"Yes, I know."

"A regular minx."

"Oh, much worse than that."

"Do you truly not know who I am, to tease me so? I am The Hawk, the blackest sheep the Hartes have ever birthed."

"Oh, pooh, to say it as though I ought to shudder and run. I will have you know, my lord, that in Newcastle I am called The Circe and I am by far the most nefarious of all the Pritkins."

FIVE

The Circe? Hawkworth stretched full-length upon his bed and studied the cherubs who gallivanted about the woodland glen that covered his bedchamber ceiling. They call her The Circe? he thought amazedly. She is the most nefarious of all the Pritkins? "I did never know," he murmured, "that Pritkins were ever nefarious. And it is not she whom Tolly means to wed. It is her sister Sarah."

He attempted to visualize Sarah, but he could not. He thought she might be taller than Priscilla, but he did not remember that with certainty. "I do not even remember the color of the chit's hair," he grumbled to himself. "How could I have sat beside her at nuncheon and not so much as noticed the color of her hair?"

"It is short and blond and almost as curly as your own, my lord," offered Strange as he wandered into the room.

"It is?"

"Indeed. And her eyes are a most lovely brown. She is, in fact, a very pretty young lady, if I may say so. What do you wish to wear to dinner, my lord?"

"She looks just like Miss Priscilla Pritkin? How could I not notice if that were the case? Is she just as tiny, too, Strange?"

"Who, my lord?"

"Tolly's Miss Pritkin. Miss Sarah Pritkin. She looks exactly like her sister?"

"Oh, is that whom you were attempting to recall? I thought 'twas the other Miss Pritkin you strove to visualize—the one first took your notice."

"No, Strange, I *know* what Miss Priscilla looks like."

"Just so, my lord. I was mistaken. Lord Tolliver's Miss Pritkin has hair the color of honey and blue eyes and is vaguely taller than your Miss Pritkin. She comes, I believe, near to the height of Lord Tolliver's shoulders. What shall I lay out for you to wear to dinner, my lord?"

"Nothing."

"Nothing, my lord? But you always change for dinner."

"I am not going down to dinner, Strange."

"Well, of course you are," urged Strange gently. "This is your home, my lord, and all of the guests will expect to see you at the head of the table."

"Not so. They do none of them wish to see me at all, Strange. They will, in fact, heave a collective sigh of relief when I do not join them in the drawing room before dinner and an even greater sigh when I do not come barging in to take the head of the table in the midst of the meal. They are none of them truly friends of mine. We would do best, you and I, Strange, to ride for London tonight."

"My lord, we cannot. You have not forgotten why—"

"No, I have not forgotten why we came. And we shall not return to London, because it would be a dastardly thing to do, to desert Sidney before he even arrives. But I will not go down to dinner either. I shall have a tray in my room and perhaps sketch a bit. I have not painted anything at all since I did this ceiling. Perhaps I will begin upon my sitting room wall, eh? No, better than that! We shall decide, you and I, which chambers will belong to Sidney and I shall begin upon one of his walls."

"Do you mean to keep him in this wing, then?" asked Strange, a flicker of sincere hope in his fine gray eyes.

"I have been thinking about it, Strange, and I cannot see why I should not."

"No, my lord, there is no reason at all why you should not. All of Hawkworth Aerie belongs to you, and you may quarter Master Sidney and Sir Godfrey as well, if I may say so, wherever you please."

"Just so," muttered Hawkworth. "Wherever I damn well please."

Dinner proved to be a long, tedious affair and Priscilla gave thanks when at last Lady Hawkworth arose and led the ladies from the dining room. Priscilla had fully expected to see The Hawk at the head of the table, but he had not joined them, and she did take note that a number of the ladies and gentlemen appeared greatly relieved when it became obvious that he had no intention of doing so.

But perhaps he will join us in the drawing room, Priscilla thought hopefully. I cannot have frightened him off just by—just by—no, of course not. I ought not to have kissed him, but certainly he, of all men, will not hold such outrageous behavior against me. And no one else has the least idea that we were even together this afternoon.

"Why do you frown so?" Sarah asked, taking her sister's hand and leading her to the window seat. "Sit here with me for a moment and tell me what disturbs you, Priscilla. I have not seen such a pucker between your brows since Harry dropped your locket into the well."

Priscilla grinned at that. She had been merely eleven and Harry three and the locket had been but a trinket given her by her mama to put around her doll's neck. "I have not thought of that in a considerable number of years, Sarah," she grinned. "I thought it lost forever."

"And the following year, up it came in Winstead's bucket," smiled Sarah.

"Indeed. A most amazing thing, was it not?"

"But what makes you frown now, Priscilla? You did not truly smile even once at dinner."

"I did. I smiled whenever Mr. Radshaw spoke to me, and whenever Mr. Carter spoke to me as well."

"But not a true smile. I was watching."

"You were? I thought you to have eyes for no one but Lord Tolliver."

"Even I cannot stare at him all the time," giggled Sarah. "It would be most unacceptable. Tell me what troubles you."

"Only that his lordship did not dine with us."

"Lord Hawkworth?"

"Yes."

"Oh, but Priscilla, you should rejoice that he did not. Everyone else was rejoicing. Even Lady Cecily, who has known him since she was a child, was relieved that he chose not to make an appearance."

"Why? Does he eat with his fingers? Or shout at people down the table? Or invite his dogs in to dine and toss great hunks of meat onto the floor for them?"

"Priscilla, shush, someone will hear you."

"Well, and I do not care if they do hear me. This is his home. Certainly he ought to have dined at his own table."

The gentlemen had obviously not lingered over their wine, for they entered at just that moment and in a moment more, Lord Tolliver had sought and discovered Sarah and strolled to the window seat himself, and Priscilla, knowing herself wished to Jericho, gave up her position beside her sister to the gentleman.

"I shall just go and see for myself why he does not join us," she murmured to herself, gazing around the drawing room and seeing not a sign of Hawkworth. "There is no one here will so much as notice that I have gone."

The Hawk was laughing. She could hear him the very moment that she opened the pocket doors. The sound of his laughter brought a smile to her lips and a sparkle to her eyes. Oh, Priscilla thought, to hear such unbridled laughter for a lifetime. How wonderful that would be. I cannot understand why he is such a pariah when his laughter alone would make him welcome in my home.

Quietly, she made her way down the corridor toward a chamber whose door stood open wide and from which a considerable amount of light flowed onto the corridor carpet. She peered around the door frame cautiously, not wishing to disturb him, and especially not wishing to bring an end to his laughter. And then she stared, dumbstruck, at the sight before her.

A number of Holland covers had been strewn about upon the floor near the north wall of the chamber and atop them, in a semicircle, stood various tables and chairs with a hundred candles or more distributed haphazardly upon them in various branches and candelabras and bowls. Some of the candles had even been melted and then stuck into their own wax upon dinner plates. And in the midst of the candles, trampling upon the Holland covers in their stockinged feet, without neckcloths or collars or cuffs, stripped right down to their shirtsleeves, their faces and hands streaked with charcoal, the Earl of Hawkworth and another gentleman gamboled about in the oddest manner.

"I have never seen such a thing in all my life," Hawkworth whooped. "It looks like a—a—humpbacked mouse!"

"It is Turnabout, my lord," replied the other gentleman, snorting oddly. "You did say to put Turnabout there."

"Yes, Strange, but bigger, grander, and looking more like a horse! Never mind, I will do it. See if you cannot draw in these flowers I have started, eh? You are much better with flowers, I think."

"Much better," replied the gentleman, nodding and snorting both. "But not good."

"Sidney will not mind, Strange. He will be pleased just to think that you took the time to draw them."

"And you will fix them when you paint, will you not?"

"Just so. I will fix them when I paint."

Priscilla watched, enthralled, as the two men switched places and the earl, a stick of charcoal in his hand, began to draw upon the wall with great swirling motions. Before her eyes the great beast that Lord Hawkworth had ridden that very day appeared upon the wall. Ears back, nostrils flaring, eyes rolling, the horse reared up upon its haunches, front hooves flailing at the air. And then, like magic, a knight in armor began to take shape upon its back.

"Oh," Priscilla sighed when the knight, with spear at the ready, was done.

"Oh?" Hawkworth turned toward the doorway. "Priscilla? What the devil are you doing, spying upon me?"

"N-no. No. I only came to see why you did not join us for dinner, my lord, or appear in the withdrawing room afterward. Oh, it is wonderful."

"What is wonderful?"

"The wall. Is there to be a dragon as well? And a maiden for the knight to rescue? Are there gnomes? There, those look like gnomes," she said, stepping into the room and pointing happily. "I have always wished to see gnomes. That is just exactly what I thought they would look like."

"She is pointing to your squirrels, Strange," chuckled

the earl. "They are squirrels, sweetling. At least they will be squirrels when the painting is finished. But gnomes are an excellent idea," he added, "just about here, I think." And in the wink of an eye three tiny, well-dressed gnomes appeared, one perched upon a giant mushroom, smoking a pipe, and the other two lying lazily beneath it with hats pulled down over their eyes.

Hawkworth pushed a lock of hair out of his own eyes with the back of his hand and left a smudge of charcoal upon his brow. "I did not come down because Strange and I are otherwise occupied. Have you met Strange? No? Miss Priscilla Pritkin, may I present my valet, Mr. Strange. You ought not be up here, sweetling."

"Why not?"

"Well, because it ain't done. You ought to be in whichever drawing room my stepmama is using tonight. You are one of her guests, after all."

"Yes, but I do not wish to be."

"You do not wish to be one of her guests?"

"I do not wish to be in the drawing room. It is deadly dull."

"See, Strange, I told you it would be deadly dull, did I not?"

"Indeed, my lord."

"Well, we are jolly here, sweetling, and I have nothing against your remaining with us."

"My lord, we are not suitably attired," declared the valet.

"Priscilla does not mind, Strange. Priscilla has younger brothers. I will lay you odds that she has seen them in their shirtsleeves at least once."

"That is not the point, my lord."

"It is not?"

"It is precisely the point," interrupted Priscilla, fearing that the valet would squelch her opportunity to remain. "Truly, Mr. Strange, I do not at all mind that you are in your shirtsleeves. And I do so wish to help with the wall. May I help with it, my lord?"

"Do you draw as well as Strange?" the earl asked, grinning.

"Indeed, quite as well as Mr. Strange."

"Well, then, I stand in need of a pond there at the corner. Not a perfectly round pond, either. One that flows over onto the connecting wall."

"We are doing two walls, my lord?" asked Mr. Strange, with an eagerness in his tone that Priscilla could not mistake.

"Well, I know we were not going to do two, Strange, but now we have an extra hand, you see. Do you not think Sidney would like the scene to cover two walls?"

"Oh, indeed, sir. Master Sidney will be thrilled."

"Yes, well, we shall see, Strange. He may not like it at all. He may not even like the country. But we shall see."

"Oh, Priscilla, he is the most romantic of all gentlemen, and so very kind and thoughtful and pleasant. I cannot help but love him." Sarah plopped down before the hearth in the sitting room they shared, her face beaming above the high collar of her flannel nightgown. "And I played for him while he sang. He has the most magnificent tenor. Everyone was enraptured. And he led me out onto the balcony in the moonlight. Just for a moment, Priscilla. There could have been nothing wrong in it, for his mama and the others were right there behind us in the drawing room. He led me out onto the balcony and he declared that he loved me with all his heart and soul."

"And did you make him a declaration of equal significance?" Priscilla asked, coming to sit beside her sister upon the brocade settee. "Did you, Sarah?"

"Oh, yes. I vowed I would love him until the day I died."

"And did he ask you to marry him?"

"No, but he will, Priscilla. He must gain Papa's permission first. You were right. He means to accompany us back to Newcastle when the party ends. Oh, I am so gloriously happy."

"Yes," laughed Priscilla, "so I see. You would fly to the heavens if you could."

"I have already done so. But where were you? Where did you go? I had no idea that you intended to leave us for the entire evening. When you did not return by the time I went to play upon the pianoforte for him, I did begin to worry, you know. And I did think to discover you conversing with Cecily or other of the young ladies when we returned from the balcony. Did you have the headache, dearest?"

Priscilla studied her sister's sweet, blushing face a moment, then gave a nod. "But it has almost disappeared now," she assured Sarah with a smile. "I am so very happy for you, Sarah!" And feeling the least bit guilty for lying to her sister, she took Sarah into her arms and gave her an energetic hug.

One ought not lie to one's sister. Especially, one ought not lie to Sarah, Priscilla thought as at last they parted and she slipped into her own bed. But I could not possibly say to her that I had spent the entire evening in Lord Hawkworth's wing of the house drawing pictures upon a bedchamber wall. Sarah would have fainted dead away. No, more than that, she thought with a grin. She would have screamed first, when I revealed the state of dress that he and his valet were in, and then she would have fainted dead away.

"But I do not care in the least," she whispered into the night. "I had the most wonderful time and he is the most incredible artist I have ever known. Of course, he is the very first artist that I have ever known. And to think, that marvelous landscape in the corridor is his own work, and I am to have it for my own in payment for my able assistance."

She closed her eyes and saw him, charcoal in hand, outlining the form of the captive maiden for whom the knight was poised to fight the dragon. His dark curls were all askew and his face smudged and his nose wrinkled up in the most endearing manner as he concentrated. And just as it had at the time, Priscilla's heart once again spiraled upward into her throat and her breath came in short gasps and she began to feel warm all over. Very, very warm.

Oh, dear, she thought, opening her eyes to stare up at the flickering of firelight upon the ceiling. Is this what it feels like to fall in love? No, it cannot be. He is most unacceptable. Even I know that. Papa and Mama will have apoplexies should I so much as suggest to them that I have developed a particular fondness for such a one as The Hawk.

SIX

Hawkworth descended to breakfast the next morning in a remarkably pleasant mood. Mr. Butler was pleased to direct him to the sun room, where his stepmama had decided that breakfast would be served during the house party, and he murmured a "good morning" to Mr. Crosby and Lord Dugan.

"No one else has arisen as yet, eh?" he queried politely, helping himself to a slice of beefsteak, shirred eggs and a tankard of ale at the sideboard.

"Late evening," Mr. Crosby replied. "You did not come down to dinner, Hawkworth."

"Do not say that you wished for my company."

"Not at all. Had a splendid time without you, Hawk," Crosby grinned. "Always do. Cecily was in a dither, expecting you to make an appearance in the drawing room afterward, but she did settle down eventually."

"When are you going to marry that chit?" asked Hawkworth, taking the seat at the head of the table.

Lord Dugan guffawed as Crosby's face tinged with red.

"Well, he has been playing at devotion with Cecily for two full years now, Dugan. Ought to marry her," Hawkworth continued, cutting a piece of the beefsteak. "Cannot keep the chit on a string forever."

"Just so," nodded Dugan. "Just so. Exactly right, Hawk."

"Yes, and you, sir, have been doing the same to my stepmama. I cannot think why she would wish to marry anyone again. Two husbands should be enough to turn any woman sour upon marriage. But all the same, Dugan—"

Crosby chuckled as Lord Dugan paused with a forkful of eggs partway to his mouth. "Odd role for you, Hawk," the elderly gentleman managed around a cough and a grunt. "Cupid."

"Not so. Not Cupid. Interested in marriage, merely."

"Yes, so long as it is not you doing the marrying," Crosby offered.

"Rumors that Tolly is thinking of taking the leap," Hawkworth ventured. "With Miss Pritkin. Is it true?"

"His mama apparently thinks so," nodded Dugan. "Already treating the girl like a daughter-in-law. Quiet little thing, Miss Pritkin."

Hawkworth's eyebrow cocked. "Quiet?"

"Aye, and shy as well," Crosby acknowledged, pausing to sip at his tea. "But she is pretty and as rich as Croesus."

"Rich? The Newcastle Pritkins are rich?" Hawkworth lowered his fork with a piece of beefsteak still upon it and stared down the table at Crosby.

"Great Aunt Somebody died and left the two girls a fortune to share between them," mumbled Crosby. "Not that Pritkin himself will cut up cold when he dies because he will not."

"Does Tolly know about this inheritance?"

"Everyone knows, Hawk," Dugan offered. "Written up in all the papers when it happened."

Hawkworth literally trapped Priscilla as she and Sarah strolled from their chambers into the second-floor corridor. "Come with me," he murmured, catching her by the arm from behind. "I must speak with you."

"Oh!" squeaked Sarah. "My lord, what do you think you are doing? Unhand my sister this instant!"

"Great heavens, what a start!" laughed Priscilla. "I did not so much as see you standing there, Lord Hawkworth."

"No, I was leaning against the wall. I have an overwhelming need to speak privately with you, Priscilla. Go back and don your riding habit and we will go for a canter, just you and I."

"How dare you take such liberties," declared Sarah. "My sister is Miss Priscilla to you. And she will not do any such thing as to ride off alone with a gentleman of your—of your—reputation!"

"Sarah, hush," Priscilla murmured, studying the handsome face that stared down at her. Hawkworth's turquoise eyes did not sparkle the least bit and his lips lingered in a straight line, not even one corner of them twitching upward. "It is something serious, my lord?"

"Most serious."

"Very well, I will be a few moments only," she nodded, turning back toward her chamber door.

"Priscilla, no!" Sarah squealed.

"Do not panic, Miss Pritkin. I have no intention to ravage the girl, I assure you," Hawkworth muttered, catching Sarah by the arm to keep her from following Priscilla. "No, and I ain't about to pillage her either."

"Oh!" Sarah huffed, her cheeks reddening at his words. "To say such things to me! Begone and cease plaguing Priscilla or I will tell Arlin that you are taking liberties with my sister and he will—"

"What?" asked Hawkworth softly.

"He will—he will—call you out!" declared Sarah, peeling his hand from her arm finger by finger.

"Tolly? Oh, my dear, you put much too much faith in your splendid beau's portion of courage. Tolly would not call me out if I were to bed his intended the night before his wedding."

Sarah's hand flashed upward and connected mightily with Hawkworth's cheek, her lace gloves imprinting a pattern of reddening eyelets upon it.

"Yes, well, I did not intend to suggest that I would actually do such a thing, my dear," Hawkworth drawled, ignoring the sting of the slap completely.

"You are a Philistine! And why you have taken it into your head to terrorize my sister when you have barely a nodding acquaintance with her—"

Hawkworth could not help himself. He grinned. "Terrorize?" he drawled. "Terrorize your sister? I merely requested that she ride with me, Miss Pritkin." The Hawk was unaccustomed to having a peal rung over him by anyone, much less so diminutive a being as Sarah Pritkin. The absurdness of it tickled him immensely.

She is taller than Priscilla, but still, she barely comes up to my stickpin, he thought. And I will be wildly surprised if she weighs seven stone. But she is as plucky as a bantam rooster.

"Requested that she ride with you?" Sarah glared. "No, my lord. You demanded that she ride with you and *alone*. Proper young women do not ride off *alone* with any man, much less a perfect stranger with a reputation for roguishness."

"If that is all," drawled Hawkworth, "I will take one of the stable boys with us. Will that satisfy you, Miss Pritkin?"

"No, it will not! You have no business to go riding with Priscilla at all. What can you possibly have to say to her that you cannot say right here in this house? You rode with her from the Bear and Bell to the Aerie and have not seen or spoken to her since. And now you discover some reason that she must ride out with you into a countryside foreign to her and with only a stable boy to attend her. And *your* stable boy at that!"

"Why, Miss Pritkin," drawled Hawkworth, stuffing his

hands into his pockets and leaning one shoulder against the wall. "I am amazed at you."

Sarah stared up at him, puzzled.

"To think that such an upright and gently bred young woman would even think—" He ceased to speak and shook his head sadly from side to side. "To tell the truth, I find it appalling," he murmured then. "Horrifying, in fact, that such thoughts could enter such a charming mind."

"Thoughts? What thoughts? Of what do you speak?"

"You know precisely of what I speak, Miss Pritkin. That I should take your sister out into a *foreign countryside*, with only *my stableboy*. Come, Miss Pritkin, even such a lackwit as I know what such words imply. And that a young woman with such a sweet face and such delightful manners should suggest that I plan to assault Priscilla in a place where she cannot possibly find aid—well, pull your mind up out of the gutter, Miss Pritkin, do. It does not become you to have it residing there."

"How dare you!"

"If I intended to assault your sister, my dear, I would not take her out into the countryside to do it. It is messy, to say the least. And cold. Especially in February."

"Oh!"

"Oh, indeed," commented Hawkworth with an elegant cock of an eyebrow. "I ceased to dawdle about with maidens in bushes when I was sixteen. I discovered, you see, that I much prefer silk sheets and a warm fire to dirt and stickers and a north wind whipping down out of the hills."

"A north wind whipping down out of the hills?" queried Priscilla, opening her chamber door and stepping out into the corridor, looking quite lovely in a habit of deep blue velvet with a matching hat perched saucily upon her golden curls. "It will be wickedly cold then, will it not? Are you certain you wish to ride, my lord?"

"More certain than ever," Hawkworth replied with a long, studious look at the vision before him. "And there is barely a wind at all. Your sister and I were merely discussing—possibilities," he said with a half smile and a wink at Sarah, who gasped to see it.

He offered Priscilla his arm and she took it despite the consternation upon Sarah's face and allowed him to lead her off in the direction of the main staircase.

He led her down the hillside in silence, the horses picking their way around boulders and bushes, rabbit holes and loose gravel slides, Priscilla frowning down in concentration at the treacherous ground over which they traveled.

"We ought to have taken the drive," Priscilla sighed at last, looking up to discover that they were still very near the top and had a great way yet to descend.

"No, do you think so?" Hawkworth replied. "But where would the adventure be in that? Anyone might gain the meadow by way of the drive."

"You," Priscilla pointed out, "are not riding sidesaddle. A sidesaddle is an adventure in itself."

He laughed and the sound of his laughter wrapped itself like a comforting wool muffler around Priscilla's heart. Truly, I do love to hear him laugh, she thought upon the instant, a smile rising into her eyes.

"You are not quite ready for this particular adventure, eh? Well, but you were game to attempt it without the least protest when we began. I know just the thing," Hawkworth offered, bringing his mount to a halt upon the edge of an outcropping and dismounting. "Come here. Let me help you down."

Priscilla could not imagine what he intended, but did as he bade her, relishing the strength of his hands about her waist as he lifted her to the ground. He did not release her, but kept his hands upon her waist and stared deeply into her eyes.

"What?" she asked when he neither moved nor spoke. "What is it you wish?"

His face grew somber and the brilliance of his turquoise eyes took her breath away. "Do not ask that particular question, my little Circe," he murmured. "I may answer you true, and then both our souls will be lost." He released her then, slowly, and turned away for a moment. When he turned back, he was smiling again. "Come up before me on Turnabout," he said, grinning and taking one of her hands into his own. "You will be a deal more safe with my arms around you and we will reach the meadow in better time. Sammy will bring the mare down with him and you may remount her in the meadow."

Before she could protest, he brought her up beside Turnabout, set her sideways upon his own saddle, and mounted behind her.

"All you need do, sweetling, is relax and gaze at the countryside," he whispered in her ear. And then they were flying down the hillside, soaring over boulders instead of picking their way around them and crashing through bushes and underbrush without the least regard for rabbit holes or gravel slides. In less than three minutes they had reached the bottom of the hill and Hawkworth's great beast was carrying them eagerly across the meadow toward the stream. And then he was not.

Priscilla cried in delight as Turnabout's headlong rush ceased and he reared upon his haunches and whinnied and pawed at the air. He dropped back to earth and spun in place, turning a complete circle with only the barest movement of his rear legs. Then he turned the same tight circle in reverse. And then the enormous horse began to dance, prancing first one way and then the other, making figure eights and great wide arcs, waltzing through the high brown grasses with prideful, bouncing steps.

Exhilarated, excited, her cheeks red with the wind and her hat long since blown away, Priscilla leaned her golden curls against Hawkworth's strong, broad shoulder and laughed and laughed. Secure within his arms, she called out to the horse, urging him on. "Spin, dance, waltz, you angel," she called out to him. "Oh, you are the most wonderful horse. The most amazing horse. I positively adore you!"

"Hush, or he will never stop," Hawkworth murmured in her ear, his warm breath sending thrills of the oddest anticipation through her.

"Never say so," she answered back. "Surely it is you who are making him do this. And you may bring him to a halt at any time you wish."

"No, not I, sweetling. All this exuberance is Turnabout's alone, I assure you, and I have very little power over him at the moment. We shall never reach the stream at this rate, much less cross over into the wood. We will be gamboling about this meadow until spring."

"Let us do it, then!" declared Priscilla with enthusiasm. "Let us gambol and frolic and dance about the meadow until the grass is green and the flowers blooming! Oh, it is wonderful!"

Hawkworth, enchanted with her enthusiasm and bewitched by the featherweight of her in his arms, did nothing to quiet the beast's curious and joyful frolic, allowing the great horse to do as he pleased until at last he saw that Sammy had reached the meadow with the mare in tow and was riding toward them.

"Turnabout," he said then in a most authoritative voice. "Cease and desist, do. Priscilla's mount has arrived."

He did nothing but speak, Priscilla noted with amazement. His hands did not tighten upon the reins, nor his knees send a signal. He merely spoke and the horse listened, and in a moment the dancing that had seemed to her like a celebration of life slowed and then stopped. Hawkworth leaped to the ground and lifted her down beside him. Taking her hand into his own, he led her in Sammy's direction, and when they reached the stable boy, he lifted her up into the sidesaddle, gave the mare's reins into her keeping and then whistled. In an instant, Turnabout was beside him and he was swinging up onto the horse's back.

"He were dancin' agin, m'lor'," grinned Sammy. "I do enjoy ta see 'im dance."

"Someday, Sammy, you will dance with him."

"Me, m'lord?"

"Yes, indeed. You and Turnabout, larking about the meadow, waltzing with the flowers. And I shall sit here and watch the two of you and think how wonderful life is, eh?"

"Aye," the little boy nodded. " 'Tis wonnerful, life."

"It is," nodded Hawkworth. "Every moment of it."

"Every moment of life is wonderful?" asked Priscilla once they had started off again and the stable boy was quite far behind them. "Do you truly believe that to be so, my lord?"

"Yes. Even the blackest moments, when you look back upon them, turn out to be in some way wonderful."

"Well, I cannot imagine that."

"Likely because you are not old enough to have endured a truly black moment. Little dips and twists and dawdles are likely all that you have known, sweetling, though some of them have seemed most black to you. But even small aggravations are somehow wonderful, if only we have the faith and courage to see them properly. They add flavor and spice to the great adventure of our lives and give us a reason to go on, always forward, always rejoicing in what may come to meet us."

Priscilla stared at him, her lips parted in amazement.

"What?" queried Hawkworth. "Close your mouth, sweetling, or something quite unpalatable is like to fly in."

They rode to a small glade in the midst of the wood, where Hawkworth helped her to dismount and guided her to a small outcropping bathed in sunlight. "There is something we must discuss, Priscilla," he began, shedding his coat and spreading it upon the flat, worn rock for her to sit upon. He saw her nicely settled and then sat down beside her, his long legs crossed Indian style. "You are an heiress. You and your sister both."

"Yes."

"How great of a fortune do you share?"

"You have brought me here to speak of money?"

"No, not money. Not exactly. Is it a large fortune?"

"It is—significant," Priscilla managed, suddenly suspicious of him for asking.

"Just so. I feared it might be," he murmured, leaning forward and picking a stone from the ground, beginning to toss it nervously in his hand. "There is something I must say to you."

"What, my lord?"

"It is about Tolly—and about your sister, as well."

"About Sarah?"

"Indeed. She is in love with Tolly?"

"Yes."

"You are certain of it?"

"Indeed. I am very certain of it. He rides back with us when we return to Newcastle for the purpose of gaining my papa's permission to pay his addresses to Sarah, and Sarah is overjoyed that he intends it."

Hawkworth stared off into the woods and said nothing further. His hands worried at the stone and he sighed.

"What is it?" Priscilla demanded at last, tugging at his sleeve. "You did not insist that I accompany you just so that I might sit upon a rock and watch you stare at trees."

"It is merely that— No, it is not merely anything. It is

not a subject that may be introduced by such a word as merely. Tolly struck his mistress," he said in a quiet, worried voice. "Viciously. It is not the first time he has done so. I came riding home to confront him on Jane's behalf. And now I discover that he intends to marry your sister, and that she is rich."

Priscilla stared at him, bewildered, and could not think of one word to say.

SEVEN

"He has given me his word," Hawkworth murmured, dropping the stone and turning to face her, reaching out with one finger to trace the delicate line of Priscilla's jaw. "He has given me his word that he will never raise his hand to a woman again. He claims to love your sister, that she is the woman of his dreams."

"And do you have reason to doubt his word?" Priscilla asked.

"Yes. But it is not merely that which worries me. This, sweetling, is your sister's life of which we speak. Were she not an heiress, were she simply Miss Pritkin of the Newcastle Pritkins and Tolly claimed to love her— But she *is* an heiress and Tolly has spent his whole life plotting ways to achieve a fortune with which to restore his estate. I cannot think but that your sister—that she is not his love, but his fortune."

"No, Lord Tolliver loves Sarah. He truly does."

"You are certain? Because if he does not love her, if he thinks to marry her only for her money and they do not—get along—he is like to— But I will call him out if he does. I made that clear enough. He does not doubt me."

Priscilla sat stunned. "You would call out your stepbrother?" she murmured after a long silence.

"If he raises his hand to any woman again, yes. And I

will aim for the heart, too, should the woman he abuses be your sister. But it will be too late then for Sarah. Her happiness will already have been ruined. A man may beat his wife in England any time he pleases, did you know? And Sarah will be his wife, and he will have her fortune, and—and if I make her a widow, it will be I who am the criminal, not Tolly."

Hawkworth shook his head. "Devil it, but my thoughts run wild! Tolly would not harm the woman he loves, do you think? But does he truly love Sarah? Is it your sister or her fortune for which Tolliver's heart beats so fondly? I do not have the answer, sweetling, nor do I know anything to be done but to warn Sarah of him. And I cannot do that. She will not accept any such warning from me. No one would. My words are always suspect in the face of Tolliver's righteous propriety. And I— What I thought was—that perhaps *you* might warn her."

They rode back in silence, this time taking the drive up the hill to the Aerie. Priscilla left Hawkworth at the main entrance to the rambling structure and hurried up the staircase to change from her habit. She must hurry. She must don a morning dress and then discover where Sarah had gone. It was more than likely that wherever Sarah was, Lord Tolliver would be beside her.

It was so. Priscilla discovered them, along with a number of other members of the house party, in the music room attempting to form themselves into an orchestra. Sarah rose from the pianoforte the moment Priscilla appeared and crossed to her, taking her arm and urging her back out into the corridor.

"Are you all right, dearest? That fiend did not harm you? If you had not come back within another ten minutes, I was set to tell Arlin all and get the gentlemen to go in search of you. Priscilla, you are trembling. What is it? Tell me at once. He *has* harmed you! Oh, I knew I ought not to have given in to your will."

"No, he has done nothing," Priscilla cried in a hushed little voice. "Sarah, I must speak to you privately. Come away with me to some empty chamber. You must and at once."

With fright and questions in her eyes, Sarah hurried with her sister down the corridor. They turned into the very first empty room they discovered and closed the door tightly after them.

"Now," Sarah said, taking a seat in the armchair behind the table in the armaments room, "tell me all, dearest. Everything. All that happened, all that he said. Whatever it was, there can be no shame in it upon your part, Priscilla. I am convinced that you did nothing improper."

Priscilla, trembling still with the fear that Sarah would not believe a word of it, paced the length of the room, her glance darting from floor to wall to ceiling and back again as she said what she must say.

"It is all a sham," Sarah declared when Priscilla had ceased to speak. "How you can believe that such a perfect gentleman as Arlin would—would— You are foolish beyond belief, Priscilla. If anyone is guilty of cavorting about with mistresses and striking them viciously, it is that villain, Lord Hawkworth!"

"No, Sarah, he is not a villain. I vow it to you."

"You cannot possibly vow it to me. You do not even know the man, Priscilla, and yet you take his lies to heart. How can you?"

"But I do know him, Sarah. I have spent time with him, and I believe him to be speaking truth."

"Well, I do not. He detests Arlin and wishes to ruin his happiness by sending you to me with such a message. The man is an ogre and rightfully a pariah and I shall not listen to his slanderous phrases, nor will you from this moment on. We are going home, Priscilla, the very first thing tomorrow morning. I will not have that rogue come near you again. Not ever again!''

Nothing would change Sarah's mind. That evening, as Priscilla laid her head at last upon her pillow, their bags were already packed and waiting to be carried down to the coach the first thing in the morning.

Priscilla woke to a scratching upon the door between her bedchamber and the sitting room she shared with Sarah. Rubbing at eyes still scratchy from tears, she tumbled from her bed and made her way barefoot across the thick carpeting by the light of a dying fire. "What is it you want, Sarah?" she mumbled as she turned the knob and tugged the door open.

Hawkworth stood in his shirtsleeves, one hand upon the door frame, staring down at her. One cheek was streaked with blue paint and the front of his shirt stained with green and gold and red. A fine reddish brown had taken up residence in a splotch upon his chin.

"I want to know that you are all right," he whispered. "I went down to dinner only to see you again and you were not there. The headache, your sister told everyone, all the while glaring at me as though I had been the cause of it. Does your head ache? Am I the cause of it? Did you tell Sarah about Tolly? I had to wait until everyone was asleep to come here, lest we be discovered together and your reputation sunk forever."

Priscilla seized him by the arm and tugged him into her chamber. She closed the door behind him and locked it. "Sarah does not believe a word of it because it comes from you. And she has determined that I am in danger from associating with you and so has declared that we must leave the Aerie tomorrow morning."

"It is already tomorrow morning," Hawkworth whispered, taking her flannel robe from the chair and holding it open for her. He then bent down and searched beneath the bed for her slippers. Finding them, he urged her to sit upon the mattress and placed them upon her feet. Then he crossed to the grate, stirred the coals and added more.

"Come here, closer to the fire. You will freeze way over there." He pulled the one large chair in the chamber up before the blaze and Priscilla, doing as he bade her, left the bed and went to sit down in it.

He sat cross-legged at her feet and blinked up at her. "I did think that she might believe you," he whispered, brushing a dark curl back from his brow. "I knew she would never believe me, but I hoped that you might— Perhaps we are wrong to fear the worst, sweetling. Perhaps we ought simply wait and trust in your sister's loving nature and good judgment to find Tolly out or to bring an end to his—to his—ill manners."

Priscilla sniffed the merest bit and rubbed one eye with her fist. "I do not think that Sarah has good judgment," she murmured sadly. "She is too easily swayed by the opinions of others. She does never open her eyes and see for herself."

"No, do not cry, sweetling," Hawkworth whispered, gaining his knees, tugging a handkerchief speckled with paint from his pocket and dabbing at two slowly falling tears. "Why do you say she is easily swayed? She struck me as a young woman of definite opinions."

"Yes, but the opinions all belong to someone else. She would not berate you so else, when she does not know you from Adam."

"She berated me, did she?"

"She called you a villain and an ogre and a pariah."

"But that ought not be held against her good judgment, sweetling. I am all of those things."

"No, you are not! You are funny and kind and noble."

Hawkworth shook his head and returned to sitting

cross-legged upon the floor before her, his back to the fire. "I may be humorous from time to time, sweetling, but I am neither kind nor noble. I would not be sitting here with you now if—"

"Balderdash," sniffed Priscilla.

"Well, we shall not argue the point. I admit that I rather like the idea that *you* see me as better than I am. I never thought that anyone would do that, and to have such a beautiful Circe as yourself do so is the most remarkable thing. I have been thinking all evening about what to do, sweetling, and I have got a workable idea at last. At least, I think that it will work if you will assist me in it."

"I shall not be able to assist you in anything, Hawk," Priscilla whispered sadly. "Did you not understand? Sarah and I both shall be gone shortly after the sun rises, and I do believe that Lord Tolliver intends to accompany us."

"Yes, but that is all for the good, sweetling. It plays right into my plan."

"It does?" Priscilla stared at him, all thought of tears immediately displaced by hope and curiosity.

"Yes, and if all goes as it should, we will know for a fact if Tolly loves your sister or if it is merely her money attracts him. And we can test whether he intends to keep his word about never raising his hand against a woman in anger again, but you must help me the slightest bit."

Hawkworth cursed himself for a fool as he made his way through the darkness to the stables. Men had been hanged for less than he intended to do once this day's sun had risen. If it had been anyone else but Miss Priscilla Pritkin's sister—truly, she was the most enchanting miss, Priscilla, and she had the most unsettling effect upon him. He had not known such a woman for facing a man down since Marjorie.

Marjorie. Ought not think of Marjorie now, he told himself as he set about saddling Turnabout. Not the time. But little Miss Pritkin had brought her to mind that first evening when she had put her hand to her lips instead of to her eyes when she walked in upon him in his bath.

Hawkworth smiled to himself at the memory. His heart beat a bit more loudly in his ears. "The Circe. The most nefarious of all the Pritkins," he murmured and then he chuckled. Devil, I could learn to love such a one as Miss Priscilla Pritkin. She would not shrink from the adventures of life. Once offered to her, she would live the adventure with me to the fullest.

"If I have a life to live after this day's work," he mumbled, leading Turnabout out into the yard and swinging up upon the great beast's back. "If I am not shot or forced to hide out upon the continent for the rest of my years."

No, I will not hide upon the continent, he thought. Sidney will detest the continent. Well, but if I am able to keep Tolliver and Sarah from recognizing me, all will go well enough and I shall not need to worry about what will become of me or Sidney either. "I wonder," he murmured then, "what Priscilla will think of Sidney?"

Bah, he thought then, she will not think of Sidney at all, because when all is ended, she will go home to Newcastle and I will never see her again, much less have the opportunity to introduce her to Sidney.

The possibility of never seeing Miss Priscilla Pritkin again gave him pause. It produced a familiar and detestable ache in the area of his heart, his stomach and his loins. He moved about in the saddle in a futile attempt to relieve it. "It is a bit of undigested brussels sprout or the result of that final sip of brandy," he muttered. "Nothing more." But in the depths of his soul, he knew it was much more. It was the precise aching that had plagued him after Marjorie's death, a mixture of need and longing and hopelessness that had taken two long and terrible years to subside. And now, at the mere thought of losing Priscilla's company, it had returned full-force.

"Damnation!" Hawkworth mumbled and urged Turnabout into a gallop. "Damnation, but I prayed never to feel that wretched aching inside of me again!"

Priscilla could not sleep. She tossed and turned beneath the counterpane alternately joyous and fearful. When she closed her eyes, Lord Hawkworth's face—all ridges and valleys like his lands—and his remarkable turquoise eyes, alternately alight with sparking hope and frozen cold in thought, appeared before her and sent her heart to racing. But when she opened her eyes, the shadows upon the ceiling above her bed gave rise to the most spine-chilling visions of the morrow, visions of pistols flaring and horses galloping wildly out of control—and the most frightening vision of all, the vision of The Hawk tumbling from his mount to lie dying in the ditch beside the high road.

"Why would you do such a thing?" she murmured. "Hawk, why would you court such danger for two women you have only just met? It is not as though Sarah and I have the least right to depend upon your assistance. Sarah has done nothing but berate you and fling your reputation in your face. And I—I have been nothing but a considerable bother with all my peeking about and interference in your pastimes. And we are neither of us your responsibility, regardless of Lord Tolliver's intentions toward Sarah. Surely, you cannot think yourself responsible for Lord Tolliver? He is a grown man and responsible for his own actions."

I shall not allow him to do it, she thought then, turning upon her side and staring at the wall. I shall confess all to Sarah the very first thing in the morning and we shall not leave this house at all. We shall remain right here until the end of the house party as we planned. Surely if I tell her what Lord Hawkworth plans to do—oh, surely the fact that The Hawk is willing to put himself in such danger for her sake must make Sarah believe in him and take his warnings to heart. The mere thought of it must bring Sarah to trust him. Yes, that is precisely what I will do. I will tell Sarah all.

"No, I cannot," she whispered then to the empty room. "I cannot because not even the fact that he places his life in jeopardy will weigh with Sarah. Society has named him a rogue and a villain, and Sarah always believes what all the *best* people say. She will see his attempt to save her from abuse only as proof of The Hawk's own villainy. She will say that it is a plot hatched for The Hawk's own benefit, that it is not meant to be a sham at all, that he truly intends to profit from it. Oh, Sarah, why are you so easily swayed by proper manners and polite utterances? Why can you not this once open your eyes and your heart and *know* who is true and who is false?"

Priscilla rolled once more onto her back and nibbled upon her trembling lower lip. He is The Hawk after all, she thought to herself encouragingly. The Hawk will not allow himself to be thwarted. No, and he will not allow himself to come to any harm either. He will know precisely how to do what must be done, and he will do it splendidly. I must merely perform my part and all will go well. "Oh, please God," she whispered, "please. Lord Hawkworth has made himself more dear to me than any gentleman I have ever known. Please watch over him and protect him when he—when he—rides down upon our coach and abducts us all."

EIGHT

The first pistol shot rang out as the Pritkin traveling coach rounded the bend and started down the hill into the Savory Gap. Inside the coach, Priscilla jumped and hit her head against the top of the vehicle. She had been waiting for what seemed an eternity for the coach to be set upon, and still that first pop of a pistol had frightened the wits out of her.

The coach lurched forward as the driver urged the six prime bays into a run. Sarah screamed. Tolliver poked his head out of the window and drew it quickly back inside. "Highwaymen!" he exclaimed. "Where the devil did highwaymen come from? There has not been a coach attacked upon this road for years."

"We shall be murdered in our own blood!" cried Sarah in horror. "Oh, Arlin, we shall never live to be married."

"Hush," Tolliver mumbled, giving Sarah's knee a pat. "Is there a pistol in here somewhere? Must be a pistol."

"It is under your seat," Sarah advised him. "But Papa has never needed to use it."

"Well, I expect I need to use it," grumbled Tolliver, attempting to reach beneath his seat in the wildly bouncing coach without losing his balance and tumbling to the floor. "There is nothing here," he proclaimed at last.

"It must be there," insisted Sarah. "It has always been there. Oh! Oh, Arlin!" Sarah screamed and jumped right across into his arms as a great explosion echoed through the coach.

"It is the groom upon the box firing his blunderbuss," Tolliver explained, setting her to the side. "Seize hold of that strap, Sarah, do. And hold on tightly. Are you all right, Miss Priscilla? Do not release your grip upon the strap or you will be bounced about wildly, I promise you."

"Arlin, what are you doing?" Sarah cried, as Tolliver knelt down between the two seats, nearly slamming his head against the door in the process.

"I am looking to see if that pistol is under this seat. Calm down, Sarah. No one is going to murder us. I promise you that. Ought to have brought outriders with us," he added under his breath. "But why? No highwaymen between here and Newcastle since Hawk and Archie sent Langhorn running for cover. Damnation!" he shouted. "Nothing! Are you certain there is a pistol?"

Before Sarah could assure him that there was, the blunderbuss above their heads fired again and the driver's horse pistol popped loudly. Hooves thundered directly behind the coach, and then a rider upon an enormous gray was directly beside the window and passing them. In a moment more the coach began to slow bit by bit until at last, within a hundred yards, it halted.

Priscilla peered from the window to see the man on the gray riding back toward them, a horse pistol trained upon John Coachman and the groom. She saw him free one foot from the stirrup and kick at the coach door. Could it be The Hawk? There was no possible way to tell. His face was covered with a red wool muffler and his hat pulled down over his eyebrows, and the sun was shining from behind him, casting him into silhouette so that not even the color of his eyes was visible to her. But it must be Lord Hawkworth, though he did not ride Turnabout. Turnabout was a bay with a white blaze, and this horse a solid gray without one marking. Well, of course he would not ride Turnabout, Priscilla thought then, disgusted with herself for not having thought of it sooner. Lord Tolliver would have recognized Turnabout the very first thing.

Two more men, pistols at the ready, joined the highwayman as he kicked at the door with his boot again. "Be ye in there, m'pretties?" he called in a gravelly voice that did not sound at all like The Hawk's. "Come out, m'darlin's, an' let me lay me daylights upon ye. Ain't no use ta be hidin', sweet things, when we've caught ye fair an' square."

Sarah shuddered in her corner of the coach, a sight which sent a pang through Priscilla's guilty heart. But then she reminded herself why she had hidden the pistol in the boot the first thing this morning and why she had agreed to this outrageous plan in the first place, and with a lift of her chin, she reached across to the opposite corner and gave Sarah's knee an encouraging pat.

"They will not dare harm us," she said boldly. "Do not fear, Sarah. It is merely money and jewels that highwaymen covet. We shall give them what we have and they will send us upon our way. Open the door as they have requested, Lord Tolliver, and help me down."

They stood in a little line before the highwaymen—Tolliver, then Sarah, then Priscilla.

"Keep yer daylights fixed on the box, Bob," growled the one upon the gray. "I don't be lookin' ta git me 'air parted wif no pistol ball from that deerection. Come now, m'pretties, an' show ol' 'enry wot ye got." He swung from the saddle and strolled directly up before Sarah, his gloved fingers tugging out the necklace of diamonds and sapphires she wore from beneath the collar of her pelisse.

"You keep your hands off me!" cried Sarah at once, backing away. "Do not you touch me. I am Miss Pritkin of the Newcastle Pritkins and I will not be soiled by such hands as yours."

The highwayman took three steps back from her at once and, placing his hands upon his hips, stared silently from the shadows beneath his hat brim. "Ye be jokin'," he said at last. "One o' the Newcastle Pritkins? Them morts what done inherited all o' that money? Aye, an' I suspect this un be yer sister, eh?"

"Indeed she is," declared Sarah.

"Ah," sighed the highwayman. "Ah, yes. The Newcastle Pritkins. We 'ave foun' us a treasure, m'hearties," he bellowed then. "Two treasures! Down, down, coachman. Down, both a' ye, right this minit," he ordered, his pistol pointing steadily at the coachman and the groom. "Bobby, climb up on that box an' take the reins, m'lad. Gilly, take this," he added, tugging a red and yellow neckcloth from one pocket, and a scrap of muslin and an old stocking from the other. "Blindfold the lot of 'em. We 'ave changed our plans, we 'ave. We ain't goin' ta steal nothin' off these dashers. No, we ain't. We is goin' ta take 'em pris'ners."

"Prisoners!" shouted Tolliver. "Who the devil do you think you are? I will see you swinging from a gibbet before the week is out, you fiend. I vow I will."

"Aye, likely, but not afore the week be out, m'dear. I reckon as 'ow it'll take at least that long afore Lord Pritkin o' Newcastle kin come up with the blunt ta pay fer his precious daughters, an' ye'll be me pris'ners until then. 'Ave ta wait a bit, dearie, fer the swinging. Goin' ta be rich as Croesus, we are, Bobbie," he added with a growling laugh. "Goin' ta in'erit two whole fortunes, we are. Ever bit of 'em! Git 'em inside, Gilly. Git 'em inside. An' tie 'em up with them bits o' rope ye bin a savin' of. An' then cover up their beamers. We don't want they should know where we be takin' 'em, sweet'eart. We don't want 'em ta know that atall."

"Of all the stupid things to say!" Tolliver exclaimed from his corner of the coach, his hands tied behind his back and his eyes covered with a most odiferous piece of muslin. "To announce to the fiends that you and Priscilla are heiresses!"

"Well, I—I did not think," sniffed Sarah. "Who would guess that they would be so bold as to—as to—"

"Were they not bold enough to ride down on our coach in broad daylight?" Tolliver hissed. "It might have entered your mind that they would also be bold enough to hold you to ransom."

"Do not speak to Sarah in that manner," Priscilla protested. "She did not intend to get us abducted. She made a mistake."

"Some mistake," mumbled Tolliver. "Where the devil are they taking us? We have been banging about inside this wretched vehicle for an hour already."

"An hour? Do you think so?" Sarah ventured timidly. "I thought it seemed a very long time."

"They will take us to their hideout, of course," Priscilla offered. "I expect it will be some forlorn little cottage in the midst of a forest somewhere."

"Bah! A wet, stinking cave more like," spat Tolliver angrily. "They'll not be concerned with our comfort, I promise you that. We shall spend a week or more in Hades—if we are lucky and they do not kill us all before the week is up."

Sarah gasped. "They would not dare!"

"Yes, m'dear, they would dare. They have already committed a hanging offense, you see, so the threat of the gallows will not deter them now."

Priscilla heard Sarah sob and felt herself to be the greatest wretch. How could she have agreed to put her own sister through such agony as this? It had seemed a reasonable idea, somehow, when Lord Hawkworth had proposed it, but now it seemed only cruel and unfeeling. If only she could lean over and whisper in Sarah's ear that there was nothing at all to fear, that their captor was none other

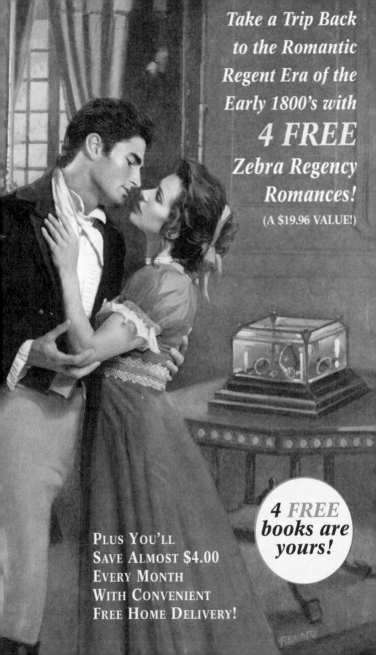

We'd Like to Invite You to Subscribe to Zebra's Regency Romance Book Club and Give You a Gift of 4 Free Books as Your Introduction! (Worth $19.96!)

If you're a Regency lover, imagine the joy of getting 4 FREE Zebra Regency Romances and then the chance to have these lovely stories delivered to your home each month at the lowest prices available! Well, that's our offer to you and here's how you benefit by becoming a Zebra Home Subscription Service subscriber:

- **4 FREE** Introductory Regency Romances are delivered to your doorstep

- 4 BRAND NEW Regencies are then delivered each month (usually before they're available in bookstores)

- Subscribers save almost $4.00 every month

- Home delivery is always **FREE**

- You also receive a **FREE** monthly newsletter, *Zebra/ Pinnacle Romance News* which features author profiles, contests, subscriber benefits, book previews and more

- No risks or obligations...in other words you can cancel whenever you wish with no questions asked

Join the thousands of readers who enjoy the savings and convenience offered to Regency Romance subscribers. After your initial introductory shipment, you receive 4 brand-new Zebra Regency Romances each month to examine for 10 days. Then, if you decide to keep the books, you'll pay the preferred subscriber's price of just $4.00 per title. That's only $16.00 for all 4 books and there's never an extra charge for shipping and handling.

It's a no-lose proposition, so return the FREE BOOK CERTIFICATE today!

Say Yes to 4 Free Books!

Complete and return the order card to receive this
$19.96 value, ABSOLUTELY FREE!

(If the certificate is missing below, write to:)
Zebra Home Subscription Service, Inc.,
120 Brighton Road, P.O. Box 5214, Clifton, New Jersey 07015-5214
or call TOLL-FREE 1-888-345-BOOK

Check out our website at www.kensingtonbooks.com.

FREE BOOK CERTIFICATE

YES! Please rush me 4 Zebra Regency Romances without cost or obligation. I understand that each month thereafter I will be able to preview 4 brand-new Regency Romances FREE for 10 days. Then, if I should decide to keep them, I will pay the money-saving preferred subscriber's price of just $16.00 for all 4...that's a savings of almost $4 off the publisher's price with no additional charge for shipping and handling. I may return any shipment within 10 days and owe nothing, and I may cancel this subscription at any time. My 4 FREE books will be mine to keep in any case.

Name_____

Address_____ Apt._____

City_____ State_____ Zip_____

Telephone (   )_____

Signature_____ RG0799
(If under 18, parent or guardian must sign.)

Terms and prices subject to change. Orders subject to acceptance by Zebra Home Subscription Service, Inc.

than The Hawk himself and that he would do nothing at
all to hurt them. But Sarah would most likely exclaim aloud
at it and spill the beans to Lord Tolliver. Then they would
not only know nothing of Lord Tolliver's true intent toward Sarah, but the affair might well end with the step-
brothers meeting over pistols at dawn.

And that will not do at all, Priscilla thought, jouncing
about in her own little corner of the coach, her hands
tied and her eyes covered exactly as were Sarah's and
Tolliver's. Lord Hawkworth does not wish to kill Lord Tolliver merely to be certain that he will not strike Sarah,
no matter how great the aggravation, and to discover
whether or not it is Sarah's money Lord Tolliver loves.
Certainly Lord Hawkworth will not keep us confined for
so long as a week. And he will not keep us tied and blind-
folded either, she told herself silently. That would be most
villainous of him, and he is not a villain.

As the coach continued to jog along a track that grew
rougher and more uneven with every turn of the wheels,
the possibility that perhaps she did not know Lord Hawkworth as thoroughly as she thought began to nibble at
Priscilla's mind. After all, she had known the gentleman
less than a week. And despite the fact that she had come
to cherish him in the oddest way, what did she actually
know about The Hawk? Nothing. She knew nothing except that he was handsome and humorous and a pro-
foundly talented artist. The more she was tossed about
inside the vehicle, the more Priscilla began to suspect
that perhaps Lord Hawkworth's tales about Lord Tolliver
owed more to ill feelings between the two than to truth,
and that The Hawk's interest in Sarah and herself might
be prompted by something far more sinister than a concern for their welfare.

Priscilla told herself over and over as the vehicle
bounced along that she was more than foolish to doubt
Lord Hawkworth's good intentions, that even though he

acted roguishly at times, at heart he was a gentleman and would never think to hold them to ransom for real.

"He is a dear, kind, gentle man," she muttered into the silence of the coach at last.

"Who?" asked Sarah at once. "Of whom do you speak, Priscilla?"

"Of—of—Lord Hawkworth. Certainly beneath all his bravado, he is kind and gentle at heart."

"Teal?" Lord Tolliver exclaimed in amazement. "Teal, kind and gentle? Truly, Miss Priscilla, you are overset by our predicament or else such foolish thoughts would never enter your head. What makes you think of Hawkworth at all?" he added in a gruff tone.

"I—we—that is to say—"

"What, Priscilla?" Sarah's sobbing had subsided completely. "That is to say what?"

"Only that the highwayman, you know, the one apparently in charge, he reminds me of Lord Hawkworth somehow. That is to say, his height and the manner in which he sat his mount. And I expect that set me to thinking of his lordship, and remembering all I have heard tell of his—his—exploits—so to speak. And I cannot quite believe that I have heard the entire truth of any of them, for he has been quite charming to me in the little time I have come to know him."

"Teal was birthed a rogue and will remain a rogue until the very day he dies," grumbled Tolliver. "He is not now, nor has he ever been a dear, kind, or gentle man. And if you have not heard the entire truth of his exploits, Miss Priscilla, I will only say that the part of the truth you have not been made privy to is most likely the worst part of what he has done and not the best."

"Then why do you not break with him completely, my lord?" Priscilla asked, hoping that Lord Tolliver would not be able to provide her with an acceptable answer. "Surely, if he is as villainous as you say—"

"Well, I cannot do that," sighed Tolliver. "Teal does not mind that I attempt to avoid him whenever I can, but he would actually *care* if I broke off the relationship completely. And since Mama and I depend upon his largesse, I do not wish to aggravate him to any great extent, you know. However, one day, I will restore my father's estates and take Mama away from this place and then I need not fear my name will be connected with his ever again."

"Together we shall refurbish Holbrook," declared Sarah adamantly, "and then we will bring your mama to live with us. And you need never see nor speak to that evil man again."

"You are not like to have enough money left to refurbish a stable after this," Tolliver pointed out. "Or have you forgotten that we are in the midst of being held to ransom? I shall fall more into Teal's debt than ever if he must forfeit monies to ransom me as well, though the fiends do not at the moment appear concerned with my identity. Bah! You have thrown us into the midst of a hubble-bubble, Sarah. Why could you not remain silent!"

"Will you marry Sarah even if her inheritance is forfeit?" Priscilla asked.

"Priscilla! How dare you!" cried Sarah. "Is it not dreadful enough that we are captives in our own coach and Arlin with us? How dare you infer that Lord Tolliver is no better than a fortune hunter? Next you will say that the highwaymen are secretly under Arlin's command!"

"I promise you, those ruffians and I are unknown to each other," growled Tolliver, "and had that pistol been under the seat where it should have been, we would all of us now be safe and far from here—wherever here is at the moment."

"Perhaps, but that does not answer my question, my lord. Will you marry Sarah even if her inheritance is forfeit?"

"Priscilla, really!" hissed Sarah. "That rascal, Lord

Hawkworth, has put this into your head. You must set such suspicions aside at once. You did never once doubt Arlin until you met that villain. I knew you ought not have gone riding off with the man."

"You went riding with my stepbrother, Miss Priscilla? When was that?" asked Tolliver very quietly.

"Yesterday morning," Sarah informed him before Priscilla could utter one word. "And he filled her head with the greatest nonsense, saying that you had a mistress and that you struck her viciously and that you wished to marry me only for my fortune. And that you would beat me once I was your wife."

"He did not!" Priscilla cried, confused. "The Hawk never said that Lord Tolliver would beat you, Sarah. He only feared that he might."

"Thunderation!" roared Tolliver. "If I live through this present unpleasantness, I vow, I will comb Teal's hair with a hatchet! What the devil business has he to be spilling such tales to a gently bred young woman, and my sister-in-law-elect at that! He has not a particle of sensitivity! Not a particle!"

Priscilla's heart stuttered upward into her throat, and she tugged at the cord that bound her hands, wishing to remove the blindfold from her eyes and to pin her gaze upon Lord Tolliver. He had not denied a word of the tale about his mistress! He had not pledged his love for Sarah despite the loss of her fortune. He had neatly avoided answering anything at all. "Did you have a mistress whom you struck, Lord Tolliver?" she asked, longing to see the answer in his eyes. "You do not say."

"Priscilla, hush!" cried Sarah. "There is not a word of truth ever falls from lips so villainous as Lord Hawkworth's. You are not to discuss this any farther. It is most improper and it is none of it to do with you!"

NINE

The Hawk paced restlessly beneath the naked limbs of the oaks and elms along the high road, stepping from time to time out onto the road bed itself and staring at the horizon. Where the devil were they? Even the worst of coachmen driving a team of slugs ought to have gotten as far as Curly's Knot by this time. He tugged his watch from his waistcoat pocket, flipped it open and muttered to himself. Almost noon and not even the sound of a coach approaching. What the deuce had happened? Perhaps they had broken an axle or lost a wheel. With a curse and a sigh, Hawkworth stepped up into the saddle and turned his horse's head back toward the Bear and Bell, hoping to discover the coach along the way. If he did not, he must assume that they had not taken the high road at all, but chosen to go by way of Anderson Pike. "And I will never catch them now, if they have taken the pike," he mumbled disconsolately. "I will have missed every opportunity. Damnation, but Tolly does never do what one expects of him! I will need to ride all the way to Newcastle to stop that blasted wedding."

Unless, of course, he is not marrying the girl for her money, in which case I need not feel honorbound to stop the wedding at all. That thought gave The Hawk some pause, but then he shook his head in disbelief. "Of course he is marrying the girl for her fortune," he muttered.

"And once he has it in his hands, she will not be safe
from him. Though why I care, I cannot imagine. Having
Tolly out of my hair would be the greatest of blessings,
and once he has put Holbrook back upon a paying basis,
perhaps he will get his mama out of my hair as well."

But then a vision of Miss Priscilla Pritkin, her delicate
lips tilted upward, her eyes sparkling, presented itself for
his inspection and he knew immediately why he cared.
"She is a veritable treasure," he murmured. "And anything that hurts her sister will cause her immeasurable
grief. If Tolly does one thing to cause Priscilla grief, I will
see him drawn and quartered."

It was the most amazing thing to feel such passion as
flowed through him at the thought of Miss Priscilla Pritkin unhappy. Damned if he was not losing his heart to
the girl! But that would never do. He had lost his heart
once before, to Marjorie, and because of it, he dared not
so much as think of little Miss Priscilla in any terms other
than those of friendship. No, he would be more than
foolish to allow Priscilla to increase her hold upon his
heart. He would be begging for anguish and despair.

Because, even if I grow to love her to distraction, she
will never marry me, he thought then. There is not a
gently bred woman in all of England will be brought to
marry me once word of my plans for Sidney get about.
And they will get about. Tolly will spread the tale everywhere. "Where the devil is Tolly?" he asked himself
aloud. "I am almost back to the Bear and Bell and not
a sign of the Pritkin coach. Damned if they have not taken
the pike!"

Pondering how he could possibly carry out his plan on
Anderson Pike and how long it would take him to catch
up with the Pritkin coach, Hawkworth turned his mount
into the stable yard at the little inn and dismounted.

"My lord, you is here!" exclaimed the stable boy who
ran forward to catch the horse's reins.

"I told you I would be back shortly, Carey. I would never think to take this nag and leave Turnabout with you, else."

"Yes, m'lord, but ye din't say when. They will be happy as hens you is here."

"Who?"

"The men what jus' comed a bit ago. One of 'em be a coachman an' t'other be a groom an' they come awalkin' in. Mutterin', they were 'bout bein' robbed, m'lord. An' they were fair afrighted-like. Comed from the Aerie, they said, an' got as far as Savory Gap afore they was set upon."

Hawkworth turned without a word and strolled hurriedly into the Bear and Bell.

" 'Orrible 'enry be at it agin!" cried Archie the moment he spied the earl. "I thought we run 'im off three summers ago!"

"Horrible Henry?" Hawkworth asked quietly. "How do you know, Archie?"

"Stopped a coach at Savory Gap, 'e did," Archie continued, ignoring the question. "Took the whole thin', Hawk. Coach an' horses an' passengers an' all! Right off down the lef' fork ta the low road. Seems as like the ladies was heiresses er somethin' and now 'enry be fixin' ta hold 'em fer ransom. Lef' nothin' but the coachman an' the groom, 'enry din't, an' they had ta walk all the way 'ere. I done give 'em each a tankard an' set 'em in the private parlor fer a bit. That shaken up, they was. Well, an' I couldn't be havin' 'em shakin' about m'public room, could I now? Comed from yer place, they said. Lef' the Aerie this mornin'. Ladies was yer guests, I reckon."

Priscilla stared about her in horror. How could he? How could Lord Hawkworth have chosen such a vile place to keep us? she thought angrily. Certainly he cannot intend us to remain for any lengthy period in this—this—cellar! With a sniff, rubbing at her wrists which were now free of the cord, Priscilla sat upon a three-legged stool and glared at the dank, dripping stone walls that surrounded her and the moss creeping down them and across the broken floor. Five listless tallow candles stuck by their own wax to barrels lit the cramped little room, sending the smell of butchered hogs sickeningly into the air.

"Gawd, what a place!" Tolliver exclaimed, stomping back and forth across the crumbling stone floor. "We shall all be dead of a congestion of the lungs by the end of the week."

"Surely they do not intend to keep us here for an entire week," Sarah declared uncertainly. "They would not dare."

"Well, of course they would dare," grumbled Tolliver, his back to her as he paced. "Why do you insist upon repeating such an annoying phrase, Sarah? They will dare and they do dare and they will go on daring to do whatever they wish with us. And it is all because you could not refrain from informing them of your importance. Had you pretended to be just an ordinary miss and handed over your jewels, we would all be safely on our way to Newcastle by now."

Sarah sobbed. It was a most plaintive, heartrending sob. Priscilla could not bear to hear it. She rose at once and crossed to where her sister huddled in a wreck of a chair with one arm missing and pieces of stuffing hanging out. "Do cease blaming our plight upon Sarah and think of some way to get us out of here," she demanded of Tolliver, settling upon the one remaining arm of the chair and placing a supportive hand upon Sarah's shoulder. "You are an intelligent man, are you not? You attended university. Think of some way for us to escape this place."

Tolliver snorted. "No classes in escaping abductors at

Oxford, m'dear. Quite sorry about that." And then he halted his pacing and stared thoughtfully at the wall.

"What?" asked Priscilla. "Have you thought of something, Lord Tolliver?"

"Teal," murmured Tolliver. "Teal would know what to do in a situation like this. Likely he has been in such a situation as this once or twice in his life."

"But Lord Hawkworth is not here," sobbed Sarah.

Priscilla gave her sister's shoulder a supportive squeeze as a tremendous surge of guilt boiled up inside her. Lord Hawkworth is nearer than you think, dearest, she thought dejectedly. Much nearer. I ought to tell you exactly how near, only I cannot. Lord Tolliver would hear and then—and then—well, there is no telling what might happen then.

"Must attempt to think like Teal," murmured Tolliver. "I shall succeed in getting us out of here if only I think like Teal."

"C-can you?" asked Sarah.

"Well, I have never attempted it before, but it cannot be all that difficult to think like a barbarian."

The Hawk tied Turnabout's reins to a tree limb and made his way stealthily through the stand of oaks toward the ruined abbey. The neighing of the coach horses reached him upon the wind, and he trod slowly and lightly through the underbrush making less noise than a wily shrew until he caught sight of the coach. So, he thought, Archie is correct. Henry Langhorn has returned. Damnation, what a time he chose to do it, too! But at least it is Henry and I need not go chasing about searching out some other miscreant's hidey-hole. Not but what I shall have the devil of a time to slip past Henry and his men and into that miserable cellar. That is likely where he has them stowed. Damnation, but I did not like that place even when we were children. Mayhap Tolly has figured out where he is, though. That will give him some hope to escape, if he recalls that crumbled stairway and is near to it.

The Hawk took a deep breath and then backed carefully out of sight of the coach. He turned and made his way over the ruins until he came to a spot marked only by a fading T scratched into a piece of the rubble lying at his feet. His eyes searched the surrounding area hopefully. "Ah, there you are, sweet thing," he murmured at last, and then eased himself down onto the loose pile of rocks that had once been the ceiling of the monks' dining hall. Careful not to set even one of the rocks tumbling, he slid cautiously behind a wall that threatened to collapse at the least touch and wiggled as quietly as he could through a gaping aperture, landing with the slightest of skidding sounds amongst a pile of jagged stones and splintered beams that littered a long, underground corridor. Off to his right he could smell a fire burning. Laughter snatched at him, and he nodded. Henry, all right. And in a jolly fine mood. To his left lay a dank, dark, dismal tunnel pierced only spasmodically and very weakly by sunlight from the holes amongst the rubble of the ceilings and the floors of the upper levels.

Hawkworth squinted, attempting to adjust his eyesight to the gloom, and then stepped to his left, away from the laughter. He kept himself in the deepest of the shadows, lest Henry or one of his fellows should think to gaze in his direction. He paused for a moment once his vision had thoroughly adjusted and withdrew a fine Italian blade from the inside of his boot. "Just in case," he murmured to himself. "Just in case."

Priscilla watched the frown deepen upon Lord Tolliver's face and felt Sarah trembling beside her and wished for near the fiftieth time that she had not agreed to this despicable plan of Lord Hawkworth's. Oh, it had not sounded despicable when he had explained it to her. And her part had been quite simple—merely to dispose of the pistol and not spill the beans to Sarah and Lord Tolliver. But she had thought—she had thought—that Lord Hawkworth meant to abduct them and carry them to some reasonably hospitable place, not this cancerous hole in the ground.

I have been all wrong about him, she thought sullenly. He truly is the brute everyone names him or else he would not even know of the existence of such a vile place as this. I shall tell Sarah and Lord Tolliver all and beg their forgiveness, and we shall simply pound upon that door until The Hawk deigns to come to us and then walk right out of here. We shall demand that he drive us back to the Aerie and we will set out again for Newcastle on the morrow.

"S-Sarah," she began in a nervous whisper, "there is s-something I m-must— Whatever can that be?"

"Someone sliding the bar on the door," Lord Tolliver hissed, jumping to his feet. "Stay where you are, both of you, and do not so much as glance in my direction. I shall get us out of here. I vow it." And giving Sarah's knee a quick pat, and nodding supportively at Priscilla, Lord Tolliver scurried into the shadows and pressed himself against the wall beside the door.

"No, wait," Priscilla began, but just then the door was tugged open, scraping and scratching over the debris in the corridor as it did and Lord Hawkworth took a hurried step into the room. He saw Priscilla and Sarah and took a second step, and in that instant, before Priscilla could call out to warn him, Lord Tolliver pounced upon his back and drove him to the floor.

"No!" Priscilla cried, as Hawkworth's head struck the

stones and his dagger went skidding unnoticed across the floor. "Lord Tolliver, no! It is Lord Hawkworth!"

"Teal?" Tolliver muttered, pushing himself off Hawkworth's back. "Surely not. You are mistaken, Miss Priscilla. Come, we must hurry," he added, striding to Sarah and taking her hand. "The others may come to search for this one at any time."

"But it *is* Lord Hawkworth," murmured Sarah, allowing Tolliver to help her from the chair she had never left. "I saw his eyes when he stepped in as clearly as though the sun were—oh!"

"Oh, what?" asked Priscilla, as she knelt down beside The Hawk. "Oh!" she exclaimed then as an enormous hand seized her by the shoulder and yanked her to her feet.

"Be still, lady," ordered Horrible Henry, his arm closing about Priscilla like a vise. "An' do not ye think o' comin' fer me, me fine gent, er I'll put a ball through this mort I got 'ere. Kind o' ye ta take this bloke down fer me," he laughed evilly, rolling Hawkworth's limp form aside with one shove from his enormous foot. "Drop that lady's hand, lor'ship, an' step away from 'er. I've no yearnin' ta put a end ta yer days as yet, but I will. I will. An' ye cease yer squirmin', me pretty, er I'll swing ye up agin that wall an' put a ceasin' to it meself," he added with a growl at Priscilla.

But Priscilla did not cease in her attempt to free herself from his grasp. She fought him all the harder, twisting and kicking and biting at the man who attempted to keep Tolliver and Sarah in his sight while overcoming the woman in his grasp.

Terrified for Hawkworth and desperate to go to his aid, Priscilla kicked a boot heel into the villain's knee. The man yelped and loosed her. The unsteady and unreliable horse pistol in his hand trembled and then Lord Tolliver shouted, "Sarah, watch out!" and abruptly there was the smell of gunpowder and a loud popping sound and Priscilla, shocked, watched Lord Tolliver fall into Sarah's arms as Sarah screamed.

And then, most unaccountably, the highwayman took a step backward and stumbled and fell, and Priscilla heard a great whack as Lord Hawkworth, dizzy but game, having tugged the man to the floor, landed a fist solidly upon the man's jaw.

"You are all right!" Priscilla cried joyously. "Hawk, you are all right!"

"Quickly, Priscilla," Hawkworth ordered, gaining his feet and attempting to ignore both pain and dizziness as blood trickled in a most grisly manner down across his brow and into his eyes. "Take your sister's hand and lead her out into the corridor. Go to your left. There is another chamber just beyond this. Go just inside and wait for me. I will bring Tolly."

"No, no," Sarah sobbed as Priscilla seized her hand. "I cannot leave him. He saved my life!"

"Come, Sarah. Lord Hawkworth means to bring Lord Tolliver with us. Hurry, dearest. Some of the other men will have heard the shot and will come to see what has caused the uproar!"

Moments after Priscilla and Sarah had reached the darkness of the adjoining chamber, Hawkworth was with them, his dagger once again within his grasp and Tolliver, with a neckcloth tied tightly about his shoulder, leaning heavily upon him. "The ruins," Priscilla heard Lord Hawkworth whisper. "We are in the abbey ruins, Tolly. In the cellar beneath the monks' study."

"Must go up," Tolliver murmured, and then groaned.

"Indeed we must, and quickly too." Hawkworth pushed Tolliver up against the dank wall and held him there with one hand. "Priscilla," he hissed. "You and Sarah must take hold of Tolly for a moment. I cannot keep him standing and find the passage at one and the same time."

"Passage?" asked Priscilla, catching Lord Tolliver below one shoulder as Sarah caught him beneath the other.

"Was a staircase," Hawkworth mumbled as he disappeared into the darkness at the far corner of the room. "No one has been here since we covered it up, Tolly. Henry and his men have not made a move to clear the entrance," he announced, and then Priscilla heard only the sound of large chunks of rock scraping and tumbling and clunking against one another.

"The others are coming," gasped Sarah. "I hear them."

"And we are going," Hawkworth replied, appearing before them out of the gloom and once again taking Tolliver into his own charge. "Straight across the room, Priscilla. There is a gap in the wall and a faint light at the end of it, far above. You cannot see them well, but the stairs are there. You must feel your way up rather than attempt to see it. Go, Priscilla! Now! Lead your sister out and run directly into the closest stand of trees."

"But how will you—'

"I will bring Tolly. Just go!"

TEN

They did not come. Priscilla and Sarah huddled amongst a group of elms, well hidden in the shadows, and waited, breathless, for Hawkworth and Tolliver to emerge from the top of the ravaged staircase and scuttle across the ruins to them, but they did not come. Nor did any of the highwaymen appear. Around the two girls the wind bustled amongst the leaves and grasses. Overhead, the clouds parted and boiled and drew together again. One moment the sun sparkled and the next it was not to be seen. But in the shambles that was Swarthsford Abbey, all seemed frozen in time.

"Something has gone very wrong," whispered Priscilla at last. "I am going back inside, Sarah."

"And me. Whatever you may think to do alone, we will be able to do twice as well together."

"Then find a stout stick and I will do the same. If we must go into battle, at least we shall have weapons of a sort."

They descended into the ruins as cautiously as they had exited them, this time with the flickering sun at their backs and nothing but silence and shadow before them, until at last they were deep within the bowels of the ancient corpse that was Swarthsford Abbey and the sound of heavy breathing and the scudding of boots against stone reached their ears.

"Can you see anything?" Sarah whispered, peering over Priscilla's shoulder as they reached the bottom of the staircase. "What is happening?" she hissed as Priscilla gasped and stepped out into the room.

Hawkworth, struggling out from beneath the body of the last of the highwaymen, froze immediately at the gasp. "What the devil are you doing back down here?" he asked, shoving the corpse from him. He gained his feet and instinctively swiped the bloody dagger across his thigh to clean it. He took a step forward. "Are there more of them up top? Priscilla, answer me. Could you not get out? Are there more men up there with whom I must contend? I vow, I did not see so very many when I arrived.

"Tolly is there," Hawkworth added, acknowledging Sarah and pointing with the tip of his dagger to the place where he had laid Tolliver near the wall and attempted to hide him from view behind a jumble of fallen rock. "It was all I could think to do to keep him from more harm. The first of the ruffians came upon us only moments after you departed and the others before I could safely get Tolly up the staircase."

Priscilla could not drive the vision of him, dirty and bloody and surrounded by dead men, from her mind. She was safely back at Hawkworth Aerie, Lord Hawkworth having driven her and Sarah and Lord Tolliver there himself in the Pritkin traveling coach, but each time she closed her eyes or stared out a window or studied a flickering fire, The Hawk appeared before her in all his devastating gore. He had strolled among those bodies as though they were no more than the fallen beams and building blocks of the abbey itself, ignoring them, stepping over them, shoving them out of his way as he attempted to get Lord Tolliver, herself and Sarah to safety. Surely he was everything people named him. She could not deny it now—uncivilized, a rogue, a black sheep covered in blood. All. Beneath his charming smile and his glorious eyes and his handsome form, beneath his genius and his passion, lay the soul of some pagan prince.

"Priscilla? Are you not coming?" Sarah asked quietly. "Arlin has specifically asked that you be present."

"Oh, yes. Are you certain he is well enough? It has been a day and a night merely."

"His mama says that he demands to speak with us."

They were the last to join the little gathering around Lord Tolliver's bed, where that gentleman lay propped up by pillows and looking very pale and exhausted. To his left his mama sat upon a chair, and to his right Lord Hawkworth stood with his back to the bed, staring out into the late afternoon sunlight.

Lady Hawkworth abandoned her chair to Sarah and urged her to sit and take hold of Lord Tolliver's hand. "He is most flustered, Sarah, and will not cease to demand your presence and Priscilla's as well. I cannot think what—"

"I am not flustered," Tolliver interrupted. "I am tired and sore and remorseful, but not flustered. Ah, there you are, Miss Priscilla. I thank you for coming. I could not say all I must without you to hear."

Priscilla went to stand beside Lord Tolliver's mama at the foot of the bed. The poor lady was wringing her hands nervously and gazing with worried eyes upon her son, and Priscilla's heart went out to her.

"I was rude and inconsiderate," Tolliver began, glancing at Sarah from beneath half-lowered lids. "I am ashamed to have spoken to you as I did in that dreadful place."

"You were overwrought," Sarah offered softly.

"An excellent excuse, but inappropriate. I have been proud and selfish and insensitive all my life, and the rudeness and inelegance I displayed were quite in character

for me, I assure you. Gad, but I have been the greatest
of oafs! I am so very sorry, Sarah. Truly, I am. I have
never been so sorry for anything in all of my life."

"This is nonsense," murmured Sarah. "You merely
spoke truth. It was I who placed us in a most untenable
position and—"

"No, no, listen to me, Sarah. I am not speaking of our
time in the abbey merely. I have been a villain and a
beast and a dolt for as long as you have known me. You
do not know all, Sarah. You do not comprehend."

"There is no need to bare your soul, Tolly," muttered
Hawkworth, refusing to face anyone in the room. "I vow
to you that I am satisfied and will hold my tongue forever
upon the subject. Do not do this thing."

"I will do this thing," Tolliver declared. "It is not because of you, Teal, but because I will have Sarah understand. Yes, and Miss Priscilla as well."

At the window, Hawkworth exhaled audibly and his
head bowed.

In the bed, Tolliver sighed and took a firmer grasp of
Sarah's hand. "There is no acceptable excuse for all I
have said and done. Teal is not the black sheep in this
family, Sarah. I am. My papa gambled and drank and
treated my mama abominably and he lost everything—his
fortune, his unentailed lands, and my mama's love."

Lady Hawkworth made the tiniest sound—a most an-
guished sound—and Priscilla took that lady's hand into
her own and gave it the most consoling squeeze. Whatever it was that Lord Tolliver wished to say, his mama and
Lord Hawkworth already knew and both were obviously
distraught by it.

"The thing is, Sarah—the thing is—I do *not* wish to
follow in my papa's footsteps. I d-do not drink and I d-do
not gamble and I am careful of my reputation."

"Yes, dearest, I am aware of that," Sarah murmured.

"Dearest. Still you call me dearest. Sarah, I have done

worse than my papa. I have sought to better myself by marrying your inheritance. Oh, gawd, I am a fortune hunter, Sarah, and nothing more. All my attentions to you, all my sweet phrases and longing looks were lies. I wished to marry you because I must marry you in order to gain your money. How vile! The very saying of it turns my stomach. I had no thought for you, Sarah, for your happiness, only for myself."

Priscilla, clasping Lady Hawkworth's trembling hand, felt her own heart tremble as she watched tears begin to trail, silently, down Sarah's cheeks. She longed to say something, anything, to ease her sister's pain, but she could think of nothing at all.

"Far too scrupulous as usual," muttered The Hawk then. He turned from the window and leveled his gaze upon Sarah. "If you do love Tolly, then you must come to accept, Miss Pritkin, that he is far too scrupulous in regard to some things. He does love you. A gentleman does not leap in front of a young woman and put his own life at risk on her behalf if he does not have some strong feeling for her. At least—Tolly does not."

"Yes, but—" Lord Tolliver began painfully.

"Enough, Tolly. You will talk yourself into a fever and Miss Pritkin into the vapors with all this nonsense. Not to mention the grief you are imposing upon your mama. We do not generally get along, Tolly and I, Miss Pritkin. I am a brute and Tolly most elegantly civilized. There is little understanding passes between the two us. But I know what it is to love, and I promise you that whatever went before, Tolly loves you now, with all his heart."

"I th-thought he did," managed Sarah, attempting not to give way to her tears. "I th-thought he loved me."

"Indeed. You, Miss Pritkin, have proved a good deal more insightful than I. You knew Tolly loved you when I doubted him considerably. Apparently, Tolly did not even know himself until he saw a pistol waver in your direction.

And if he said nasty things to you while you were held captive—which he has admitted to me, by the way—he did so only because of his confusion over his own feelings, I expect. He did not wish to see your fortune gone, you know. It pained him to think of it."

"But he did not strike out at you, Sarah," Priscilla offered abruptly. "He did not once raise his hand to you as Lord Hawkworth feared he might."

Hawkworth's gaze fell instantly upon Priscilla. "Just so," he nodded, the sticking plaster upon his brow peeping out at her from beneath his dark curls. "And he might have done, had he not come to care so exceedingly for you, Miss Pritkin."

"I would never hit Sarah," Tolliver declared. "Never! Not if it were the only way to save my own life! And I am thoroughly ashamed that I ever, ever hit any woman."

"How much my stepmama and I owe you, Miss Pritkin," said The Hawk, returning his gaze to Sarah and smiling the tenderest of smiles. "You have driven the beast right out of Tolly. Something I could not do with all my threats. Whatever you decide, we are all beholden to you for that."

Lord Tolliver opened his mouth to speak again, but closed it immediately as the most outrageous howling and the pounding of running feet drew all eyes to the open doorway. In a matter of seconds a tremendously large bloodhound came snuffling into the chamber and, lifting his nose from the carpet, gave one last bloodcurdling howl and leaped in his own lethargic bloodhound way upon Lord Hawkworth.

"Sir Godfrey an' me has founded you all by ourselfs!" cried a little voice gleefully. "We did not even needs Nanny to help us, Papa!" And ignoring everyone else in the chamber, a curly-haired, giggling little boy dashed madly across the room and threw himself upon The Hawk, sending his lordship, the hound, and himself tumbling, amidst laughter and giggles, directly to the Aubusson carpet.

Priscilla could not drive Lord Hawkworth from her mind. She and Sarah and Lord Tolliver and Lady Hawkworth had spoken long and solemnly once The Hawk had taken the boy and the dog away. Sarah and Lord Tolliver were speaking still, striving to know one another all over again, honestly and with their eyes wide open. Lady Hawkworth had gone to attend to those of her guests who remained—Lord Dugan and Lady Cecily and Mr. Crosby merely. But Priscilla could not bring herself to join them in the winter drawing room. She could not because visions of Hawkworth still assailed her at every turning and drew her mind away from every conversation. And so, she sat alone before the fire in one of the smaller parlors and pondered the odd meanderings of her heart.

"My stepmama was not mistaken. Here you are."

Priscilla started at the sound of his voice.

"Do I frighten you now so very much that you jump at my words, Priscilla?" he drawled, crossing the room and taking up a stance before the hearth, one arm resting along the mantelpiece.

Priscilla could not look at him. She could not. She kept her eyes lowered as she spoke. "You do n-not frighten me at all. What makes you think—"

"I saw the look upon your face when I stood in the ruins amidst five dead men, wiping their blood from my blade."

"Well, I was—"

"Appalled. Do not deny it. But Henry Langhorn and his cronies would have it no other way. Archie and I sent them dashing off to fairer climes three years ago. Apparently, they determined I was jesting when I warned them not to return. I was not. Had I been able to take them alive, Priscilla, they would all of them have hanged. But I could not take the risk of attempting to capture them with Tolly wounded and you and your sister threatened."

"N-no, of course you could not."

"No. You will not smile for me ever again, will you, now that you know what a heartless savage I truly am?"

"You are not a heartless savage!" Priscilla exclaimed angrily. "How dare you to say such a thing! You saved our lives!"

"Yes. I hope you will remember that at least, when you see me standing over those corpses in your nightmares. If you had not come back down into that place—"

"We had to come back down. We waited and waited and you did not come up. I was certain you required assistance." At last she lifted her gaze, her eyes resolutely meeting his. "I would have gone into Hades to give you aid."

"You did," he murmured. "You escaped Hades once and then stepped right back into it. You are the most splendid, courageous, alluring woman. Will your sister give Tolly a second chance, do you think?"

"Yes, I am certain of it."

"Good. He has had a difficult time of it, Tolly. It is not at all easy to know yourself the son of a reprobate and the stepbrother of a rogue. I will give him enough money to restore his estate as soon as I have sold off a number of investments. My father began investing sums on Tolly's behalf when first he and Tolly's mama married. I have continued to do so. There will be enough profits soon to restore Holbrook Hall to its former glory. I should like to think that your sister will rule the place. She will do it honor."

"How can you?" Priscilla asked suddenly.

"How can I what?"

"Speak of Sarah and Lord Tolliver and their making a

match of it and not—not—say a word to me about—about—"

"Sidney?"

"Yes—Sidney."

"Sidney is four and my son by a barmaid named Marjorie, whom I loved with all my heart. She would not marry me. She was older than I and most conscious of the disaster such a marriage could bring. I did not care a fig, but she—well, she died of the influenza nearly a year ago. I have been keeping Sidney with me in London."

"You have?"

"Indeed. And I shall keep him with me here now, no matter how extraordinary people think it. Sidney is not some nasty accident to be avoided. He is my son. He will not grow up like Archie into a barely educated innkeeper who has never known his father except by reputation. I do not care if no gently bred woman will ever marry me because of him," Hawkworth added in a most arrogant tone. "Sidney stays with me and will be loved and educated as suits the son of an earl."

Priscilla noted how Hawkworth's shoulders straightened and how his chin rose stubbornly and how his eyes flashed as his hand fisted upon the mantelpiece. The very sight set her heart to overflowing with love for him and respect and pride. Her lips tilted upward. She gave a little shake of her head. "You are the most determined man I have ever met," she said with a lilt of laughter. "You will be a rogue and a black sheep and continue upon your own path regardless of anyone or anything."

"Yes, I will."

"I know," Priscilla nodded, her brown eyes beginning to twinkle in the most engaging manner. "It makes me love you all the more. What a scandal it will be when I accept your proposal of marriage and take Sidney to my heart as fully as I do my own sons."

"Wh-what?"

"You heard me, Hawk. Must I state my case more clearly? I love you. I have loved you since first you kissed me in the corridor. And I shall go on loving you until you give in and offer for me. Neither mills nor mud nor corpses nor illegitimate sons shall sway me. I am quite determined to be a rogue myself, and if you never see fit to marry me, I shall never marry anyone at all."

A great silence fell into the space between them. Priscilla could not believe that she had said the words. What must he think of her? But it was truth. She did not care a groat what anyone thought—her papa and mama and Sarah, polite society, all could either accept it or turn their backs upon her—she would have The Hawk or no one. She must have The Hawk. Every murmur of her heart, every whisper of her soul told her that it was true.

Hawkworth lifted an eyebrow. He removed his arm from the mantelpiece. He took a step toward her and then another. He held out his hands to her and she placed her own within them. And then he pulled her up out of the chair and into his arms.

"You are the most audacious brat," he whispered into her ear. "Are you quite certain you wish this thing? Because I am quite certain that I love you, minx. I knew the moment Tolly said he was to marry Miss Pritkin and I thought he meant you."

And before she could so much as answer him, his lips were upon hers and Priscilla was laughing and kissing him at one and the same time.

TEMPTATION

by

Jeanne Savery

"She's a looker under all that drab material," said Locke Talmidge, Lord Brant. He stared out the light traveling carriage's window, world-weary eyes feasting on the young woman.

Martin Herrick cast no more than half a glance toward the pedestrian. "She's a dowd."

Brant slid a faintly sardonic look toward Herrick. "You haven't an eye in your head if you cannot see she'd pay for dressing."

Herrick, yawning, missed the look. "You should know," he muttered, faintly resentful of his taller friend's success with the ladies. He yawned again. "Wake me when we arrive."

"Stay alert," replied his lordship once he'd controlled his own urge to yawn. "It's no more than a couple of miles now." He gave a thought to Miss Tenacious Smythe walking in all their dust. *Poor Tenny. I wish it were proper to have offered her a ride.* "You'll see some of the horses soon. I can't offer to race them, but you'll enjoy them," he said to his friend.

"Good horses?" asked Herrick, suspiciously.

"Hmm? Oh yes. His lordship has perfected his stock for over three decades." *Except she'd have refused to get into the carriage because it is me, not because it is improper. . . .*

"Can't have," argued Herrick after turning the notion over this way and that.

That caught Brant's attention. "Why not?"

"Three decades? I'd know the stables," said Herrick.

Brant chuckled. "No you wouldn't."

"Why not?"

"Because he don't sell them."

"Is that why you come here? The horses?"

Brant evaded an exact answer. "I very much admire the work he's done." Lord Brant loved Falcon's Pride and admired his uncle's horses; that he more than admired the neighbor's daughter was something so sensitive, so private, he couldn't bring himself to reveal it. Given his reputation, he rather doubted he'd be believed. He sighed gently.

"There, Marty," he said. "The first pastures."

"Mares." Then Martin added, accusingly, "None are in foal."

"A *program,* Marty. He's got a bee in his bonnet about raising equine intelligence. He's careful which he breeds for the next generation. There is one stallion I'd like you to see. . . ."

And a particular young lady. Lord Brant pretended to study the horses. More than advice concerning the stallion, he wanted Marty's support as he nerved himself to ask for Miss Smythe's hand. But if he couldn't bring himself to reveal his intent, then how could he expect help? *More than likely,* the sour thought intruded, *I'll not need it. If Tenny treats me as she has been, I'll once again put off testing my luck.*

"You want my advice?"

"Yes. Too, I enjoy your company, Marty."

Thinking of the sort of larks he and his friend had enjoyed, Brant turned. "Marty," he said, "we must behave. My great uncle is not utterly straitlaced, but he has a touch of the Methodist in him, so keep your paws off the maids. If you want a woman, take yourself off to the village inn."

Herrick's brow arched. "And take a closer look at that drab walking along the road?"

Brant quickly suppressed a sudden and surprising panic. "You leave that one alone. She's gentry."

"Gentry?" Herrick looked at Brant with disbelief. "Dressed worse than—than my aunt dresses her house-maids? I don't believe it."

A muscle jumped in Locke's jaw. "Believe it."

Herrick shrugged. "Tavern maids, then. Is that all the entertainment you can offer? Besides the horses?"

Brant recalled that Martin didn't care for country pur-suits.

"I can take a gun out perhaps?" asked Herrick. "A rod?"

"Anytime," said Brant encouragingly. *I should have come alone. I'd have done so if I'd not been worrying about Tenny. . . .*

"Bosh and tush. Can't bear to sit about waiting for a fish stupid enough to take a bite at m'bait, and I shoot about as well as your gentry miss could do!"

The words reminded Brant of the time he had invited Herrick to a deer stalk in Scotland. He grinned, his teeth white against his tanned skin. "I'd forgotten how bad a shot you are, but find another comparison. That young lady has a stable full of brothers. They taught her which end of a gun you point!"

"You know her?" asked Martin, curious about the warmth he heard.

"Of course. Gowned as she was, how do you think I knew she'd pay for dressing?"

"Your well-known percipient eye, of course!" retorted Herrick. "Are those your uncle's gates?"

Tall, wrought-iron gates, a stylized falcon centered on each half, stood tightly closed in a high wall. At a halloo from the driver, a lad ran out of the gatehouse and, with effort, tugged them open. Lord Brant tossed a coin to the boy and got a cheeky grin for his pains.

"We've arrived," he said, his satisfaction obvious.

"You like it here!" said Herrick, amazed at the discovery. *"You really like it!"*

"Yes," agreed his lordship softly. "I really like it." He stared at the long, low, two-story house built of golden Cotswold stone hauled north early in the previous century. "I really do."

Lord Brant had returned.

Miss Tenacious Smythe, returning from a visit to an old and rheumatic lady in the village, wrinkled her nose against the dust raised by the passing carriage. She glared at the equipage which, neatly designed, didn't deserve such a look.

Miss Smythe knew her world would be in turmoil until he went away. How dare he cut up her peace? How dare he change from her childhood hero, to something other than the delightful friend he'd later become?

How dare he turn into an unrecognizable monster?

Not that he had changed by one hair. Miss Smythe gritted her teeth. All that had happened was that she now knew him for what he was and could no longer allow herself to dream dreams of the man she'd *thought* him to be.

It wasn't fair of him to disappoint her so!

Realizing how very silly a thought that was, Miss Smythe compressed her lips against a smile. Her heart and mind in conflict, as always when she thought of Locke Talmidge, she was glad to see her second-oldest brother coming along the lane toward her, driving their eldest brother's curricle.

She needed distraction.

"I've been looking for you," said Matthew sternly. "In

fact, we are *all* looking for you. Once again you went off without telling anyone where you'd be, which you *know* you are not to do."

But not a lecture!

"Especially not when a gazetted rake resides in the neighborhood!"

How, wondered Miss Smythe, *did they know of Lord Brant's arrival when he'd only just driven through the village?*

Only later did it occur to her that Matt referred to an entirely different rake.

"My lord," said Lord Brant, formally introducing Herrick and his host, "my friend, Mr. Martin Herrick of the Rutland Herricks." Locke turned to Martin. "You will be glad to know my uncle, Lord Asten."

"Rutland, hmm?" said the old man without rising from his chair. "Believe I once heard tales of a Herrick from that branch." Lord Asten frowned. The frown turned to a scowl. "Now I remember. *Sinjin Herrick.*"

Herrick rolled his eyes. "My black-sheep cousin. Last heard of, he'd taken himself off to India. Ages ago, my lord. I didn't know him myself—"

Herrick hoped to lighten his host's ill-humor.

"—Before my time. Er, tell me—"

He spoiled it.

"—did he actually climb the wall at midnight to get into the Tower precincts? On a bet?"

Lord Asten bit back a sound which might or might not have been a laugh. "That and any number of other tomfool stunts. Not perhaps a true black sheep, m'boy, but wild to a fault! Like my nephew." Asten glared at Martin. "I suppose you are another like Locke here," he growled.

"Can't be," said Martin promptly.

"Why can you not?"

"No one measures up to Brant," said Herrick with honest admiration. "He's a nonpareil. Maybe someone rides better, but he won't shoot well. Or perhaps there is someone as good at cards, but he cannot drive. Locke can do *everything.*"

"Bah! You should say he knows more ways of wasting time than anyone else." Asten eyed Locke consideringly. "You do mean to stay a while, do you not? This isn't another of your dashes in and out as if this was a stop for the Royal Mail and you'd only a moment before you must be off again?"

"I've nowhere to go and nothing to do," said Locke promptly. "I'll stay as long as you wish."

"Well then, I—" The moment was lost when the double doors to the salon opened. Asten peered around the edge of his chair. "Yes, Tempest?" asked his lordship rather crossly.

The butler, a man far more stately than Asten could ever be, stared down his nose. "Dinner, my lord, is served."

"About time." The elderly man struggled to rise.

When Martin moved to help him, Locke quickly shook his head. "No," he mouthed and watched, helplessly, as Lord Asten finally made it to his feet. He handed his uncle a pair of canes and, moving at a snail's pace, the younger men followed their host from the salon.

Dinner was long, involving many courses which Lord Asten picked at, eating a mouthful of this, a bite or two of that. He drank a glass of wine and then had it removed, a goblet of chilled water replacing it.

Herrick was more than a trifle disconcerted to see his own wineglass disappear. He glanced at Brant, who was experiencing the same oddity. "Water?" mumbled Martin, staring at his clean glass. *"Water?"*

"Good for you," said Asten in a tone which forbade contradiction. "Comes from a special spring." He turned to Brant. "Now then, boy. The mares in the boxes. You'll check them and tell me which should be bred."

Brant lay down his fork. "Bred to which stallion, Uncle?"

"That, too, is up to you." The elderly man grinned sourly when his nephew looked more than a trifle rattled by the notion. "I've three at the moment." He glared. "As usual, you've got 'til your birthday to make up your mind, m'boy." He glanced down as a footman served him from a tray. "Tempest, what is this mess?" he demanded.

"A fricassee of veal, my lord, with tarragon sauce."

"Bah. Frenchified nonsense. Besides, I've finished." He pushed back from the table but, before rising, looked at his guests. "You stay. Eat more if you want. The young, I seem to recall, are always hungry." He sighed. "Been a long time now since I enjoyed my food. A long, long time . . ."

He was still muttering as he left the dining room. The two young men, who stood until he disappeared, reseated themselves. Lord Brant smiled at the butler. "Do you think, Tempest, that you might bring back that bottle of claret? Poor Mr. Herrick will expire of thirst if you do not!"

"Very well, my lord."

Later, Lord Brant waved away the sweets and port wine but watched indulgently as his friend selected a portion of nearly everything offered. "I have never understood how you eat so much and remain so thin." Brant toyed with his wineglass.

"Hmm?" Herrick looked up from his plate on which rested a slice from a Chantilly cake, a goodly portion of the trifle, a petit four, and a cinnamon-flavored glazed pear. "I'm hungry. Would have liked another slice off that ham before it disappeared, and I'd have taken another partridge if it had been offered. Didn't quite like to ask. Would have seemed greedy when your uncle ate so little. Might not have taken so many sweets if I'd had another partridge."

Lord Brant tipped his wine, watching the thin trace of color on the side. He had yet to finish a single glass of the wines offered since his uncle's departure. When Herrick drained his glass yet again, Lord Brant sighed. *It will be,* he thought, *too bad if Martin means to make a night of it.* Brant hoped for an early bed.

Tempest set brandy on the table and departed.

Herrick sipped at his. His brow arched. *"Finally.* A reason for leaving town for this godforsaken place!" One disparaging glance out the window and he closed his eyes, a pained look on his face. "There's nothing here, Locke!"

"Pastoral scenery does not induce swoons of ecstasy?"

Herrick groaned and Brant grinned, his smile a devilish slash across his tanned features. He took pity on his friend. *"I* left town at my great-uncle's request," he said. "I asked if you would care to rusticate for a time. Remember?"

"Thought you had a mill in mind," grumbled Herrick. "Or a private race." He finished his brandy and poured another. "Didn't say anything about duty visits to elderly relatives." Suddenly he looked up. "Locke, how *do* you mean to entertain me? Tell me I need not resign myself to doing the pretty by the old gentleman each and every day."

"Since my uncle raises horses, I doubt"—Brant played with the brandy he had yet to sip—"you'll have difficulty finding entertainment."

"Not quite dark yet," said Herrick. He squinted through his glass toward the uncurtained windows. "Might take a toddle down to the stables? Might run our peepers over those mares you're to judge?"

"An excellent notion." Locke promptly set down his glass.

"Think Asten means to leave his stud to you?" asked
Herrick as they strolled a gravelled path toward an arch-
way cut in a tall hedge.

"I . . . don't know."

Herrick laughed at Brant's unexpectedly wistful tone.
"You *hope* so, is that it?"

"I have said I admire his stables," said Lord Brant.

"He'd be a fool to leave it elsewhere," said Herrick
scornfully.

For that belief, Brant gave his friend a smile of gratitude. They passed through the hedge and stopped. Herrick, staring at the layout of buildings before them,
whistled softly.

"My uncle is extraordinarily proud of the design. He'll
enjoy showing it to you."

"He's spent a fortune on all this." Herrick's eyes narrowed. "This choosing the mares . . . that's a test?"

"I've done it every year for a decade," said Locke, not
exactly answering the question. "Sometimes I come reasonably close to his notions. Sometimes not."

"So that's why I'm here. You want my help."

"No." Lord Brant gave fleeting thought to Miss Tenacious Smythe who, for nearly three years now, was never
far from his thoughts. Even on his increasingly rare visits
to his mistress, it was Tenny's face he'd see in his mind.
"No, it is something else entirely. I'll tell you when I've
finished this year's work"—*Or maybe not?*—"perhaps." A
short-legged man, Asten's head groom, came trundling
toward them. Brant was glad of an excuse to change the
subject. "Bolton! How are you?"

He introduced Herrick who, after they'd exchanged a
few comments, was accepted by the groom as another
horseman and then ignored. Bolton and Lord Brant indulged in a general discussion of the Falcon's Pride stables before Brant asked about Rebel's Star.

Bolton looked around, lowered his voice. "His lord-ship's thinking of getting rid of the Rebel line."

Brant, his mouth tightening, glanced toward Herrick who, a little apart, stared into one of the loose boxes. "I want Herrick to see Star." He raised his voice. "Martin, come away from that creature and see an animal in which I've taken an interest."

Herrick tore himself from the mare and they crossed to where the stallions were housed.

"Have him out, will you, Bolton? Once Marty's seen him, I may as well ask his advice. Not," he added, "that I'll have the opportunity to try what I want to try. . . ."

Herrick watched the stallion's oddly flowing action. Once the animal's paces had been shown, he ap-proached, introduced himself to the horse, and then went over him. Finally he backed off. "Bolton, you said Lord Asten is thinking of getting rid of this animal. Does that mean," he asked, amazed, "that he thinks the other stal-lions are better?"

"For his purposes, yes," said the groom.

"Hmm. Don't believe it."

"Now you've seen him, what would you say to mating him to Beauty Flying?"

"Beauty Flying. Beaut—ah! Beauty Flying! You mean that black of Lady Hangerville's? The one with the odd gait? Hmm." Marty's lower lip protruded and he once again studied the stallion. "Just realized! This horse runs in that same odd way. . . ." Herrick frowned.

Finally, after they discussed the proposed mating, Brant said, "You put Star away, Bolton. It was a long journey. Last night and most of today. I'll see the mares tomor-row."

"Very well, my lord."

"Excellent stock," said Herrick as they strolled away. "How long you say your uncle's been breeding 'em?"

"Three decades or so." Brant yawned a bone-cracking

yawn. "Marty, I'm nearly asleep on my feet. We should have started yesterday morning and stayed overnight on the road."

"We had invitations to the Summerwood ball. Not so bad starting out after the ball. Besides, I slept most of the way. You didn't?"

"No." Brant studied his nails, then glanced at Herrick. "I invariably get into a fret when I come to Falcon's Pride. I love it, you see, and I always fear it will be my last visit."

"You mean your uncle would forbid you the premises?"

"I mean"—Brant stared blindly over a paddock—"if he decides to leave it away from me, if I've no hope of it ever being mine, I don't think I could bear to come again."

Brant spoke with such simplicity that Herrick was deeply impressed. "The old man won't find a better horseman in all of England. Not our age."

"That's nice of you to say, Marty, but although I know horses and I know my uncle's plans"—his face twisted in a quick grimace—"I don't necessarily want what he wants. Like mating Star to Beauty. He'd say it was a waste of time, not forwarding his plan." Brant yawned widely. "You slept, but I did not. And I didn't get all that much sleep the night before, thanks to that winning streak I was on." He shrugged his tight coat into a more comfortable position. "Sat at the tables far too late."

"Regret it?"

Brant grinned wickedly. "Regret owning Stillman's pride and joy? How could I?"

Herrick stopped short. "That estate on the Thames near Reading? He actually wagered Still Waters?"

"Yes."

"Lucky devil."

"No." Lord Brant's teeth flashed again. *"Sober* devil." His lordship said it a trifle smugly but then yawned again.

"Blast it. I'm asleep on my feet. Marty, I've got to go to bed. . . ."

"You toddle along. Bolton will saddle me a horse and I'll ride into the village. Wouldn't mind looking over the maids at the inn there. Do it before *you* do. Once the maids see you, I'll only get your leavings. As usual."

"You'll have your choice. I don't indulge that particular passion while visiting my uncle."

"Don't want to dirty your own kennel, hmm?"

"Don't sneer, Marty." Brant did not laugh. Thinking of Tenny, he couldn't even smile. "Besides, I've visited *your* home!" He cast a sardonic look his friend's way. "When home, you behave like the angel you are not!"

Marty's volatile emotions turned toward humor. "Got me there, right and tight! See you at breakfast, Locke."

"Or later. If I sleep now, which"—he yawned another gaping yawn—"I must, as I'll be up at dawn. I'll see the mares before I see you."

Herrick handed the Falcon's Pride gelding over to a groom at the small inn in North Deighten and strolled toward the inn's side door. The door opened into a short hall with private parlors on both sides.

Herrick heard the clear tones of a woman's voice coming from one of the parlors. Very pleasant sounding. He wondered if the woman would be half so lovely as the voice and, hearing a few words which piqued his curiosity, decided he'd find out.

He crossed his arms and leaned against the wall across from the door, which stood slightly ajar.

". . . so do not pretend you do not understand," the woman said, her tone indicating a degree of impatience. "You know I cannot go."

"Then you can forget the new schoolhouse," said a grating voice.

One could *hear* a sneer contorting the man's face. But what, wondered Herrick uneasily, was Liviston doing in this godforsaken corner of England?

"The schoolhouse is for the children, my lord. It is badly needed and you, my lord, would not miss the few sovereigns it would take to build one."

"I deny that."

"That you would not miss them? But you have so much!"

A derisive laugh was the response to that.

"You must have," repeated the woman.

Liviston ignored her. "I've told you what you must do to get your schoolhouse. If you do not, then you may forget it."

"I cannot go with you to the next assembly in Harrogate. You have not thought, my lord, how it would look."

"You, Miss Tenacious Smythe, are more of an innocent than I knew. What," he said gloatingly, "do you think the local biddies will say when they discover you have spent this past half hour alone with me here in the inn?"

"Nothing at all. Because I have not."

"Nonsense. Look at us, my beauty." The purring sound of a sinister male voice came slightly nearer. "We are here. We are alone . . ."

"Stay where you are, Lord Liviston. I said we are *not* alone and we are not. Mary!"

"What the devil!"

Herrick wondered where a maid had been hidden that Liviston had not noticed her.

"Mary, we must leave. His lordship is either incapable of understanding the importance of what I ask, or he is more selfish than I had heard. Good evening, my lord."

"Just one little minute."

"Yes, my lord?" There was a bright hopeful sound to her voice. "You've changed your mind, perhaps?"

"About you? Of course not. I'll have you, willy-nilly, so

you may as well cooperate and come to me without a struggle. Because it will be the worse for you if you do not."

"Threats, my lord? With a witness?"

"Who would believe the word of your half-wit maid?"

"Mary is not a half-wit!"

"She can't talk, can she?"

"She does speak. Just not often. But she can *write*. And, what is more, she has a very good memory. She will write out this whole conversation," said the lovely voice gently. "Now I must go. Good evening . . . *my lord!*"

Marty, hearing the chit's sudden alarm, shoved the door open. "Ah! There you are. Come along like a good girl," he said crossly. "Your family sent me to bring you home, you know. Ah! You here, Liviston? Didn't know you lived hereabouts. Well?" He glared at the chit. "Come along, girl. Haven't got all night!"

Very slowly, Liviston released the young lady's arm. With somewhat more haste than grace, she retreated into the hall, her maid following. Herrick was about to do likewise when Liviston spoke.

"Herrick!"

He turned.

"I won't forget this."

"Will you not?" Herrick forced a slow smile, although he felt more than a trifle sick. The notion that he'd put himself into Liviston's bad books didn't set well. But then, neither did the notion that he might have slunk off and, saving his own skin, left a young lady to his lordship's less than tender mercies. "Neither will I, my lord."

Marty retired from the room just as Liviston was pouring himself a brandy. Irritated that he could not do likewise, but must go after the young woman, who was obviously in need of a keeper, Marty stalked out. Hearing her lovely voice, he followed the sound until they were well beyond the village and, with luck, beyond any gossip's eyes.

"Miss," he called.

She turned, startled.

"I think I should escort you and your maid home. Lord Liviston is not a man one may trust. If he knows you walk this way, he may follow."

The chit bit her lip. "It seems I misjudged him. I wasn't aware—"

"What a rake he is?"

"*He* is not a rake. I *know* a rake," she said sternly. "The man I know is not at all untrustworthy. Lord Liviston, on the other hand, has proved himself clearly evil."

"Evil?" Marty felt a twinge of unease. "Don't know if I'd go *that* far!"

"I would," she said firmly and continued sternly. "Sir, I do not know you. How do I know I may trust you any more than I may trust his lordship?"

"I'm Herrick, friend of Locke Talmidge. Lord Brant, you know? We're visiting his uncle, Lord Asten." He broke off, wondering why the chit appeared to be fighting between chagrin and laughter! "Miss . . . ?"

"The fact that you are a friend of Lord Brant is not proof I may trust you! Quite the contrary."

"Well," said Herrick, lifting his hat and scratching his head, "I don't know how I may prove it, but since you need an escort, shall we say that if you arrive home safely, that will be proof?"

"But how am I to know I will?"

Marty glanced over his shoulder. "May we walk on as we argue? If we don't, we're more than likely to run into Liviston. Or rather, he's likely to catch up with us. Frankly, I'd prefer to avoid that particular problem."

The young woman tipped her head, thinking. Her maid tugged at her sleeve and, when the young woman turned to her, pointed onward, stabbing her finger in that direction several times.

"You think we should walk on?"

The maid nodded, casting a fearful look over her shoulder.

"You are afraid of Liviston?"

The maid nodded again.

"Sensible child." Herrick smiled, and the maid blushed rosily. He turned a fierce glare on the other female. "Now, are you *half* so sensible?"

She chuckled. "Very likely not. I like a good rousing argument, you see, but cannot seem to do more than one thing at a time. I doubt I can walk and continue arguing with you!"

Disgusted, Marty shook his head. "I've no wish to fight Liviston somewhere along this dusty road. It is well known he don't fight fair."

"You think there might be fisticuffs . . . ?" Obviously Miss Smythe had not considered that possibility. "Oh dear. I have, by thinking I knew better than my brother, gotten *you* into Lord Liviston's black books as well as myself. I am sorry."

"So you should be!" Her words registered. "You mean someone told you to stay clear of Liviston and you didn't?"

She nodded.

"Headstrong wench!" he muttered to himself. "Should be paddled until she can't sit down. Maybe she'd pay attention."

Miss Smythe had sharp hearing and was not one to pretend she was deaf. "It hasn't done much good in the past," she said. "Punishment," she added when he gave her a querying glance. "I am, I am told, exceedingly stubborn but"—her chin rose—"I am determined to do what is right."

"And who determines what's right?" demanded Herrick.

She chuckled again. "I suppose I do. Right now I must find the money to build a schoolhouse. I can teach the children even without it, but we must meet in the inn and not only is the room too small, but we must vacate it if Timothy—the landlord, you know—has need of it. Too, there is no place to keep supplies, the slates, sandboxes, books and so on. I must have them carted in each day, wasting a servant's time and energy."

"Sandboxes?"

"The youngest write their letters in sand and then smooth it. One needn't buy paper or ink, you see. The older children, of course, must practice with the real thing. I can afford that much, but haven't the funds to build a school. Lord Liviston could."

"Probably couldn't," contradicted Herrick.

"But he owns—"

"Mortgaged."

"But he inherited a fortu—"

"Lost at play."

Miss Smythe was silent for a moment. "I see. It would have been ever so much better if my brother had told me the man was a pauper rather than try to frighten me to death. Which he should have known he could *not* do."

"Maybe should have done both," said Marty cautiously. "Liviston's a bad man. I don't suppose that's your brother riding toward us now, is it?"

"One of them. That's Charlie. I suppose Bill told him. Charlie, you may take that scowl off your face. I am perfectly safe."

"But she's made an enemy of Liviston," amended Herrick. He bowed. "I'm Herrick, by the way. Martin Herrick, friend of Lord Brant. We're visiting Lord Asten."

"Liviston," explained Charles Smythe civilly, "is feuding with my father. An old border dispute. It is quite in character that he'd avenge himself through my sister. Tenny," he added, turning toward her, "Bill told you not to go but, as usual, you thought you knew best. Luckily he came to me when he discovered you had disappeared." He frowned in a pensive fashion. "What, my girl, are we to do with you?"

"I am, as you see, perfectly safe."

"But will that ever again be true?" exploded Charlie. "Don't you *see*, you great silly?" he continued when she tipped her head questioningly. "You have made yourself an enemy who will stoop to anything!" He sighed when she shook her head. "That settles it. You will have to remain at home unless one of us can take you wherever you wish to go."

"But, Charlie, how can we manage?" she asked in earnest tones. "I must be at my school each morning, and there is my work for the vicar, and you know I *never* know when I'll be called out because of illness among the poor, and—"

"Stop," he ordered but she continued listing the duties which kept her moving round the region. Charlie interrupted again and told her to come along so he could toss her up on his mount. "You will be still, Tenny!" he insisted, this time reinforcing his demand by covering her mouth. "When we get home, I will take you to our father. *He* will decide what is to be done with you."

"You know that isn't true, Charlie," said Miss Smythe, still earnest. "As is usual, *Grandmother* will decide."

Charlie grimaced. "You will obey whoever it is, do you hear?"

Miss Smythe heaved a huge sigh. "I must do what I feel is right." Saying no more on that head, she turned to Marty. "I am sorry to have caused you trouble, Mr. Herrick. I do not feel guilty, since I did not know you'd overhear and come to my rescue, but I *am* sorry it happened."

"Er, well, yes. Never mind. Since we are so close, I think I'll just go straight on back to Falcon's Pride now . . . good night."

A much subdued Marty strolled across the meadows toward Asten's place. He didn't feel quite comfortable leaving the gelding at the inn, but, equally, he didn't wish to chance running into Lord Liviston again. Especially not a Liviston deep in his cups, which the man would be by now. At least, he ought to be well up in his altitudes if he'd emptied that decanter as he appeared intent on doing!

Dead drunk would be all right, of course, but *belligerently* drunk would not!

Brant woke the next morning, as he'd expected, at a ridiculously early hour. If he were not so wide awake, he'd drop back into the dream.

Or perhaps he should call it *The Dream?* The dream which had recurred regularly for nearly two years now? Such a wickedly delightful dream it was, too.

Unfortunately, the odds were strongly against its coming true.

To force the dream from his mind, he stared greedily at the scene beyond his windows. How unlike London, where his view, if he were daft enough to look, was no more than a soot-blackened brick wall. Here at Falcon's Pride he never allowed the drapes to be drawn. It was a special treat to wake to the morning sun and watch the young stock cavorting in the paddock beyond the side lawn.

A groom appeared, buckets dangling from a yoke across his shoulders. The colts and fillies heard him whistling and raced toward the long trough into which the groom poured the grain. Brant chuckled when a filly nipped a colt which, startled, moved away. The filly, looking smug, slipped into the vacated spot near where the groom stood. He wondered if his uncle had noticed that particular filly and, rising, moved to the window where he continued to observe her.

He checked the sun's position. Hmm. The grooms would have been up and doing for some time. He dressed quickly and, unshaven, took the back stairs to the kitchen, where Cook made him a sandwich of newly baked bread and lovely, thin slices of ham. Brant thanked him and strolled on, taking his first bite as he entered the scullery on his way to the back door.

In the dim and steamy workroom off the kitchen, he noticed a young girl up to her elbows in hot water. He glanced back, saw no one could see him, and, removing a scrap of ham, told the chit to open wide. Happily chewing the bite he stuffed into her maw, she returned to her scrubbing.

Brant reached the stallion's stabling and leaned, for a time, on Star's half-open door. Then, duty bound, he studied the other two stallions, thoroughly reviewing their bloodlines before returning to the boxes in which the chosen mares were housed.

"Morning, Bolton. Is this a bad time?"

"My lord, any time's a good time for *you*," said the bandy-legged groom, smiling broadly. "We'll have 'em out of there in no time at all," he added once he'd given orders. "You'll have no trouble this year. Myself, I think it's obvious what his lordship has in mind."

"You work with them all year round, Bolton. I'm expected to judge them after only the shortest acquaintance. I've never understood how my uncle can believe it possible."

"You do better than the others," said Bolton.

The offhand comment revealed what Brant had long suspected. The sure knowledge that there was competition for Falcon's Pride settled like a rock in his chest.

"Ah!" added the groom. "Now there's a likely lass." He nodded toward the first mare out of her box.

"You say that about all of them," teased Brant. A frown settled on his brow as he studied the mare, which a young groom encouraged into a trot at the end of a lead. Brant spent over two hours with the mares. At first he kept them together, testing their paces. Later he dismissed all but one groom, who put each horse through the tests his uncle had made traditional. As expected, each mare passed.

His eyes narrowed. How *did* his uncle decide among them? Every year it was the same: He'd end by guessing! Or . . . perhaps *not*, this year? *This* year he'd dreamed up a new test. Just maybe he'd argue his choices for a change, justifying them as he'd been unable to do in the past.

"Enough for now," he told the groom. "I'll be back later and then I mean to saddle them up."

"Saddle . . . ?" The groom gave him a wary look. "We don't ride the breeding stock, do we?"

"We do this year. I'll talk to Bolton myself, so you keep a still tongue in your head!" He pretended to glare; the young groom grinned.

Brant strolled through the gardens. Turning a corner of the house, he arrived at his uncle's library, where low-silled open windows allowed him entry. "Uncle?"

"Hmm?" Lord Asten looked up from the papers spread over his desk. "Locke. You were not at breakfast." He eyed his nephew's unshaven chin and frowned. "A trifle late, are you not?"

"Not." Brant grinned at his uncle's questioning look. "I've been up for hours. The one you call Number six. What was her lineage?"

"Bolton couldn't tell you?"

"I sent Bolton off after the first parade."

The two men settled into a long discussion of lineages.

Brant mentioned the filly he'd watched from his window
that morning. His uncle, brows arched, said he'd keep
an eye on the youngster. Both enjoyed the talk a great
deal, although Asten wasn't as certain of Locke as he
wished to be. Was the lad truly as interested as he
seemed? Was he dedicated to the goal? Would he continue the work?

Asten sighed softly. "So you see, boy, the Rebel's line
isn't showing so well as we'd hoped. Not at all so well."

"I am sorry to hear it." Brant debated with himself.
He shrugged. "Uncle, I know you don't want to see any
of the horses bred for any purpose other than your own,
but . . ."

"But you have a mating in mind for Star?" asked Asten
coldly.

"Yes."

"With what goal?"

"Action."

Asten cast a startled look toward his nephew. "What?
Not for speed?"

"Racing is a chancy business, and I have no desire to
take part in that game. But Rebel's Star? The offspring
might be special. Both the dam I have in mind and Star
use unusual leg action. If possible, I'd like to bring it out
in a line of horses. Uncle, the ride one gets is so soft, so
smooth, so"—he frowned, then shook his head—"I don't
know how to explain it. But those are the only two horses
I have ever seen use it."

"The mare?"

"Beauty Flying. Lady Hangerville bought her off a man
who brought her across the Atlantic from what's called
The Piedmont."

"Odd action, hmm? Takes a lot out of the animal,
hmm?"

"In actual fact"—Brant mimed a nonchalance he
didn't feel—"they appear to have *greater* stamina."

Asten's brows climbed his forehead. "Impossible."

"I believe it."

"Never watched Star for his action . . ." Asten stared at his nephew. "Need to see it myself," he said.

Brant drew in a deep breath. "Uncle, would it be impossible to have *two* programs in progress simultaneously?"

"Two breeding programs?"

Asten stared down his nose at Brant who wished, not for the first time, that he knew how to read his uncle.

Finally the elderly man spoke. Impatiently. "Later. I've work to do and, for now, you stick to planning what you'd do with those mares. Locke," he added in a more kindly voice as his heir, mouth set in a grim line, walked toward the hall door, "I will think about this other thing."

Brant swung on his heel. "You will?"

Asten grinned a tight little grin. "I said I would, did I not?" His look changed to an especially stern expression. "But *you*. You've a courtesy call to pay, do you not?"

"The Smythes." Brant felt his ears warm at the thought of seeing Tenny. "We'll ride over as soon as Martin is up and presentable." He rubbed his chin, which grated softly against his fingers. "I must prepare myself as well, of course. Can't pay calls in all one's dirt, after all."

"It is my understanding that Miss Smythe spends her mornings in the village. Teaching or some such tomfoolery. I suggest you escort her home. It will give the two of you time to become reacquainted."

A muscle jumped in Brant's jaw. "You are as mad as a York hatter, Uncle, if you believe you can make a match between me and that chit. She is far too knowing, or so she thinks, to have to do with the likes of me!"

"Then perhaps—" Once again Lord Asten glared down his nose at his nephew, which was quite a trick since he was seated and Brant not. "Perhaps it is time you changed your ways."

"You'd have me give up my London rooms and live elsewhere? Here perhaps?" asked Brant with as little emotion as he could manage.

"It's a thought," said his uncle, looking anywhere but at his heir.

"Here?" Brant looked disbelieving. One of his dearest dreams about to be realized? "You'd allow that?"

Asten stared at the work littering his desk. *"Allow* it?" he asked musingly. His brows rose slowly. "Oh yes. I believe I'd *allow* it."

"Then I'll do it."

Asten's head jerked up. He stared at his nephew.

Brant expelled a short, sharp bark of a laugh. "Ah! You didn't mean it."

On the words, Brant exited the room, too upset to remain where anyone might see how disappointment settled tightly inside him, contrasting far too sharply with that all-too-brief stab of elation. Tense in every muscle, he dashed up to his room, where his valet was laying out fresh linens.

The valet gave one glance to his master and, tactfully, looked away.

Steam rose gently from the ewer standing on his wash table. Brant went directly to it and pressed a damp cloth to his eyes. Unobtrusively, the valet set a screen around the washstand. He waited and was rewarded when Brant threw his cravat over the top. His shirt followed and boots clumped, one after the other, to the floor. Then Brant's unmentionables were hung over the top and his stockings flung aside.

"When you have finished, my lord," said Williams, hearing vigorous splashing, "I will shave you. You will wish to look your best when, as is usual with you, you visit the Smythes."

"Oh, yes. Definitely must look my best," muttered Brant, half cynically, half resignedly.

He grimaced into the cloth with which he scrubbed his face and neck. As if looking his best would change Miss Tenacious Smythe's stubborn mind. Blast the—the—*tenacious* chit! That reminded him of how her name had been chosen. A premature babe, her grandmother had said, but particularly tenacious of life so that her father insisted that be her name! The memory slid away as quickly as it came, his thought returning to Miss Smythe.

He scowled. Tenny had liked him well enough before Bobby started nattering about his reputation. Which was no worse than that of any other man-on-the-town! One day he'd find an excuse to bloody Bobby's nose, because it must have been Bobby's blethering that led to Miss Smythe's stubborn refusal to so much as speak with him.

What could a man do?

Lord Brant told some of this to Herrick as they rode into the village a little later, giving his friend the first hint of his serious interest in Miss Smythe. They walked into the inn and heard the sweet sounds of young voices raised in an old and familiar hymn. They waited. When the final amen trailed away, his lordship opened the door and strolled into the makeshift schoolroom. He looked around at a sudden scrabbling from one corner.

"Oh. Bobby," he said, not entirely pleased. "You here?"

Robert Smythe relaxed back onto the high stool on which he'd been sitting. "Tenny's got herself into another bumble-broth," said her fond brother in an exasperated tone.

"Tenny can speak for herself," said Miss Smythe. "Although not to *you.*" She turned her back on Brant. "Good day to you, Mr. Herrick. I hope you are feeling well this fine morning?"

"You know Martin?" asked Brant, looking from one to the other.

"Last night," growled Bobby, "he rescued her from one of Liviston's plots. The little idiot thought she could pry money from his lordship for a school! Now Grandmother says we must bear-lead her until we know his bloody lordship's left the region." Bobby yawned, patting his mouth with his hand. "It's going to be one big bore," he said, rolling his eyes. "*I've* been assigned the job of seeing her to and from the village each day."

"It won't hurt you," snapped his sister. "Perhaps you'll learn your letters. Finally."

"I know my letters," returned Bobby without heat. "It's putting them together to make proper words that stumps me. They keep getting mixed up, you see. And that's a bore too." He looked out over Miss Smythe's head toward her interested students and told them, "I don't know why I can't learn to read, but I can't. At least not well. You do better, hear? It's a very good thing if one can read. Now," he continued, standing up, "all of you. Take yourselves off until tomorrow."

There was a scramble and clatter as the children left the room.

"This is *my* school, Bobby!" Miss Smythe's hands settled against her hips. She softened. "Although I do appreciate your telling them how important reading is, sending them off like that"—she scowled—"Well, it's the outside of enough!"

"Merely told them it's time to go, which it is. You coming, Locke? Mr. Herrick?"

"Thought we'd stop by and do the proper by your grandmother," said Brant, but he was looking at Miss Smythe who, very carefully, was *not* looking at him. "Are you riding or walking?"

"Neither. Drove her in. Charlie let me take his curricle!" Brant grinned. "Feeling lucky, was he?"

Bobby, the sort who could laugh at himself, grinned. "Must have. But I neither overturned it nor scratched it, so maybe I've improved?"

"While I'm here, we can work in a lesson or two. If you want."

Bobby sobered. "Thanks, Locke. I'd appreciate it."

Miss Smythe stood with arms crossed, glowering. "If you two have quite finished, then I believe it is time we go."

"I already said that," said her brother, and led her to the door. He was startled when his sister didn't step forward. In fact, she stepped *back*, pushing against him. He noticed Lord Liviston then and forcibly put her behind his own back.

Brant took in the scene at a glance. "Liviston," he said, his voice icily polite.

"*You.* What the devil are you doing away from London?"

"One might ask you the same."

"Repairing lease." Liviston jerked at his cravat. "Trotting too hard. Needed to recoup."

Brant chuckled, a low, harsh, unfunny sound. "It will be difficult to make a recover, will it not? Impossible, perhaps?"

His change of meaning, referring to Liviston's gambling debts rather than his health, was not appreciated. "None of your damn business!"

"Tut-tut, Liviston." Herrick wagged a finger back and forth. "Lady present."

Liviston looked beyond them to where, her face a trifle pale, Miss Smythe stood near her brother. "Lady? *Lady?*" He laughed. "That *baby-minder?*" Moving on down the hall, he continued laughing in that nasty way.

"Why does he think me less than a lady? Does he feel my teaching puts me beyond the pale?" Tenny frowned.

"Surely he cannot mean that helping others is a lowering sort of thing."

"I doubt if he thinks of it as helping," suggested Brant, "but in his eyes you've demeaned yourself by associating with the lower orders. He isn't worth a thought, Tenny. Don't allow him to win you over to his way of thinking."

"As if I would. Come along, Bobby. If we do not return home in good time, it would be very like Charlie to order everyone out to search for us. He is such an old worrier."

"Since you've run afoul of Liviston, Miss Smythe," said Herrick, politely, "then very likely he has reason."

"You too?" She glared.

"Tenny, come along now," ordered her brother, tugging at her. "You may argue all you wish once you are in the curricle. Locke and Mr. Herrick can ride alongside."

"Oh, dear. A moment, please." Miss Smythe turned back to pack up her school supplies, which she'd forgotten at Brant's unexpected appearance. She wore a rueful look. "It is such a bore that I cannot argue and do anything else at the same time," she said, as she efficiently packed a crate.

Soon they rode along the lane, not hurrying, but not exactly dawdling either, and Miss Smythe argued with Brant.

They reached a point where the lane wove its way around a hill and alongside a tumbling stream before turning sharply to cross a bridge. Since she was losing her argument, Miss Smythe checked the tiny watch she wore pinned to her bodice and suggested her brother speed up a trifle. "Charlie will, as I said before, be fit to be tied if we do not arrive promptly."

Brant dropped behind the curricle to ride beside Herrick. They rode without speaking for a minute or two when, suddenly, Brant leaned forward. Then he yelled, "Bobby, pull up!"

But Bobby, singing a rollicking song, did not hear him.

Herrick, too, saw the wheel wobble. The two men looked at each other and then, urging their horses to a gallop, rushed forward on either side of the curricle. Coming alongside the mare, they reached for her harness and pulled her up.

"Why'd you do that?" asked Bobby, angry. "I was doing just fine!"

"*You* were doing fine, gudgeon, but the *carriage* is about to lose a wheel."

"*Charlie's* curricle? I don't believe it." Smythe handed his sister the reins and climbed down. "By all that's holy, you have the right of it!" He push back his hat. "How could . . . ?" He broke off, biting his lip.

The three men had the same notion at the same time and stared at each other.

"Perhaps you could take Tenny up behind—" Bobby began just as three masked men tore down the hillside. Grim-faced, he turned to climb back into the curricle as Miss Smythe reached to the floor and lifted a shotgun. Her face as grim as her brother's, she placed it at her shoulder and took aim.

Herrick and Brant, about to move in on the marauders, thought better of getting between the gun and Miss Smythe's target. But the sight of the gun was sufficient. The masked men curved to the side and back up the hill, disappearing over the top.

Very slowly the four on the road relaxed.

"Masked?" questioned Herrick.

"Highwaymen?" said Miss Smythe. "Here? They must be desperate indeed if they think there are pickings hereabout."

"It has yet to occur to you," said Brant gently, "that the 'pickings' they meant to acquire was you yourself?"

"Me? Oh." Miss Smythe turned bright red. "You mean

Liviston, do you not?" She frowned. "But *he* wasn't with those men. I'm certain he was not."

"No. He's waiting for them to bring you to him. An abandoned house, perhaps. Or a barn. Or, from what I know of his financial situation, they might deliver you to his traveling carriage on the road to the coast. He would steal you away to the continent"—Brant caught and held her gaze—"and abandon you there when done with you."

"*Evil.* I *said* the man was evil. How dare he plan such nastiness for me? For anyone?"

"*Now* will you believe you must take care?" demanded her brother. He trembled at the thought of what might have happened.

Miss Smythe suddenly turned a hard stare on Brant. "How," she asked, "do you know what his lordship might do?"

"I have an imagination," said Brant. "It is *not* something I'd do myself, if that is what you think."

"Bah."

"Locke," said Herrick as he nervously glanced here and there, "your gelding is stronger than mine. You take Miss Smythe up. One shotgun is not sufficient to hold off three men and they may realize it."

"Bobby, can you ride that mare?" asked Brant, gesturing toward the carriage horse the younger man was unhitching.

"She won't like it but she'll take me. Tenny—"

"I'll wait for you," she interrupted.

"You will not wait for me. You will go with Locke. Now."

Fortunately, Tenny realized the sense of it and, for once, decided she must not argue. Brant helped her seat herself sideways before him.

"All right?" he asked.

Tenny nodded.

It was a lie. She wasn't feeling at all well. In fact something was very wrong. She felt quite breathless. The masculine arm around her waist, a muscled thigh under hers, her arm and shoulder pressed against his chest . . . she had never been so lightheaded in her life. Miss Smythe bit her lip and stared at nothing at all, wishing she could stop the odd sensations which crawled over her from wherever she touched Brant. And no matter how stiffly she held herself, she could not avoid a certain amount of contact.

What did it mean? What was she feeling? And why?

She didn't like it . . . did she?

Surely not. It was so strange, this odd, waiting feeling. *Waiting for what?* she wondered. *Oh dear, I'm not about to faint, am I?*

"You aren't about to faint, are you?" asked Brant, noting her pallor.

"No—"

His breath was warm against her ear, adding still another new sensation to the collection with which she already dealt with the greatest of difficulty.

"—of course not," she insisted.

Or perhaps I will, she decided, as she experienced the faintest of pulls in her hair and realized it was his whiskers snagging on a strand or two. *Oh, dear, how curious . . . how very unsettling.*

Brant, for his part, was doing his best not to react to having his tenacious Tenny in his arms, but it was a losing battle. He had wanted her there for so long. So very long. It was easier when he was in London, where he could occupy himself in one manner or another with the things one did in town, but even there the dream returned again and again to plague him. Here at Falcon's Pride it came more often. Every night, in fact.

The Dream. The dream which concerned Tenny.

His Tenny, if she'd ever admit her feelings for him.

Because she did feel something for him. She would not treat him as she did if she did not. She'd treat him as she used to do, in an easy, sisterly fashion. Laughing at him or listening with that solemn, serious look she got when interested in something. Or he'd watch her plan mischief, her eyes twinkling and her lips setting in that tight little smile they'd get when she thought to trick him.

What she would *not* do was ignore him in quite such an ostentatious fashion. And, he thought with satisfaction, she would not tremble as she did now, while held close to him!

"Damn and blast it all," muttered Lord Brant. He wished he were more like Liviston and could simply ride off with her to a romantic tryst. He'd seduce her gently, teach her how wonderful love could be. There was another difference between himself and Liviston in that, if he *were* to do so, he'd never let her go, never wish for another woman to take her place. Liviston *would*. Brant breathed one more soft curse.

"I am sorry to be such a burden," said Miss Smythe, her voice cold.

"You are no burden at all. I didn't mean you to hear that, but since you did, I must explain." Brant thought quickly. "I was upset to discover Liviston here." That was true enough. "He and I do not see eye to eye and, as much as I can, I avoid him." That too was true, if not all of it.

"I am told you are both rakes. You should have a deal in common."

Both rakes? She thinks I am the same as that snake? "As with every other sort of person," retorted Brant, "there are different kinds of rakes."

He saw her jaw tighten, a rejection of his words. How to explain . . .

"Tenny, you recall the old vicar in North Deighten? A hunting parson, was he not? One who spoke the shortest of homilies? Nothing at all like the current man who, my uncle tells me, is a great bore who will not shorten his

sermons by one jot or tittle, even when he knows the
scent runs high and the hunting men are restless." He
glanced down at her, wondering if she understood.
"There are, likewise," he continued gently, "different
sorts of rakish men. Liviston is a man I'd not wish asso-
ciated with anyone I admired or loved or respected. He
is not to be trusted, Tenny."

"Miss Smythe, my lord," she said in a rather strangled
tone. "I have not given you permission to use my name,
let alone my family's pet name!"

That was too much! "I have called you Tenny for nearly
the whole of your life. I was unaware I had need of your
permission at this late date."

Miss Smythe felt her ears heat. It was true and she was,
perhaps, being a trifle childish, but she had been unable
to recover from her disappointment at learning Brant was
nothing more than a here-and-therian, a heedless soul
whose whole mind and effort was bent on seeking amusement.

And not always *acceptable* amusement—assuming she'd
understood half Bobby's monologue.

"Ten—er, Miss Smythe?"

"I am foolish to demand that you change after all these
years, my lord. I give permission to use my name as you
have in the past."

"Thank you, Tenny."

He felt her swallow. Hard. She was, he realized, truly
upset with him. He wondered what had set up her back.
Surely something beyond Bobby's naming him a rake!
Perhaps Bobby could tell him . . . ?

But no. Bobby was not particularly sensitive to the nu-
ances of people's emotions. He would have to ask Charlie,
and that would be far more difficult. Charlie, with his ten
years' superiority, had always had a way of looking at one
as if one didn't exist. Still . . . he'd do it. And then, once

he knew what was wrong, perhaps he could make progress with his Tenny.

Permission to use her name was, he decided, progress of a sort. One could not be utterly distant while using an intimate name! His arm tightened every so slightly as he looked ahead to where Charlie and Matt stood before the front door, and he realized he'd soon have to give up this closeness. "You are almost home, Tenny. You'll be safe now."

"Until I must go out again," she said.

"If there is any way you can manage it, I hope you will curtail your activities. You are in *danger*. All who admire you must worry about you."

"I must do"—her firm little chin rose a notch, her hair again pulling against his slightly rough beard—"what I must do."

"Then I ask," he said gently, "that in each case you think seriously whether you truly *must* do something or if someone else might do it for you."

"Bah," she said.

"Trouble?" asked Charles as Brant pulled up. He stared not at his sister, but at Brant.

"Liviston tampered with your curricle. Three masked men rode at us when we stopped because of a loose wheel. Tenny chased them off with the shotgun."

"She *fired* it?"

"If *she* had," said Miss Smythe, dryly, "she'd have gone tail-over-top over the back of the curricle and ended up in the road!"

Lord Brant chuckled. "Very likely true. I am glad those men didn't think of that!"

"Hired by Liviston, you think?" asked Charles, ignoring the few bantering words between Lord Brant and his sister.

"There cannot possibly be three highwaymen so stupid they would wait along that stretch of road," said Brant and struggled with the bereft feeling he experienced when Charles lifted his sister to the ground. "It is nothing more than a lane going nowhere. They must have been Liviston's men."

"Blast it." Thoroughly disgusted, Charles looked down at his sister. "Tenny, I am going to brick you up in a tower and feed you through a hole in the wall too small for you to crawl through. I know of no other way to keep you safe."

"Bah." Tenny turned on her heel and stalked into the house.

Charles sighed. He glanced up at Brant. "We serve luncheon soon. You will stay?"

"I would like to," said Brant, politely, "if we will not put your grandmother out too much."

"We?" Charles swung around and saw Herrick approaching with Robert. "Ah! Mr. Herrick. He and I met yesterday when he was escorting Tenny home."

"After her ill-advised meeting with Liviston." Brant nodded. "A harebrained notion that, that he'd build a school in the village."

"Tenny's latest project." Charlie sighed ruefully. "She always has a project, you know. A few have been wild or foolish, but most seem to fill some need. Draining that swampy area near the old cottages at the far end of the village, for instance. She talked Lord Asten into that year before last, and I'll be damned if she wasn't right. Since the job was finished, there has been very little of the sorts of illnesses with which nearby cottagers were plagued."

"This, you think, is one of her wilder projects?"

Charles grinned. "No. Only her belief that Liviston would fund it!"

Brant smiled. Perhaps they had reached an age where they could be friends? He hoped so. He had always admired Charles. From a distance. James and Robert were his special friends, the two nearest him in age. Matt, like

Charlie, had felt himself above them and William, still younger than Tenny, had been too young to join their games. But now . . . ? Well, he'd see.

"I'd like," he said, before he lost his nerve, "to have a talk with you? Later?"

"After we eat, I ride in the Pride's direction to check a flock. You might ride with me."

"An excellent notion. Assuming," said Brant, his brows arched, "I can rid myself of Herrick."

"Ah. A private conversation." Charles rubbed finger and thumb against the bridge of his nose. "I assume he's a horseman since you've brought him to visit your uncle. I'll send him with Matt to check a mare we have in foal."

"You always were perceptive," said Lord Brant. "I'm counting on it, actually."

The rest of Brant's stay at the Smythes was something of an anticlimax. There was, of course, no way it could be otherwise when he'd held Tenny in his arms for nearly a mile and had no hope of being anywhere near so close to her again that day.

Or the next.

Or perhaps ever again. Now *that* was a sobering thought. "Hmm?" he responded to the Smythe matriarch. "Yes, I mean to stay a while. My friend will leave in a week or three, but I plan a more extended visit."

"Very good," said Mrs. Smythe. She stared across the room to where her granddaughter entertained Mr. Herrick and hoped the man would stay far less than two or three weeks! He was a distraction to a long-cherished plan. Mrs. Smythe thought that Locke—Lord Brant, she should say, although, since she'd known him before he was in breeches, it was hard to call him that.

She blinked. Where had she got to in her thoughts? Tenny chuckled at something Mr. Herrick said.

That was it. Mr. Herrick must return to London before he turned the chit's head. Locke was the proper man for her granddaughter. As should be obvious to anyone with eyes. He doted on the chit, but he was a sensible man. He wouldn't allow her to run off in all directions doing no one knew what!

He'd keep her busy and he'd keep her happy.

Mrs. Smythe sighed. She did so want her granddaughter happy, and the little nitwit had *not* been for some time now. It occurred to the good lady to wonder why, and her eyes narrowed as she stared tensely at the girl. *Why-why-why?*

"I'll ask Charles," she muttered.

"Poor Charles," said Brant, grinning. "It seems everyone has questions for him."

She had forgotten Brant and cast him a startled glance. "You too?"

"Hmm."

Mrs. Smythe waited for Brant to elaborate. He did not. "For myself, I want to know why Tenny is unhappy. It has been months now since she lost that—that—"

"That bubbly quality one finds in good champagne?"

"Yes. An excellent description! You too have noticed?"

"She was changed when I visited two years ago. I have never known why"—a guess didn't count as *knowing*—"so if you discover the reason, will you tell me? Perhaps I could help to lighten her world again?"

"Oh, yes." Mrs. Smythe cast him a sharp glance. She chuckled, her whole huge body quivering and jiggling. It was a jolly sound and drew eyes. "Yes, indeed. A huge new candle to light up her world! I do hope so. Oh yes, I certainly hope so." And she went off into more jolly chuckles, drawing smiles and outright laughter from others, although no one, including Lord Brant, had a notion what she'd found so amusing.

"Grandmother?" asked Miss Smythe, curious.

"Never you mind, girl. Just never you mind. You'll do now," she finished complacently. "Oh, yes, dearie me, you'll do!"

Miss Smythe's quick mind arrived at an unacceptable suspicion. Although it explained her grandmother's behavior, she could not believe her relative wished her wed to a man who was certain to make her unhappy. She pushed the notion aside.

When they were ready to leave, Brant caught up with Miss Smythe and grasped her hand so she could not escape. She refused to look at him and he was forced to lift her chin before she'd meet his gaze. "Do not underestimate Liviston, Tenny. He has lost all pretense of owning to the title gentleman."

Tenny, who had expected something far different than this earnest request that she have a care for herself, took a moment to recover, staring at him rather blankly.

"Believe me, he will stoop to anything to have his way," he said. Tenny frowned. "My friend, if I am wrong about him, then you are, of course, in no danger. But what if I am correct in my belief?"

"I see. You would have me act as if the worst is possible in order to prevent what *might* happen."

"Is that not sensible?"

She sighed, looking away. "I cannot refute the logic."

"Then please employ your brothers as escorts when you must leave your home. And perhaps both they and you should be armed. I know you are an excellent shot and, although I do not think you capable of killing a man, you might, if necessary, wound him."

"But how would I live with myself if I were to miss my aim and kill someone?"

Brant stared down at her. "You would know," he said slowly, "that it is a perfectly moral thing to defend oneself and that, if while doing so, someone died, you'd not blame yourself but would put the blame squarely where it belongs. On Liviston."

Her lips twisted. "That sounds too easy. I'd have pulled the trigger."

He grinned suddenly. "*I* see what you would do. You seek to argue the point not so that one or the other of us is proven correct but so you need not actually think of the deed itself. If you merely talk about it, you think it isn't quite real." He sobered and tweaked the chin he still held. "But Tenny, your danger *is* real."

"So you say but"—she tossed her head, freeing herself, then she crossed her arms—"I have known Liviston all my life. I cannot believe he would harm me, someone he must have known in the cradle. No one could!" she ended on a triumphant note, dropping her hands to her sides.

"You believe that, assuming you'd been foolish enough to go with him to the next assembly in Harrogate, he'd have done no more than take you there, enjoy a pleasant evening dancing and conversing, and then deliver you home?"

Tenny pulled away from him and turned her back to him. "You are horrible."

"Because I force you to recognize that the world is not always a pleasant place?"

She spun around. "I *know* the world is far from perfect," she said hotly. "Do I not labor to ease the burdens of those in need? Do I not nurse those who fall ill? Do I not nag those in a position to do something so they help those who can't do for themselves?"

"Ah! But those are Other People. You must accept that you yourself, who grew up in a kind and generous household, might also, through no fault of your own, be made to suffer. And to suffer, my dear, in ways you cannot guess."

A pained look, a shake of her head, and Tenny walked

off. She began by walking, but soon broke into a little run and, lifting her skirts slightly, took the stairs at a pace not at all in the manner in which she'd been taught.

"A very good try," Charles told Brant as they rode away from the manor. "I am only sorry you did not manage to wring a promise from her she would take one of us whenever she is forced to go somewhere. She is the most stubborn chit, but she does keep her promises!"

"Perhaps I broke through that terrible complacency to a degree. At least I hope I did."

"It is not so much complacency, I think, as innocence. She has never suffered a hurt beyond the skinning of a knee. Small things, soon mended—except the one time she broke an arm trying to climb up to where Thomas had found a robin's nest with the eggs still in it." Charles stared straight ahead, his expression glum. "Liviston would hurt her in such a way that it could never be mended."

"Does she know . . . ?" began Brant, but trailed off. His ears burned.

Charles grinned. "You would ask if she has been told what goes on between a man and a woman? I can't know what Grandmother has taught Tenny, but I doubt she has allowed my sister to reach such a great age completely unaware of the way of things. I'd guess Tenacious will not go completely unsuspecting to her wedding night!"

"Her wedding night . . . she is wooed?" Brant almost choked on the words.

"Oh, yes. Suitors have run tame here ever since her sixteenth birthday. She'll have none of them. Locke, I have sometimes thought . . ." Charles shook his head. "No. I do not know, so I must not say it."

"Which"—Brant rather desperately hoped he knew what it was Charles sometimes thought!—"brings me, I think, to what I would ask. Why has she turned against me, Charles? We were once the very best of friends. I think she rather more than just liked me. And then, between one visit and the next, she changed. She will not speak to me unless forced to do so. She does not even look at me if she can avoid it. I know Bobby bragged about my reputed way of life. Perhaps he said things a young girl would dislike, but surely it is something more than that."

"I don't know. I can ask." He glanced at Brant, who stared straight ahead. "It is important?"

Brant's ears, which had faded to a normal color, once again turned a bright, aching red. "I have long wished to wed her," he said, biting off the words. "Then, when I returned to my uncle's two years ago, meaning to ask for her hand, she had turned into such an ice maiden that I didn't dare put it to the touch. I hoped she'd get over whatever it was which separated us . . . but she hasn't and, frankly, I'm desperate!"

"I'll see what I can discover." Charles grinned a quick slashing grin. "But given it is my stubborn sister, I promise nothing. Locke," he added, soberly, "this business with Liviston. You must know him better than we, since he has spent the last decades in London. At least, elsewhere than here at Highacres. Such as it is. A *disgrace*, Locke!" he added, distracted by thoughts of the deterioration on the Liviston estate.

Brant nodded, unsurprised. "I haven't a notion if a new owner will do better, but there must soon be one. Liviston is so far up the River Tick he'll never make a recover. Even if he sells up, which I'm sure he means to do, he'll not cover his debts. He's a desperate man, Charles. I think that, soon, he'll leave the country. When he does, he must not take Tenny with him!"

"I will talk to Grandmother. Perhaps she can make the chit see sense! Grandmother won't mince words. She may shock Tenny to the point of frightening her." Charles shook his head. "My brothers did not do our sister a favor when they taught her to be so fearless!"

"You taught her good things, Charles, which have made her the woman she is. I'd much rather she be fearless than a little mouse so nervous of her shadow that she is tongue-tied and jumps at the least unexpected sound!"

Charles gave him a look. "Yes, all very well for you to say. In ordinary times I might even agree, but at the moment I very much wish she were the latter! She might still be in danger, but we could expect her to do as she's told. It would be far easier to protect her!"

"I will do what I can," said Brant, slowly, "but it is difficult. I, too, am in Liviston's bad books. Last autumn I caught him mistreating a young female. I rescued the girl and he—hmm, did not thank me for it."

"Tell me about it."

"She was far too young to pander to Liviston's demands. Evidently she'd refused him . . . something, and he beat her." A muscle jumped in Brant's jaw. "She survived it."

Charles swore softly. Then, "Exactly where did this take place?"

"Where were we?" Brant looked at Charles, something in his tone calling more attention to the words than they deserved. "A house party. The girl was a maid, born on the estate." His voice was a trifle drier than usual.

"Ah!" Charles grinned sardonically. "I assumed it must be a house of ill repute. Which is just the sort of thing to turn Tenny up cold!"

"I ceased patronizing those houses years ago. The very best are well run and the women pretty much safe but I prefer to choose a mistress from among those who have had no opportunity to become diseased."

"A mistress."

"Bachelor fare! Don't act the prude, Charles. I am

aware of the two girls in the village who accommodate those of you in need of relief!"

"I'll not deny I know them as well as the next man hereabout, but I wasn't thinking of myself. I was thinking of Tenny. Again, she'd not approve. She would object to the notion that the man she meant to marry had a mistress in keeping!"

"Once I am destined for parson's mousetrap, I mean to sell my Chelsea house. I want no marriage of convenience." Brant barked a sharp laugh. "I wonder why we don't say a marriage of *inconvenience* because that is exactly what that sort of arrangement so often becomes. Some more inconvenient than others, of course."

Charles chuckled. "We have digressed, have we not? You mentioned that you, too, have become an enemy to Liviston. Will he try his tricks on you?"

"It is not impossible. Assuming we are correct that he has hired those men to take Tenny, he is likely to tell them to do me damage if they've the opportunity." Brant grimaced. "Thank you for reminding me."

"Yes, well, if you cut across the hills here, you'll avoid the road and be less likely to meet up with them. I'll request that Grandmother give Tenny a sharp talking-to. We'll meet as often as we can, Locke. Ah!" Charles looked around at the sound of hoofbeats. "Here is your friend. He will ride with you, of course, but do take care. Don't forget to watch your back!"

When Herrick and Brant had passed beyond the hearing of the Smythe men, Herrick asked, "What did he mean, watch your back?"

"I have reason to believe Liviston will be after my hide as well as hunting Miss Smythe. Charles was merely cautioning me to be careful." Brant's lips compressed. "I wish Tenny—Miss Smythe I should say—would carry a pistol. Blast it, Martin! Tenny *must* be made to stay at home until we are assured Liviston has left the region!"

He growled deep down in his throat in his frustration. "Not that she will. Not that anyone *could* make her!"

"You are not paying attention, Locke." Lord Asten scowled up at his nephew from his wheeled chair. "Look at her. Tell me what you think."

Brant obediently looked at the mare, but he didn't truly see her. Finally, his shoulders slumping, he turned away. "I can't. Not while Miss Smythe is in danger. The mares can wait but she cannot. Uncle, something must be done."

Asten pursed his lips, his eyes narrowed. He shrugged, motioned to Bolton to put the mare away, and asked, "Liviston, you said?"

Brant nodded, his mind going in circles as he tried to find a means of protecting the young woman he loved.

"He's home?"

"He's in the area. I assume he's at Highacres."

"Do you think he may finally be brought to sell?"

"I would not be surprised. He's rolled up, and Highacres is the last thing of any value left him. Not that it can be worth much. Mortgaged to the hilt, I'd guess."

"Hmm." Lord Asten turned himself about and wheeled off toward the hedge and the house. "James!" he called. The footman detailed to push him came running.

Brant barely noticed that his uncle had left and ignored Bolton when the head groom appeared at his side. Bolton cleared his throat. And again.

Finally Locke glanced at him. "Yes, Bolton? You want something?"

"Understood *you* wanted something."

"I did? Oh!"

Well, why the devil not? Perhaps it will take my mind off my problems, and when I again try to find a solution I'll do better. I could hardly do worse!

Brant turned his mind to his new test of the mares. "You will think I've run mad, Bolton, but this is what I've planned . . ."

Bolton listened with his mouth opened. He closed it, then opened it again to ask, "You don't truly think . . . ?"

"I think it is worth a try. That a horse might reason from observation is, is it not, the sort of thing his lordship hopes to achieve?"

Bolton rubbed his chin, his stiff salt-and-pepper whiskers making a raspy sound against his calloused fingers. "All right. But if you break your neck, I'll deny knowing anything about it!"

Brant tried his test on each of the mares. Only one acted like a normal horse who had never been ridden and Locke finally gave up trying to get her properly saddled.

"What do you think, Bolton?"

"Never did like that mare. Haven't a notion why his lordship even considered her."

"She *looks* good."

"He's never been one to choose on looks, but she *was* selected by"—Bolton gave Locke a quick look—"never mind."

Politely, Locke ignored this further clue that others than himself were being tested by Lord Asten. He sighed softly. "As far as I'm concerned, she's out of it. I believe I'll recommend the mare I had to bribe and numbers two, five, seven, and eight."

Bolton nodded. "I see nothing wrong with your decisions. His lordship—well, one never knows, does one? He'll have his notions."

"This year *I'll* have notions, too!"

Bolton chuckled as Lord Brant walked away.

But before he had gone more than a few steps, Brant's

shoulders slumped and his head bowed. The tips of his fingers went into pockets at the sides of his skin-tight leathers. Bolton shook his head, watched for another moment, and then, shrugging, turned back to his work.

"What," Brant asked Herrick a little later, "am I going to do?"

"I suppose we might go reason with her."

"Mrs. Smythe will do that and far more bluntly than we may permit ourselves to do." A muscle in Locke's jaw bunched, then relaxed. "Mrs. Smythe is not a stupid woman. She knows exactly what Liviston has in mind for her granddaughter and she'll tell my Tenny far more than the poor chit ought to know of the evil men may do." The muscle jumped again in Brant's jaw. "I don't like to think of what she might do if he gets her in his clutches."

"What could she do?" A sudden suspicion had Herrick's expressive face revealing alarm. "You don't mean she would . . . you know . . . ?"

"Kill herself?" asked Brant, bluntly. "Yes. The idea frightens me. And one couldn't bring Liviston to trial for it! He'd have caused it but not be legally responsible for it."

"Responsible for abduction. Just as dead hung for that as for the other."

Brant hunched his shoulders. "This is speculation. Somehow we must see that she is *not* kidnapped. It isn't relevant that that too is a crime"—his eyes widened—"or is it!" He rubbed his chin. "Hmm. Why not?"

Locke headed for his uncle's study where he found paper and ink and an old-fashioned quill pen which, once mended, did not sputter or drip. It occurred to him to buy his uncle some new steel-tipped pens, but it was a thought which passed into and out of his mind, a fleeting reflection.

It took him some little time to compose a letter outlining the situation. When he had a clean copy, he drew out still another paper on which he wrote much more briefly. The two sheets were folded and firmly sealed. And then Locke strode out to the stables for a few words with Bolton who, after listening, whistled softly once. He called over a mature groom.

". . . And don't dawdle," ordered Bolton. "His lordship wants his runner here as quickly as may be. Not next year."

The groom grinned. He tossed and caught the small bag of coins Locke had given him for expenses and put it in his pocket. The letter was already in a flapped bag with a long strap which he had put over his head. The bag rested under his arm and, covered by his coat; it was nearly invisible.

"He'll reach your solicitor as quickly as possible, my lord. Finding a good man at Bow Street may take a bit longer."

As Bolton spoke to Brant, the rider disappeared from sight, a cloud of dust obscuring his passage along the farm lane which would shorten his route by several miles from that through the front gate and the village.

"So." Brant frowned. "What do I do until the runner gets here?"

"Is Miss Smythe in grave danger?" asked Bolton.

"Yes. You don't know Liviston."

"Know he treats his horses badly." From Bolton's point of view, one could hardly say worse of a man. "Could we be of help?" Bolton gestured around the stable yard.

"The grooms?" Locke's eyes narrowed. "Why not? Ask for volunteers, if you'd be so good."

That evening Lord Asten grumbled and groused but, secretly, he was rather proud of his nephew. Once Locke completed his plans, a squad of men surrounded Miss Tenny whenever she left home or, alternately, guarded the house. The plan was as well organized as any in Wellington's army and included a duty roster, timed so that no one lost much sleep.

The Smythes were not quite so impressed by Locke's efforts but, after Locke confided in Mrs. Smythe and she learned he did indeed wish to wed her darling granddaughter, she put her foot down and told everyone they were to cooperate.

The old lady glared long and hard at her granddaughter. "You in particular will do as you are told!"

Miss Smythe turned up her nose and left the room. Locke followed. They were well down the hall toward the back entrance when Tenny realized she wasn't alone. She turned. "You! You are the cause of all this turmoil."

"I rather thought it was you," he said gently.

"Liviston, then." She stamped her foot. "Why must men be such idiotic creatures?"

"You would say all men are the same?"

"You contend they are not, but what nonsense it is, this army with which you'd surround me!"

Locke studied her. "What would you have us do, Tenny, when you will not admit to your danger and will not promise to behave in a manner making it unnecessary?"

"Why should it concern you in any case?" she retorted, not answering his question but asking one of her own.

"Do you deny me the capacity of feeling concerned for you?"

"You are a rake. A wastrel. A care-for-nobody. It is absurd. I can only conclude you are bored and must play games to keep yourself amused!"

"I have never been a care-for-nobody, even in the wild days of my grass time, Tenny. I am not a wastrel but rather have great care not only for my inheritance from my father, but also for those who help to make me the wealthy man I am. As to being a rake . . ."

Brant stared at her, thoughtful, wondering what she knew about the more irregular relations between men and women. Her cheeks took on a rosy tint and she looked at her feet, shrinking very slightly away from him. He recalled it was likely she knew a great deal most unmarried girls would not.

"I contend I am no more rakish than any normal man," he finally said. "Ask your brothers if you do not believe me."

She lost her nervousness in outrage. "But Locke, it is exactly the things my brother told me that convince me you lie!"

"When?"

"A couple of years ago now."

"Which brother?" As if he did not already know. *Blast Robert!*

She eyed his frown. "I do not believe I will tell you."

"It would not have been Charles," he said, pretending ignorance. "He would not discuss such things with you. I do not think Matt would have done so, and definitely not William. He's still too young. Jim? Perhaps. But I believe it was most likely Bobby, who is the biggest gabble-grinder among them. He is also," said Locke thoughtfully, "something of an ass and was more of one two or three years ago—as you well know, Tenny. So, if you believed every word he uttered, you very likely have an exceedingly bent notion of my London activities. From things about which he's questioned me, I *know* he himself had unrealistic notions! On top of that, anything he said is out of date."

"You will say you do not keep a mistress in a little house in Chelsea?" she asked sweetly.

"At the moment I do," he admitted, aware the truth was always better than lies where Tenny was concerned. "Someday I'll marry. The mistress will be paid off and the house sold."

A complicated succession of emotions flickered across her expressive features and then disappeared before he could read any of them. Had he seen hope? Had he seen chagrin? But there at the end, he knew he saw disbelief and that pained him.

"You do not believe me. Why, Tenny?"

"It isn't a question of disbelief."

"I have not lied to you, so what is it?"

"You will never marry, so I understand that you tell me no lies. What you have done is admit you are a rake, have you not?"

"But Tenny, I have never denied my rakish behavior. To a certain extent, I suppose I am what you think me. But compared to Liviston, I swear I am pure as the driven snow!"

"Bah."

"Ah-ha! You have no answer to that. And don't scowl at me, Tenny." He grinned a quick flashing grin. *"Bah* is always your response when you are unable to counter a point!"

She smiled rueful acknowledgement, and he felt the cold, hard ball of tension lying deep inside himself relax a trifle.

Dared he continue? Yes, he did. He had to. Somehow he had to break the impasse they'd stumbled into. "It is possible, is it not, that on exceedingly rare occasions you may actually have gotten something ever so slightly wrong? Tenny, you have convicted me on the words of a lad on the verge of manhood, one who was at an age to believe such wild behavior nothing but fun and games, young enough to be jealous of the life he thought I lived. I am older. I know the limits one must set on oneself and, besides, I was never half so wild as you appear to believe."

"I accept that Bobby"—her words verified his belief as to her informant—"may have been jealous of you. There was a period when both my father and Charles were very angry with him, although they'd not tell me why. I guessed he was behaving badly, however, and I believe it was in emulation of *your* behavior."

Brant's brows rose. "Emulation, perhaps, of what he *believed* to be my behavior?"

"Do not quibble. He did not behave well, and it was your fault."

Locke sighed. "I dislike telling tales, Tenny, but I do know of what you speak. At Charles's behest, I had words with Bobby a few years ago. He quite eagerly described to me some of the things to which his family objected. I poured scorn over his boasting, just as it deserved. In the end he was very unhappy with me." A smile flickered over Locke's lips, lighting his eyes briefly. "I managed to bribe my way back into his good graces by giving him lessons in the proper management of a team harnessed to a sporting carriage. Much to the detriment of the paint on my curricle!"

"If you were the reason he settled down, then I must thank you, as would my family if they knew," she said in a coolly polite voice. "It does not change the fact you are a self-confessed rake."

This time she did not wait for a response but moved quickly to a stairway which led upwards into regions of the house where Locke dared not follow. His lips tightened. She believed him a rake and she did not approve. Was it possible that that was the sole reason she had turned cold?

And, if so, how did one convince an antagonistic young lady who was angry about one's way of life that the only person toward whom one wished to behave rakishly was herself?

"Uncle, my birthday is coming all too quickly. If you demand it, I will give you my decision concerning the mares, as has become our tradition since I have come to tentative conclusions concerning them. I would prefer to postpone the ordeal until Miss Smythe's problems are solved."

Lord Asten nodded. "I too would have them solved. I must ask that you and Mr. Herrick ride into Harrogate today, discuss two points with my solicitor concerning which I wish his advice, and then, to oblige me, stay on well into the evening, arriving home as late as you will."

"Uncle?" Locke's confusion was evident not only in his tone but in the eyes which blinked and the mouth which he had to remember to close.

Lord Asten smiled a tight little smile. "I have put an oar of my own into Miss Smythe's deep waters, nephew. I have invited Lord Liviston here, but I've no notion if, or even when, he'll come. From what you said of your relations with the man, I wish you gone when he arrives. I will discuss with him the purchase of his estate. Under certain—er, conditions, of course."

"That he leave the country, perhaps?" asked Locke, more than a little interested.

"Among other things. Now. I've written out my queries for the solicitor. There are certain forms I wish him to draw up."

"I will be quite happy to run this errand for you, Uncle, but"—he paused, glancing up—"the whole of the day?" Without his permission, his eyes drifted toward the window which faced toward the Smythes' manor.

"You surely do not think there is more for you to do there? Miss Smythe is well guarded. The grooms and gardeners will watch her home and will attend Miss Smythe and whichever of her brothers if"—Lord Asten raised a hand—"I should say *when*, given it is Miss Smythe. *When* she leaves her home."

"I wish to see that—"

"Charles is more than competent to oversee his sister's safety. You did your part by forming her royal guard and,

I suppose, in sending for that runner, although to my mind, that was a trifle extreme!"

Although reluctant, Locke had to agree. "You would buy Liviston off?" he asked.

"I do not consider it buying his lordship off, so much as that I can finally come to the rescue of his tenants!" Asten waved his hand dismissively. "Go. Find Herrick and take yourselves off to Harrogate!"

Lord Brant did as asked, but traveled a trifle out of his way so that he could stop by the Smythes. Tenny actually came to wish him good day and to thank him for the care he was taking of her, although she insisted it was far more caution than necessary. "Surely," she said, "Liviston cannot enter our home and steal me away from it, so your guard here is quite ridiculous!"

"Not Liviston, Tenny, but the men he hired. They might very well find a means of entering the house. Particularly in the middle of the night."

Tenny blushed and glanced at her grandmother, then grimaced before turning her shoulder.

Mrs. Smythe chuckled. "The boys have divided up the night hours and roam the house with the dogs. A villain would have grave difficulty coming in to her!"

"Then I may go into Harrogate with a light heart." Locke caught and held Tenny's gaze. A faint rosy color entered her cheeks and he nodded. "I will have no need to worry about you," he said softly.

"No, of course not." Tenny glanced at her grandmother, and the rosy color deepened. "I've no wish to find myself snared in Liviston's coils!"

He asked if there were errands he might run for Mrs. Smythe or her granddaughter and, when told no, took his leave. If it was not exactly with light heart, Locke proceeded to Harrogate somewhat eased by Miss Smythe's hints that she had finally accepted that she was in danger.

But he *was* made very nearly happy by her willingness

to converse with him. Not once had she spoken in that cold tone he abhorred. Nor had she avoided him as she'd been doing. She had, actually, come into the room knowing he was there.

Locke smiled to himself, dreamed dreams, and rode along blissfully unaware that his friend was keeping a wary eye cocked for ambush.

But there was no ambush.

In fact, Locke and Martin spent a perfectly normal day in and around Harrogate. Except for Locke's worries about Miss Smythe, it even passed with a degree of enjoyment. He saw his uncle's solicitor and waited while the man wrote out, in a large flowing hand, long responses to Lord Asten's queries. Martin, meanwhile, discovered that a play, *The Devil To Pay*, was scheduled for that evening. He'd never heard of it but bought two tickets anyway. Then, while awaiting Locke, he encountered some acquaintances, young people who were in Harrogate in attendance on elderly family members whose doctors had ordered them to take the waters there.

His friends had a picnic planned and a ride out to the River Nidd, where they meant to dine near Knaresborough Castle. They invited Mr. Herrick and Lord Brant to join them. Martin instantly agreed for the both of them. He had wondered how they were to fill the hours before the play!

Luckily, quite late, there was a good moon. The two rode gently home through the chill of the spring night and, although both were alert this time, again they encountered no difficulty.

Lord Asten had left orders that he wished to see his nephew and Mr. Herrick and that they were to come to him when they arrived home, no matter how late it might be. The large bedroom was well lit, and Lord Asten lay against his pillows, a tasseled sleeping cap set at a raffish angle on his head and a book in his hands. He laid the book aside.

"You should be asleep, Uncle," scolded Brant gently.

"You will discover that you require far less sleep when you reach my advanced years," said Lord Asten. "Besides, I knew you'd wish to know the outcome of my deliberations with Liviston."

"You were correct," agreed Locke.

"I have bought Highacres. That is the first thing. The second is that Lord Liviston has promised he'll not lay a finger on Miss Smythe. I have it in writing. And finally, he leaves the country just as soon as he can clear out personal papers and a few private possessions I agreed he could remove from the house."

"Just how long will he be?"

"No more than a week at the outside."

Locke's eyes narrowed. "I cannot believe he will so easily give up his revenge against the Smythe family."

"Easily? My dear boy," said his uncle grinning a rather cynical grin, "I assure you he did not make that promise easily! In fact, he went away for an hour or two in order to come to a decision and then when he returned he still objected to a written promise."

"But you got one?"

Lord Asten nodded toward a folded paper which lay on the small table set beside his bed. Locke, receiving permission, opened it and read. Ignoring the legal phrasing, it did exactly what Lord Asten claimed. Liviston promised he'd not lay a finger on Miss Smythe and that he'd leave the country within a sennight with no one but his valet and a groom in attendance.

"Heard a few stories about that valet," muttered Herrick. "Not at all surprised *he* wants to leave the country!"

Brant brushed the paper back and forth across his fingertips. "You were correct, Uncle, and I should not have been so rash as to call in a runner." He sighed. "When he arrives, I will pay him off and send him home."

"I have changed my mind about your runner. He will, if you've no objections to my hiring him in your stead, follow Liviston and see that his lordship actually does as he said he'd do and leaves England!"

"Very well. I too would be certain. If that is all . . . ?"

"Not quite. I have thought over what you suggested about two simultaneous breeding programs. If you can acquire that mare of which you spoke, then I will authorize you to plan and carry out your proposed scheme."

"Uncle . . . ?"

"You did not expect it? Earlier today I watched Rebel's Star run. It looks an exceptionally smooth ride, almost as if the creature floated through the air. I have no notion whether you can breed for the trait or if it is merely an accident of Star's training, but it will be interesting to try. Will you have to meet with Lady Hangerville or can you acquire her mare by correspondence?"

"I'll correspond with her. I doubt she will sell, but I am almost certain I can make arrangements to breed the mare and acquire the filly. If there is one."

"Ah. That is the problem, is it not? One must have mares! Well, do what you can and we will see. That is all. Good night," he finished abruptly, reaching for his book.

Brant and Herrick bowed their way from the room and, tired from their long day, went to their respective beds. Lord Brant, awakening at his usual early hour, lay there for some time watching the yearlings at play. It would, he thought, be quite wonderful to rise each morning to that view.

Then he smiled as he thought of Herrick's response to the notion that anyone could be happy living in the country.

The smile faded at just how much of a city man Martin had become since they'd come down from university. Yesterday in Harrogate had driven the knowledge home. His friend had glowed with renewed energy when among their acquaintances. His jesting manner settled over him and his quips and banter, his posturing, had had everyone laughing and enjoying themselves immensely. Society was Martin's natural milieu. Among friends he came alive as he had not while visiting Falcon's Pride.

Locke accepted that, if he married and settled here with his uncle, he would lose his close friendship with Martin. They would, of course, see each other during the season and, because of their long friendship, it was likely Martin would visit sometime during the year, but the closeness, the intimacy, would vanish.

Locke sighed, allowing the pain of it to enter into him. It hurt to lose a friend—but it would hurt far more to lose Tenny!

His thoughts turned to his uncle's complaisant belief that the danger to Miss Smythe was over. Recalling the exact wording of the written promise, Locke wasn't half so certain. An uneasy feeling drove him from his bed. And, once again, he dressed without shaving when he found he'd only a little cold water.

If he did remain here permanently, he must have a word with his valet about changes in his morning schedule!

The cook cheerfully provided him with a sandwich and, again, he shared it with the drudge in the scullery, winking at her as he popped the morsel into her mouth. He entered the stable yard just as the grooms, still rubbing sleep from their eyes, began their chores. He nodded to one or two grooms with whom he was most familiar, but didn't stop until he reached Star's box, where he leaned on the half door and watched the stallion munch a morsel of hay.

"You, my boy, with any luck at all, will someday be one of the most famous studs in the world!"

"He's agreed then?" asked Bolton, coming up behind Lord Brant.

"To a second program?" Brant nodded. "Lady Hangerville won't sell, I'm sure"—he shrugged—"but an agreement concerning any fillies produced is not unlikely." He checked his watch. And sighed. It was too early to ride over to the Smythes' to discover if all had gone well the day before. And to ascertain that Miss Smythe was enduring the special protection she resented so much. He didn't trust Liviston's promise. There was too much elbow room in which his lordship could shape his revenge. So, until his lordship left England, Miss Smythe must be kept close.

Which, given it is Tenny . . . At the thought, he stared glumly at nothing at all. . . . *will be difficult to accomplish!*

Locke's runner arrived late the next evening and immediately dismissed the army of grooms and gardeners which had been assigned to protect the manor. Locke demanded to know why.

"Can't catch the villain if he don't have the oh-por-tune-ity to do something to catch him *for.*"

"But with only you to guard the house, how can you prevent anyone from sneaking in the back when you are at the front?"

"Besides," said the runner, ignoring Locke's question, "there's that promise your man made that he'd behave himself. Sets up a man's back when it looks like you don't believe him."

"In other words, you agree with my uncle. You believe nothing will happen now Liviston has promised *he himself* will not touch Miss Smythe?"

The runner frowned and scratched his head. "Well now, put that way . . ." He scrunched up his lower lip and scowled. "Maybe I need a man or two? Just to warn me if someone happens to come by who don't belong . . . ?" The runner smirked. "Then, if'n they see someone, they can tell me and I'll nab 'em."

The runner did not impress Locke with either his mental abilities or his capacity to carry through a plan. His fears for Miss Smythe rose to a new high as his irritation with the runner he himself had hired climbed. As he schemed new ways of protecting Tenny, he made a mental note to have a word with his solicitor when he next visited London. Pretty obviously, the man had taken the first runner to offer his services and *not* asked questions concerning the fellow's competence!

Locke spent the day with Tenny and whichever brother attended her. He grew more impressed than ever as he watched her go about her errands. He listened to her gentle but firm manner when dealing with parish problems, observed her as she taught in her school, and felt warmed by the tenderness she exhibited when tending a woman who had recently had a baby and was not recovering as she should. It was a far less boring day than he'd expected, and only the knowledge that the runner was somewhere about, waiting to pounce if a villain showed his face, kept him from proposing then and there.

For that he wanted privacy.

He had always believed his Tenny special, but his pride in her grew and grew. Young as she was, she had cheerfully taken up the burdens usually cast upon the most important matron in a region.

By awkward chance, she *was* that matron! There were no women at Highacres—Liviston's mother was long dead and he had never wed. Lord Asten had always been a determined bachelor, so there was no lady at Falcon's Pride either. And Mrs. Smythe, the only other possible candidate for the position, was too old to bear the day-to-day burdens, although Locke suspected she gave advice and counsel to her granddaughter as necessary.

"You are unique among women, Tenny," he said.

She merely cast him a glance of disbelief which, since Bobby rode with them, Locke chose to ignore. Later, when they were seated at the Smythes' dinner table, a message arrived asking that Tenny come help a burned child. Tenny instantly rose from her seat and went for her basket of supplies. Charles, with equal alacrity and no questions, ordered three horses saddled. He knew Locke would ride with them.

The child was not so very badly scalded but, because of her fear and pain, it took some little time to apply salve to the skin, to administer a mild dose of laudanum and to be certain the frantic mother knew how to care for her daughter. In fact, the sun was setting as they left the village and started back to the Smythes'. They rode through the odd afterlight which, from now until late autumn, would linger long into the evening.

"As I said earlier, a very special woman. You don't believe me?" asked Locke when Tenny again glanced at him disbelievingly.

"I am in no way special," she insisted. "You must not spill the butter boat over me!"

"You cannot know how special."

"Bah!"

He smiled. "Aha! You've admitted the truth of what I say."

"Nonsense." But she smiled a quick smile, her teeth gleaming white for just an instant as she remembered him saying she used the word when she couldn't argue a point. Then, curiosity overcoming her belief that she should not encourage him, she asked, "Why do you think such a thing?"

"You have never left this region, Tenny, while I have met many unmarried women, both younger and older than you, who would have no notion what to do for that poor child. Or earlier today, they could not have advised that man who fears he will soon be too enfeebled to care for his wife, so that they will end their lives in the workhouse. And none I have met would teach the basics of reading and writing to village children! I know a few older women who would willingly contribute toward a salary for a teacher, but even they would not do the work themselves. You, my dear Tenny, are special indeed."

"Nonsense," she repeated. "I merely do what is right. Often I do not know, and then Grandmother advises me. Without her help I could do nothing. So you see? It is Grandmother over whom you should spread your butter!"

"I certainly praise her for rearing you to be the woman you are. But if she had had poor material with which to work, then she'd not have molded you into the excellent creature you've become. So you see, you must be special or her work would have been a waste of time!"

Miss Smythe suppressed a smile. "You are a palaverer, Locke." She grew thoughtful and flicked a quick look his way. "I suppose," she mused, "that is to be expected of a successful rake. How else could such a one succeed?"

"Ah!" Locke stifled his irritation that she had once again excused his compliments to her as nothing more than the stock in trade of the man she thought him to be. "I see I have another reason for removing from London and joining my uncle at Falcon's Pride."

Tenny swiveled her head and body so quickly that she very nearly lost her balance. Only the firm control provided by her knee around the saddle's pummel kept her in her saddle. *"You would move . . . ?"*

"He has asked that I remain at Falcon's Pride for an unspecified period of time. Since it is something I have wanted for several years now, I instantly agreed. I am not, even now, convinced he made the offer seriously, but now I have accepted, he must, at the least, pretend complacency. I must return to London at some point to rid my-

self of various obligations there, of course, but I mean to
return as quickly as can be."

For a moment Tenny was silent. Then, bluntly, she
asked. "Why, Locke?"

A light answer would not serve. Lord Brant drew in a
deep breath, hoping to find the right words. "I've several
reasons. I love Falcon's Pride as I have loved no other
place in this world. Then, my uncle grows frail. I fear his
strength is less than he will admit, that the accident which
left him crippled did damage we cannot see. I would be
there to take some of the burden from him. And finally"—he turned to look at her—"I have to believe I
can convince you I am not a hardened creature of no
account. If I am here where you may keep an eye on me,
perhaps that will not be so difficult. And don't," he added
when she opened her mouth, "ask why *that* is important.
You *know.*"

"You needn't sound so exasperated. I am glad you wish
to be here for reasons other than ingratiating yourself
with your uncle. Besides, you must see more of me as
well. In some manner you have acquired an absurd picture of the person I am. It would be well for you to live
here until you discover I am not the perfect creature you
seem to think."

"But Tenny," he said with a touch of sly humor, *"I have
never said you were perfect."*

Her eyes widened. She turned, this time more slowly
and with no danger to her position in the saddle. *"You*
are an even bigger tease than my brothers!"

His eyes twinkled and he grinned.

Tenny suppressed an answering smile. Pretending boredom, she asked, "How am I imperfect?"

"Charles," called Locke, pretending alarm, "do I
dare?"

"Dare what?" Charles had been paying them no attention, his eyes and ears alert for possible ambush.

"Dare inform your sister of the multitude of ways in which she is imperfect?"

"Has she asked?"

"Yes."

"Then she can have no objection to your listing them. But hurry. We're nearly home and you've not much time."

"Do I have time, I wonder," mused Locke, pretending to think.

Tenny glowered. "You, Locke Talmidge, are enough to make a saint curse. You are to tell me my failings! I insist."

"But do you *really* wish to know?" he asked with pretended relish.

"Of course." She tossed her head and stared between her horse's ears.

"Do remember you insisted!" he warned. "First, there is your inability to discuss anything without turning it into an argument. If that trait is kept under control, then it is an asset, of course. It makes for lively conversation. But Tenny, must *every* conversation become a battle?"

She cast him a look, her lips twisting.

"Then, secondly, there is this stubborn insistence that you and only you know what is right. Tenny, my sweet, men of great intellect have argued that question for centuries and have come to no conclusion. You, on the other hand, often say you must do what is right, regardless the danger to you or what others believe. How can you be so arrogant as to insist you have such knowledge when those great men do not?"

This time her smile faded. She gave him a glance indicating that this was a topic about which she would very quickly lose all sense of humor

"I see," he said, accepting that she would not discuss her strong ethical beliefs. He drew in a breath. "Then there is the imperfection which is most important to me." She again looked at him, and he smiled a rather wistful smile. "Your stubborn refusal, Tenny, to accept that I am not so black as you would paint me! Or perhaps," he said, a sudden insight giving him a new notion, "it is *disappointment* on your part? Your sentiments have become so unbending because you discovered I too am imperfect?"

Tenny's eyes widened in something which appeared to be shock. When she spoke, it was in a mutter he barely heard. Clearly she meant the words for herself rather than his ears. "Can I possibly be so stupid that I have expected him to be perfect?"

"Ah!" He grinned and another knot or two of the worry deep inside him came untied. "I see. What I once thought affection was merely infatuation. I suppose one tends to idealize the person for whom one feels an infatuation. Only *true* love can survive and continue to grow when the real person, the *flawed* person, is clear to one. Did you once love me, Tenny? Or did you love some dream you gave my name and then lost that mild and inadequate sort of love when you discovered I was not the person you would have me be?"

Tenny drew in a deep breath. "Locke, this is not something I can discuss until I have had time to think. And you have given me a great deal about which I must think, have you not? I will not answer your questions until I have cleared my mind of its confusion. It is far too important."

Locke glanced around. "There is also the fact that we have arrived and we've no time. Besides, my dear, you are tired, I think. I noticed it when we left the cottage. Understandable, of course. Is your every day like today? So full to bursting of duties and responsibilities?"

"Today was especially busy. Tomorrow, except for the school, I have only to plan menus for the coming week, oversee the cheese-making, teach a new maid her duties—" She frowned. "Oh, just everyday things."

He chuckled. "Everyday things which will have you trotting from sunup to sunset. Or, if today is an example, beyond sunset!" He dismounted and came to her side. As he lifted her from the saddle, he smiled into her eyes. "You are a wonder, Tenny," he said softly, caressingly.

"You are teasing again," she insisted, but the bite she would normally give such a comment was lost in something close to breathlessness.

Nor did she allow her gaze to meet his. Locke felt her tremble and that, along with her whispery tone, filled him with hope. She *would* be his. It would take effort to win her, but she was, whether she knew it or not, attracted to him and that was an advantage he'd use.

Along with every other advantage he could gather to himself!

Charles cleared his throat and, guiltily, the two turned away from each other. "Shall we go in?" he asked politely.

Locke glanced at the big round clock set into a tower at a corner of the stable yard. "Is it so late as that? I think perhaps it would be better if you send Harry out. I'll have his horse saddled, and while that is done I'll have a word with that runner. I cannot like this situation, Charles."

"We'll have a care for her."

Locke compressed his lips for a moment and then nodded. "Tomorrow, Miss Smythe?" he asked formally.

"We will be happy to see you on the morrow," she replied with equal formality.

It was sometime in the deepest part of the night when an exceedingly sleepy little kitchen maid crept into Miss Smythe's bedroom. The dog sleeping on the hearth rug woke and moved to push a snuffling nose into the girl's hand. "Hush," whispered the child and moved on to the bed. "A boy come from the village, miss," she said softly.

Tenny, who had carried on an exceedingly long and involved debate with herself once she was alone in her room, now slept the sleep of the exhausted. She didn't move.

"Miss Smythe, *please,*" said the maid.

Tenny moaned and rolled over. Her eyes opened slightly as she did so and the light of the young maid's candle caused her to blink. "Morning all ready?" she mumbled.

"A boy's come, miss. Please wake up."

The words broke through to Tenny's sleep-fogged mind. She sat up, yawning. "A message?" she asked, frowning and rubbed her face vigorously, trying to rid herself of a sleep-induced fog.

"Runned out from the village. Someun's sick, he says. He says, you come."

Tenny climbed wearily from her bed, took the girl's candle, and lit those in a candelabra. "You tell him I'll be down immediately."

Still more asleep than awake, Tenny dressed simply. She found a long, heavy cloak against the night airs and then picked up her basket, which was always set ready for an emergency.

Quietly, careful not to wake the brother who, for some reason, although she could not bring to mind what it was, sat slumped in a chair at the end of the hall, she moved to the kitchen. The dogs followed behind her, happy to see her, although rather confused that she was up and about so early. Still, they knew her, knew she belonged, and didn't raise their voices, which would have roused poor James—who would, for a very long time, not forgive himself for drifting off to sleep.

Tenny blinked when she saw who had come. "Young Bertram, are you not?" she asked the youngest son of the village layabout. It surprised her to see this particular lad, one she had never quite liked. "Who sent you?"

"You come, miss. You be needed . . ." The boy edged toward the back door.

"Come where?" asked Tenny and yawned a jaw-cracking yawn.

"You come quick now . . ." The boy slipped out the door and disappeared.

"Blast the dratted boy! How can I come if I haven't a notion where I'm to go?" She yawned again, her sleep-fogged mind not dealing very clearly with the situation.

But the message came from the village. Therefore, she concluded, she must go to the village. She swung her cape about her shoulders, told the kitchen maid to return to her tiny room off the scullery to get what rest she still could, and then slipped out the door and into the pre-dawn light. It was very dim but quite light enough that she didn't need a lantern.

Tenny, after all, knew her world outside as well as she knew it inside the house. Without hesitation, she cut across a dark corner of the garden and into the path which would cut more than a mile from the distance by road. Tenny plodded along, a trifle heavy-footed, yawning now and again, and was about to leave the path at the point where it joined the road when a dirty hand slid over her mouth and a muscled arm around her waist.

Suddenly wide awake, Tenny realized what a fool she'd been. Bitterness filled her.

"So," said a voice dimly heard.

"Fought like a she-demon, she did," said a rougher voice.

"Got the dose down her, though," said another.

"Excellent."

Tenny floated in a dream world induced by the lauda-num forced down her throat by the men who captured her. She knew she'd been captured but, at the moment, she couldn't care. The opiate had too strong a hold on her.

"Think you can manage the rest?" asked the first voice. She knew that voice. . . .

"Easy as pie," said the rough voice.

"No problem in the world," said another.

"Here is your pay, then. I'll be on my way." Tenny heard a sigh. "It is not the revenge I wanted, but it will do. It will do nicely!" Bitterness colored his words. "I only wish I could be here to see them made unhappy."

"We'll make all right and tidy." There was an evil-sounding chuckle. "Don't you worry none about that."

"I know *you've* good reason to see all carried out as I wish!"

Tenny heard horses' hooves, heard the crunch of carriage wheels. She felt confused that she didn't feel *herself* moving. But it didn't seem to matter. . . .

"So. Should we do it here or when we get there?" The new voice held more than a hint of anticipation.

"Don't want to lug her around in the altogether. Might catch her death. Then where would we be?"

"Hmm. Can't have that." The rough voice seemed to gloat. "Nice revenge on his bloody lordship, *I* think. Won't he be in a rage to find himself riveted to a drab little nobody when he could have himself any great lady in the land?"

Riveted? Tenny felt further confusion. *Didn't that mean married*? But again, it was far too difficult to concentrate and far more pleasant to merely drift along in the rosy haze the laudanum induced.

"Well, let's get at it."

"You take her feet."

Tenny felt herself lifted. She was carried for some distance and then laid down again.

"*Now*?" asked the impatient man.

"Hold your horses. We've got to get inside first."

Inside? Where? And, wondered Tenny, feeling a twinge of concern, *where is Liviston? It was Liviston speaking earlier, was it not?*

"Quiet now," whispered the man who seemed to be in charge. "We know which room we want, so no more talking."

"No need to tell *me* that. I don't want to get caught at this any more 'n you do!"

Tenny heard the tinkling sound of breaking glass. She hoped no one cut themselves since she didn't think she could manage to help just now.

The men lifted her again and carried her into a dark space. Then she felt them unroll her cape and then—the horror of it had her fighting weakly—she felt them undoing buttons and tapes. Undressing her. A flailing fist connected with one man's nose and she heard him mutter to the other.

Suddenly that awful taste was in her mouth again. Again she found herself swallowing against her will. And, very soon, she once again didn't care what happened to her.

"There, now," said one and eagerly added, "Seems a shame to waste the opportunity."

"Don't be an idiot," whispered another viciously. "He won't marry used goods."

"What'd he do to you what *you* want to see him brought down a peg?"

"You don't need to know. Now shut up and help me lift her. How such a little thing can be so heavy, I don't know."

Once again Tenny felt herself carried. This time she thought it was up a flight of stairs but, as they climbed, the new dose of the opiate took stronger hold. Consciousness slid away. Tenny didn't feel the men gently, carefully, lay her onto the edge of a wide bed. Nor did she feel her arms lifted and tied with silken bonds to the head of

the bed. Nor could she object when she was crudely
gagged. . . .

The Dream.
Locke welcomed the dream, the feel of Tenny's soft
skin under his hand, her gentle curves fitting his palm
as if made for it. For a very long time, he allowed his
fingers to explore, allowed them to roam up and down
and around, discovering the feel of her, the shape of
her. . . .

It was the most wonderfully real dream he'd ever had
of her. Slowly, lazily, he molded her, turned her toward
himself, reveled in it when he felt her respond with all
the innocence he'd expected of her. In fact, he even
thought he heard her moan, which was another improve-
ment over past dreams. Ah! The feel of her against him,
close to him, warm and soft and lovely. . . .

His lips trailed over her forehead, down, and felt the
butterfly flicker of her lashes. He moved to her temple.
Somewhere in his partially conscious mind he was pleased
that she seemed to be properly affected by his touch, his
light, teasing kisses.

Soon now he'd find her lips and truly kiss her. For the
moment he only wanted to prolong the very best dream
he'd ever had. But her moans? Somehow these particular
moans didn't fit the dream. Not such agitated gurgling
of sound. Her twisting against him was all right but, his
sleep drugged mind urged, he must stop that sound. . . .

Must stop those more and more urgent sounds.

Locke trailed kisses across a cheekbone, dropped a trifle lower . . .

. . . and ran into a barrier. That didn't fit the dream
either. He lifted his head, dropped his mouth to where
hers should be . . .

. . . and it was worse.

Locke's eyes popped open and he stared down into the wide-open gaze of a real woman. A frightened woman. He lifted away.

"Bloody hell!"

Locke rolled to his side of the bed and sat up. He pressed his palms to his eyes and then, turning his head, discovered his dream still lay there. *Not* a dream woman. The *real* woman.

He recalled the feel of her against his fingers, and heat traveled up his neck into his ears. Under the covers, she was stark staring naked!

"What the devil are you doing in my bed?" he demanded.

The odd gurgles sounded more distressed, more agitated.

"Oh. Sorry."

He twisted around, half lying across the mattress, felt under her head, and discovered where the gag was knotted. Careful not to pull her hair, he undid it, lifting it away from her face, and noted with renewed horror the discoloration at each side of her mouth. He touched her sore cheek lightly with one finger.

"You poor dear. Poor, poor dear."

Tenny pushed the wad of dirty cloth which had been put into her mouth out of the way, spitting it onto the pillow. Locke reached across her and flicked it to the floor. He leaned above her as she manipulated her tongue, pushing it into the corners of her mouth, into her cheeks, around her dry lips.

"Dry . . ."

Locke rolled back and out his side of the bed. He went to his wash table, where he filled a heavy-bottomed tooth glass from the ewer. He brought it to her and, shoving his arm under her, tried to lift her. Only then did he notice how her hands were tied. He sighed.

"Someone has had their fun with us, have they not?"

he said, as lightly as he could. He busied himself with the soft ropes. "Now." Again he moved to lift her, but now that she was free, she scrambled away from him. "Can you hold it?" he asked, extending the glass toward her. His eyes, despite good intentions, drifted to where the sheet barely covered her breasts.

If she reached for the glass, surely . . .

He sighed. "Tenny, I will turn my back and you wind that sheet around yourself. Tightly. *Please.*"

He saw her put one hand under the covers, move it over herself, and make a choked back sound of anguish as she realized that she was as bare as the day she was born. Color flooded into her face and hadn't faded when she muttered that he could turn. Silently he handed her the glass. Despite her situation, her eyes thanked him.

"I thought The Dream was especially good," he said thoughtfully.

"Dream?" she said. Even with the water to help, her voice cracked. "You thought you were dreaming?"

"An exceedingly wonderful dream, Tenny. About you. One I've had again and again the past few years. Were you not enjoying it as well?" He tipped his head. "I mean"—he smiled gently at her obvious embarrassment—"until you realized how improper it all was?"

"I—" The blush which had begun to fade rushed back. "I don't know. I think I am still a bit affected by that blasted laudanum they forced me to drink."

His gaze sharpened. "Laudanum. . . ."

"Yes. The first dose merely made me oddly dreamy. I sort of knew what was going on, but I couldn't do anything about it. I—" She frowned. "I have the notion that the men who captured me talked to Liviston, but that he flew off in a chariot or something and the one man seemed to think it was a shame to waste something, and the other said—" She broke off, remembering what the other had said about a marriage. Carefully, she looked away from Locke, down to her clasped hands.

"The other?" he asked gently but inside he seethed. Had the devils done more than put her in his bed? Had they dared to—?

"Never mind," she said primly.

Locke bit his lip as he stared down at the top of her head. The back of her neck was visible where the hair fell away from it. Naked and vulnerable. He couldn't bear it and, gently, he straightened her unbound locks. She jerked away from him, leaving him with his hand extended. Slowly he dropped it.

Blast it, he thought. *It didn't matter, not much anyway, if they had, except that it would have been terrible for her. Damnation, I'll wed her if she's been used by every demon in hell!*

"Tenny," he said urgently, "we must talk. The servants will be up and about very soon now, and we must decide what is to be—"

He was interrupted by his door swinging inward and his valet rushing into the room, a handful of women's garments dangling from his fist. The valet stared at the bed, horror growing. Locke closed his eyes, wishing he had somehow averted this particular disaster.

"Lord Brant!"

"Yes, Williams?"

"My lord—!"

"Yes?" he repeated somewhat testily. "Perhaps, if you have done staring, you might return to the lower regions of the house and sent up hot water for Miss Smythe. Are those her clothes? Then perhaps you will ascertain whether they require pressing and, if so, take care of that little problem as well?"

Williams couldn't seem to take his eyes from Miss Smythe, who had shut her own eyes, her only possible defense. "My lord . . . ?"

"You are, I think, aware that we have been worried that Lord Liviston meant to do Miss Smythe harm?"

The valet nodded, his eyes still riveted to Tenny's bent head. Or perhaps to somewhere below her head? Locke couldn't be certain. He stepped between his valet and the woman. The man was forced to look at his master instead of the remarkable view.

Williams cleared his throat. "Er . . . my lord?"

"She was kidnapped, dosed with laudanum, and placed in my bed while I slept last night. Neither of us knew anything about it until I woke this morning. We will, of course, make the proper announcement as soon as we can, but in the meantime, Williams, I would appreciate if you would hold your tongue which I know, since it wags at both ends, may be difficult for you!"

"*My lord!*"

"You would say it does not? Excellent. Now see about the water and the pressing. I will collect *my* clothing and retire to the room across the hall, leaving Miss Smythe here with a key. She will open that door only for you, Williams, and you will do the necessary with discretion and as efficiently as you can. Do you understand?"

"Yes, my lord." Clutching Tenny's clothing to his narrow chest, Williams backed toward the door. "But my lord? Sir? What am I to say to the maid who found the clothes and to your uncle who sent her to me?"

Locke groaned softly. "I might have known things were sorting themselves out far too easily. You will, please, ask the maid to remain silent. Assuming it is not already too late—"

"Which it will be," inserted Tenny, speaking for the first time.

"—and you will tell my uncle," continued Locke, ignoring Tenny's words, which were likely to be the truth, "that I shall give myself the pleasure of waiting upon him as soon as he is free to see me. Or perhaps I should say, as soon as I can get myself dressed!"

The door closed behind the valet, and Locke turned back to the bed. He and Tenny stared at each other.

"What," she asked in a rather fading voice, "did you mean? Make a proper announcement?"

"As soon as I've permission from your father, I will ask you for your hand. You will say yes. And we will post the banns. Immediately."

"We will do no such thing. Everyone will say it is because we must."

"But Tenny, love, they will be correct. We must."

Her features took on a mulish look. "I will not be forced to marry you. Nor will I have *you* forced to marry *me.*"

"You won't?" He put every ounce of disappointment into that that he could. "Not even if I *want* you to?"

"But you don't."

"Don't put words in my mouth." When he had her full attention, he added, "I definitely *do.*"

"Do not."

"Do too."

"Do not!"

He sighed. "I wonder if all frustrated lovers sound so much like children arguing over a nursery game!"

"Frustrated—"

"Lovers."

They stared at each other.

Red of cheek, Tenny sighed. "We'll discuss this when we are both less emotional, my lord. And when I do not feel quite so much like—like—"

"Like a parcel delivered by mistake to the wrong address?" he asked, trying for a lightness which didn't quite succeed.

"Not at all. Like a parcel opened by the wrong man!"

"Oh." Wary, he eyed her. "Tenny, do you mean there

is someone you . . ." He shook his head. "No. You are correct. We will discuss it later when we are both more likely to be rational. But my dear"—he took on an implacable look which was echoed in his voice—"I hope very much that you were not about to say there is some other man you love and whom you had hoped would someday unwrap this particular parcel because I do not believe I can allow it!"

He stalked to the door, opened it, and slammed it behind him. Only to stand there in the hall in his nightgown and bare feet feeling utterly chagrined. Having made his dramatic exit, he realized he must now return in order to find his clothes! Well, there was nothing for it. He sighed deeply, knocked, and reentered the room.

Tenny hurriedly scrambled back under the covers. "What is it now?" she asked crossly.

"I thought it a particularly magnificent exit," he admitted ruefully, "did not you? Unfortunately I need my clothes and so I am forced to spoil it."

It eased his mind a trifle that Tenny's eyes twinkled and she shoved a corner of the sheet in her mouth, stifling an appreciative giggle. If she could still laugh, then perhaps all was not lost.

"Liviston promised—" repeated Lord Asten for the third time.

"Liviston carefully promised that he himself would not lay a finger on her. He wouldn't count hiring men to do what they did as harming her himself. Don't you see? If he didn't touch her, then *he* didn't harm her."

Lord Asten swung his bath chair around so he faced out the windows. "I was so certain I'd spiked his guns."

"You did."

"Obviously I did not."

"But, Uncle, he did *not* steal her away to the continent.

He did *not* ravish her. You and you alone prevented that, since I obviously failed to see to it that she would not find herself placed in jeopardy. I wonder"—Locke frowned at the thought—"just how that was managed!"

A thundering knock on Falcon's Pride's front door had both Asten and Brant turning to stare at the study door. Half a moment later, that door burst open and Charles stood there. "She's gone."

"Damn," said Locke without heat. "Charles, I'm sorry. I should have sent you a message. It would have saved you one particular worry." Locke drew in a big breath. "She's here, you see."

"No, I don't see." It became quite obvious that Mrs. Smythe's ability to glower had been inherited by her eldest grandson. "Where is she?"

"Here, Charles," said Tenny from the doorway. "And perfectly all right. Nothing happened to me."

Charles swung around. He grabbed his sister and hugged her and then, holding her close, safe, turned back to the others. "Liviston is gone."

"You've been to Highacres?"

"We went there first. We were told he left in a heavily loaded carriage late last night. Tom and your blasted runner are leading a few good men toward the coast, but if Liviston has had the better part of the night, I don't suppose they'll come up to him."

Locke nodded. "It will most likely be a wild goose chase. He'll have been long gone."

"And it makes no difference in any case," said Tenny, turning out of her brother's arm. "I tell you I am all right. I think, Charles, you should take me home so I can reassure Grandmother and our father on that point." She turned toward Locke but would not, or could not, meet his eyes. "Thank you . . . for being kind, Locke." She turned, almost ran through the door, and disappeared toward the front door.

"Tenny!" Locke raced after her.

"Please," she said, still refusing to look at him. "I want to go home."

Locke sighed, unsure.

Charles called to him, and Locke reluctantly went back to the study. "Perhaps we should do as she asks. Whatever happened, it must have been upsetting."

"Charles," said Locke grimly, "tell your father that as soon as it is decent to make morning calls, I must speak with him."

"*Must* speak to him?"

"I don't know how they did it, but they put her in my bed. It was"—Locke grinned a quick, rather foxy grin—"a very nice birthday present, but unfortunately I didn't feel I could, er, properly appreciate it." His gaze fused with Charles's. "Not until she and I are well and truly married."

"You'll be coming to ask for her hand, then?" asked Charles quietly.

"Far sooner than I expected to do, but as you know, it has been my intention for some time now. Liviston, by his machinations, has merely given me an excuse to do so more quickly than I'd expected. Talk to your grandmother, Charles. I believe she supports me."

"Grandmother approves?"

"I *think* she gave me her blessing—but her words were such that I cannot be absolutely sure." One brow arced.

"If she approves, I will not object. Grandmother has a knack for knowing when a proper match is made. She has become quite famous for her predictions. The decades have proven her correct to a surprising degree."

Charles nodded toward Lord Asten, who had rolled his chair to the study doorway. Then he hurried down the hall to where his sister stood tapping her foot. Arms folded around herself as if she were cold, she stared out

the big front door, which stood open to what looked as
if it would be a very lovely day.

It was an odd image. Did the clasped arms indicate a
need to protect herself? But if they did, why the impatience revealed by the tapping toe? And Locke was certain
she saw nothing of the beautiful gardens or lovely day.
Her staring eyes revealed an inward-turning look. He
sighed softly and hoped very much that she wasn't going
to make difficulties about their marrying!

She did, of course.

By the time Locke managed to explain what he knew
to his uncle, and then again to Harry, and had time to
shave and dress in a more formal style for visiting, Tenny
had, in her tenacious way, taken the bit in her teeth and
already told her family she would not marry Locke
Talmidge if they put her on bread and water for a month.

Charles opened his mouth to bluster.

Mrs. Smythe waved him to silence. "Why not?" she
asked blandly.

"He doesn't want to marry me. He will do so only because it is the gentlemanly thing to do, and he wouldn't
wish his uncle to think him ungentlemanly!"

"Nonsense," said Charles. "He told me—"

"What Locke told you, Charles, was, I'm sure, said in
confidence," said Mrs. Smythe firmly. "Tenny, you will go
to your room where you will put yourself to bed. I will
send a maid up with a tray from which you will breakfast.
You will remain in bed this entire day. After such an ordeal, it is the proper thing to do. Perhaps, if I believe
you have recovered, you may come down to dinner."

When Tenny would have demurred, Mrs. Smythe
glared.

"*Now,* Tenacious Smythe, and no arguments!"

Tenny bit her lip, hesitated, and then, her head hanging and looking the complete picture of dejection, she

made her way, slowly, up to her room. And there she was forced to stay that whole long day.

In one way it wasn't so bad. She was glad she needn't face Locke . . . but not knowing what was going on! *That* was one of the worst ordeals Tenny, who always liked to be in the middle of things, ever had to endure!

The first thing she missed, of course, followed on the little kitchen maid's confession. Tears running down her face, she told of the late-night visitor. She named the boy who had come from the village, admitted taking his message to Miss Smythe, and admitted seeing her leave by the kitchen door.

Charles, fire and brimstone nothing in comparison to his well-roused temper, managed to contain himself until after Locke concluded his discussion with Mr. Smythe and had a brief talk with Mrs. Smythe. Only then was Locke ready to ride into the village with Charles. They couldn't find the boy, but they found his father.

"Don' know what you talkin' 'bout," mumbled the bleary-eyed man stubbornly.

After considerably more of the same, Locke left Charles and went to find the boy's rather slatternly mother.

"Don't know nothing, do I then?" she said insolently and tossed her head.

"How much?"

She blinked. Then she licked her lips. "Don' think I unnerstand you, do I?"

"How-much-to-tell-me-what-you-know?" said Locke, separating each word from the next.

Again the ugly, lip-licking greed showed itself. She eyed him, turned, eyed him sideways. "Lots?"

"I'll give you a shilling."

"Huh!" She folded her arms. "A whole crown."

Locke compressed his lips. "A crown it is." He waited. Then he realized *she* was waiting to see her money! Not thinking he'd need money, he hadn't put his purse in his pocket. He didn't have a pence, let alone a crown. He swore softly but fluently. "Charles!"

Charles supplied the needful. He handed the coin over and it disappeared down the woman's dirty bodice. "Talk," ordered Charles.

"Last night. Three men. They took Boy out and talked to him and talked to him and talked to him. At first Boy shook his head at them, but then he dug his toe in the dirt. Then he looked back here at the house, a fearful look, that it were, weren't it then?" She gave each a look of satisfaction. "And then," she said, "he nodded."

"So?"

"So that's all I know, isn't it?"

"You suggest the boy was threatened with something if he didn't agree to do what they asked."

She nodded, a smug look about her. The men glared at her, argued with her, even shouted at her, but in the end they got no more from her.

"I would suggest you and your husband show no particular signs of sudden wealth," said Charles sternly, "because that would mean you lied, that *you* were paid for what the boy did. I'd be very unhappy to discover you were willing to help evil men harm my sister, who has done nothing but good to everyone who lives within miles of here."

The woman sobered, her eyes widening. "Hurt Miss Smythe? Nobody said anything about hurting Miss Smythe!"

"When we woke this morning, she was gone."

The woman dithered. Suddenly she dug several coins from her bodice and flung them at the men. "Don't want it. Don't want nothin' to do with any of it. Not Miss Smythe . . ."

The slattern looked oddly belligerent, the belligerence tempered by what actually looked to be concern. Locke smiled. It seemed that, somehow, his Tenny had even managed to make herself a soft spot in this hardened creature's heart!

A grim look stiffened the woman's usually slack features. "I'll tan Boy's hide for him. That I will. Harm Miss Smythe? I'll learn him!" She turned on her heel and disappeared into the poor cottage in which they lived.

The door slammed and Locke winced. "We should have told her Tenny is safe and unharmed."

"If we had, she'd not be so determined to take that boy down a peg. And, frankly, I think it better his punishment be left to her," said Charles more than half seriously. "I'm likely to kill the lad if I get my hands on him any time soon. Now. What is next?"

"The vicar." A muscle jumped in Locke's jaw. "I want the banns posted immediately."

Charles hesitated. "Locke . . . Tenny hasn't agreed."

"She *has* to agree." The muscle jumped again. "My valet saw her. A maid knows about her clothes. By this time tomorrow the whole county will know she was in my bed this morning."

"You still insist you didn't—?"

"I was half asleep. I touched her. I did not *remain* asleep and I did *not*—" He used his hand, crudely finishing his sentence.

Deadpan, Charles said, "That's too bad."

Locke blinked, swallowed, blinked again and shook his head. "Charles, did you not understand me? I didn't—"

Charles kept his features sternly under control and interrupted. "You did no—er, irredeemable damage to her." His lips twitched, then were firmly bridled. "As I said, that's too bad."

"I don't . . ." Then Locke grimaced in wry understanding. "You mean she'll use that as an excuse to insist we need not wed?" His eyes narrowed. "Then perhaps I must apply a little blackmail to the situation."

"Blackmail?"

"Perhaps you are unaware"—this time it was Locke who managed an unbelievably innocent countenance—"that your sister has an interesting birthmark in a *very* interesting place." Locke's most foxy, devil-may-care grin appeared. "I wonder—" His brow quirked into a triangular shape. "Would she like the world to know?"

The crinkles at the corners of Charles's eyes showed his appreciation. "Still, I would not approach the vicar until we are assured you'll not be left at the altar!"

"She'll come around." Locke began arrogantly, but his courage failed him. "On the other hand, perhaps you are correct and I'll be seeing the vicar later." Then he grinned. "You know, Charles, with only a very little luck, this may turn out to be my very best birthday ever! Your grandmother, by the way, invited me to dinner this evening. I will see you then." He tipped his hat and rode back to Falcon's Pride.

There Lord Asten awaited him. "Before you left for the Smythes', I should have given you this, Locke, but I forgot." He nudged a slim but ornate box across his desk. A bit diffidently, he added, "I hope you will accept it and that Miss Smythe will wear it in pride."

Locke opened the box and stared at the strange ring it held. He looked at his uncle.

Lord Asten's eyes were fixed on the ring. Gold had been spun into fine strands which were then twisted together to make a golden rope and formed into an intricate knot. A small, uncut, reddish stone had been carefully tucked into the knot. "The Asten betrothal ring. It has been in the family for centuries. One cannot say it is pretty, exactly, but I find it strangely compelling."

"It is a unique ring for a unique woman, Uncle. I will offer it with all the solemnity it deserves."

"It is said that a woman who wears it will have a happy marriage." Lord Asten stared sadly at the ring. "My mother wore it."

Locke wondered why that thought made his uncle sad.
"She was the last to do so. . . ."

The older man stared over Locke's shoulder, and Locke
guessed there was an unhappy incident in his uncle's past,
the reason he'd remained unwed.

Sighing softly, Lord Asten brought his attention back
to his nephew. "Convince Miss Smythe to wed you, Locke.
It is too long now since a woman has had charge of Falcon's Pride. She is needed here." He glanced up. "At
least, I assume you mean to live here?"

"It has been my dream for some years now, Uncle. And
I will add your suggestion to my list of reasons why Tenny
should accept me."

Very gently, Locke closed the small box and, assuring
himself it would be safe, placed it deep in an inner pocket
sewn into his coat's lining. He patted his coat where the
box rested.

"Tenacious Smythe, you—you—Tenny, you *stop that.*"
Locke stood with his back to the schoolroom door, but
he heard giggles and guessed some of the children were
lurking nearby.

"Stop what?" asked Tenny, her pretense of innocence
an obvious farce.

"Stop making faces, blast and dammit. It puts a man
off."

"Which is, you dolt, the idea." Tenny's firm little chin
rose a notch. Perhaps two. She crossed the room and,
very firmly, closed the door.

Brant laughed softly. "You wretched girl."

Tenny rolled her eyes. "The man," she said to nothing
and no one, "speaks in such a lover-like manner. I do
not," she added, thoughtfully, still speaking as if Locke
were not there. "see how he ever gained a reputation as
a rake."

"Is that what you want, Tenny? To be wooed?"

She turned away, a faintly wistful expression quickly hidden from him. "Only by a man who loves me."

He watched her fiddle with the sand in a student's sandbox. "I love you," he told her. "I have for years."

Again her eyes rolled.

"You don't believe me."

"Actions, Grandmother always says, speak far louder than words."

"Then you shall have action."

Silence followed and, after a long moment, Tenny turned back. She blinked and then, almost wildly, she looked to the right, to the left, turned in a complete circle. He was gone. How had he managed that trick? Tenny folded her arms and tapped her foot. Moments later she unfolded her arms and the toe stopped tapping. She stared.

"You *didn't*," she said. "Tell me you didn't." Again there were giggles in the hall, but this time she ignored them. "Locke?"

Locke peered solemnly around an armful of blossoms. "If you are asking if I picked blooms from the lilac bush in the churchyard, then of course I did." He raised his eyes and looked at the ceiling. "First, of course, as you'll be happy to hear, I asked the owner of the grave if he minded and, Tenny, he made not a single objection."

Tenny giggled. "Not a word?"

"Silent as the grave," he said retaining his sober aspect with difficulty.

She touched a bloom with one finger. "Those particular lilacs are always the last to bloom. Sometimes, like this year, no one believes they will do so."

"They must have blossomed just so I'd have flowers to give you."

She turned away, again fiddling with the sandbox. Unlike the others, it had yet to be put into the crate which would be carted back to the Smythe manor until needed on the morrow. Brant stretched to see what she drew, just managing to glimpse a heart before she brushed it away.

"My uncle," he offered, "has invited me to live with him, Tenny. Permanently. He said, rather wistfully I thought, that it had been far too long since a woman had charge of Falcon's Pride. He would welcome you as well, my dear. Could you bear to live with my uncle? Or should I ask if I might open the dower house and we live there?" She didn't respond. "Perhaps you'd prefer the challenge of restoring Highacres?"

She couldn't ignore the implications behind that suggestion. She swung around, her eyes wide. "Highacres?"

"My uncle bought the estate from Liviston before his lordship left."

"Thank goodness."

"Hmm?" Locke blinked.

"I've been so worried about that evil man's tenants. I was sure he'd leave behind some wretched agent who would wring from them every penny they earned." She smiled the golden smile he loved. "Now I needn't worry. Lord Asten will see all is put right."

"Except for the mansion."

Her eyes lit up as her imagination took flight.

"You might see to that, Tenny. I'd give you a free hand and all the guineas needed."

The light faded and she seemed to shrink slightly. Shaking her head, she turned back to the sandbox.

Brant recalled that a fire bucket full of water stood in a niche in the hall. He retrieved it and settled the lilacs into it before moving, silently, to stand behind Tenny. He looked over her shoulder and relief filled him. She *did,* whether she'd admit it or not, love him!

Tenny finished the elaborate design in the sand, which included his initials. Brant, leaning around her, caught her hands before she destroyed her work. Holding her with one hand, he added her initials.

"Tenny," he said, swinging her around and staring into her eyes, "I wish Bobby hadn't filled your ears with all that nonsense which seems to have destroyed your trust in me." He stared down at her. "I wonder what I can—"

At this point, an altercation outside the room's single window caused them both to turn. One of the inn's maids stood, arms akimbo and feet straddled, leaning ever so slightly forward and yelling into the face of a man who yelled right back.

Brant grimaced. "You shouldn't be listening to this," he whispered.

"I shouldn't know that Bitsy wants the money she earned? I do not see why not. In fact I would very much like to go out there and tell that man a thing or two myself. In fact, I think I will." She jerked at her hands. "Let me go, Locke!"

With difficulty, Brant held on to her. "You let Bitsy deal with it. She'll get what is owed her!" His eyes narrowed. "Just what do *you* know about Bitsy and what is due her?"

Tenny colored up rosily. She turned her head and again she struggled to free herself.

"Stop that now." Brant pulled her closer and settled her firmly into his embrace. "I like you here," he said softly.

She stiffened. "Release me, Locke."

"Do you mean to run away?"

"No. I've words to say to you and I cannot do so when you—when I—" She bit her lip and fiddled with a button on his vest.

"When I am holding you and you feel . . . what you feel? Thank you, my love, for the information. I'll remember that for the future, when you wish to lecture me. For now"—he sighed and his arms opened—"lecture away."

"What—" Her brows made an angry line across her forehead. "What do *you* know about Bitsy?"

"Nothing, personally. Nothing of the nature of what I know about you." A twinkle appeared in his eyes. "For instance, that wonderfully shaped mark resting low on the side of your *bremff* . . ." His eyes laughed silently over the hands she'd pressed to his mouth. His hands went to hold her waist.

"Don't you *dare,*" she said.

"I thought it very nice," he said, pretending to pout. "Not that I got to *see* it, but I remember the heart shape of it on the ends of my—*finghff.*" He took her hand away. "Tenny," he pretended to complain, "it is very rude of you to not allow me to finish my sentences."

"It is rude of you to start sentences which will embarrass me to death!"

"But I do not wish to embarrass you."

"What do you wish?" she asked, again finding the button on his vest, turning it first this way and then that.

"I wish you to feel as I do. I wish you to have the longings I have. I wish—oh, I wish for a lifetime to show you the ways I love you and all I'd do to please you and all the things I want to teach you." He laughed softly at the scandalized look she turned up on him. "Such a suspicious mind it is! I refer not only to the loving we'll do, but to the waltz, to the places I wish to take you, the books I'll share with you, friends you'll enjoy, a season, and your presentation to the queen. And so much more, Tenny."

"Loving . . ." She stared at the button.

"Yes. I know you have not forgotten how you felt when you were in my bed and I touched you. . . ."

Tenny bit her lip. She still didn't know if she liked what she'd experienced, but she could not rid herself of the need to feel those things again!

"That sort of thing is only part of love, Tenny. Part is

sharing everyday things. And then again, sharing special things. I would like, for instance, to take you to a modiste I know in London. I would like to help the two of you plan you a new wardrobe. I would love to watch the fittings when Madame pinched and pinned the basted dress to you—" His brows rose. "Yes, Tenny?"

"It seems you know a great deal too much about the making of a gown!"

"Wipe off that frown, Tenny. You know I was a rake. I have never denied it. Has it not occurred to you," he asked whimsically, "that you will be the beneficiary of all I learned during those years?"

"Was a rake?"

"Was."

"How can I know that, Locke?" She spoke quickly before he could respond. "I won't share. I *won't.*"

"Why should you have to? I'll have you, my dear, and it is with you I wish to pursue all my rakish tendencies from now on."

"I'm not at all"—she glanced out the window to where Bitsy was very nearly nose to nose with her adversary— "like Bitsy." Tenny's hands made a hint of a reference to the woman's form.

"Bitsy is far more buxom than I have ever liked, Tenny. You sweetly fill a man's hand."

Regretfully, the hand to which he referred moved upward, proving his point. Tenny gasped, her eyes closing, but she didn't pull away. Locke lowered his lips to her temple, tasted the tender skin there, moved to blow softly in her ear. This time she did move.

Brant looked down at her bemused features. "Did you like that?"

"You know very well I did."

"You needn't sound so exasperated."

"I should not have allowed it. And I'd appreciate it if

you'd move that hand. In fact"—again she strained away from him—"I'd like it if you'd let me go."

Whatever she *said*, she didn't *look* as if she liked it when he obeyed and released her.

She sighed. "I must put the rest of these things away before the servant arrives to carry them to the wagon. I do wish we had a schoolhouse," she finished wistfully, rather idly putting the last sandbox into its crate and then moving around the room with a small box into which she put the few ink bottles and pens.

Brant followed along behind picking up papers, each with its careful penmanship. "Perhaps my uncle would give you the funds for one."

"No." Her mouth twisted into a moue. "I asked. He isn't convinced that education for the poor is altogether a good thing, you see."

"I see." Having retrieved the last paper, he read it. His brows climbed his forehead. "Tenny, this is a very good verse, but I've never seen it before. Where did you find it?"

"A poem? Is that Morten's paper? He likely made it up himself."

"Himself? But it is excellent. . . ." Locke read it again. "I've felt exactly that way when out along a country road on a spring evening when the light is just beginning to go. Tenny, do you think we might send this somewhere and see if they will publish it? The Edinburgh Review, perhaps?"

Tenny read it over his arm. "You mean you think it *that* good?"

"I have read worse in that very Review!"

Tenny smiled, pleased one of her students had impressed Brant. "I've kept several of Morten's poems, Locke, just because I've liked them. Will you," she asked a trifle shyly, "read them all and see what you think?"

"Of course." He handed her the papers and she put

them into a folder. "Tenny, if that sort of work is a result of your teaching, then I think it is a very good thing altogether. Even if Morten is the only genius you ever discover, your teaching will have been worth it. *I* will provide the money for your school." He put a hand over her lips when she'd have exclaimed in delight. "But Tenny, we have still to settle our own problem."

She sobered instantly. "You would bribe me with a schoolhouse?"

"I would not. The schoolhouse is for Morten and others like him."

She relaxed. "Yes. I am sorry. I should not have suggested you would bribe me. Locke, why do you pretend you love *me* when you know the most beautiful women in England? Sophisticated and knowing women of the *ton?*"

"Not a one of them has what you have, Tenny. At least I've not seen it if they do. And I want it. I want to bask in it all the rest of my life."

"It?" she asked suspiciously.

"That wonderfully generous heart that is big enough for everyone to warm themselves at its light. You, Tenny, have enough love in you to change the world. I want some of it for my own. You see?" he said, quickly. "I am not so selfish that I demand it all. In fact, I fear that if I were to have it all, you'd no longer be the person you are, the person I love. I must not be selfish. I will have to share you with others forever, and I know that, Tenny. I would not change that in you if I could. Which I could not."

She frowned. "You do not talk like a rake, Locke. Is this another example of not all men being the same? Can you be a rakish man and still have compassion and understanding for others?"

"Someday, Tenny my love, you will tell me exactly what you think makes a man a rake! I will tell you what I think, and we will have a rousing good argument. But for *now,*" he said quickly when her eyes lit up, "all we will discuss is you and I." He tipped up her chin and stared pensively down into her eyes. "Tenny, can you tell me how I may give you back your trust in me?"

"No."

A short bark of laughter followed that blunt admission. "Then we are at an impasse?"

"Yes."

Locke sighed. "Then I will return the Asten betrothal ring to my uncle until the time comes when we can cut the knots we've made for ourselves and you will accept it."

Tenny stilled. Every muscle, every finger, ever tendril of hair even, seemed carved from stone. Through stiff lips, she asked, "The Asten betrothal ring? You'd give me *that?*"

"Yes."

"Do you know what it means?" she asked, her eyes holding his sternly.

"I was told the woman wearing it will have a good and happy marriage."

"But to make that so for me, you'd have to give up your raffish ways, Locke. Could you?"

"I have always meant to do so when I wed—except where my wife is concerned!" He grinned at her blushes.

"May I"—she stared up at him, a wistful look to her— "see it?"

Foreseeing success, Locke took the small box from his pocket. He opened it. Tenny reached out with one finger and touched the oddly twisted golden wires, touched a bit of the stone which peered from between the strands knotted around it.

"It isn't the prettiest ring I've every seen," said Locke softly, "but I think it is the most intriguing."

"And magic."

"And magic," he agreed even though he doubted it. "Will you wear it, Tenny?"

She stared at the ring. Slowly she lifted her head. Her lip was between her teeth. "Locke, I don't know that I believe in magic."

"I do. In the magic we will make for ourselves," he added, when she looked skeptical.

She smiled. "Yes. There is that. And if the stories hold any truth at all, then we've a good chance of being happy."

The lip disappeared again. He waited, calling up every bit of patience he possessed. More words would not convince her. She must convince herself.

"I would think about it," she said finally.

Locke, deeply disappointed, nodded.

"Where, I wonder," she continued in a brisk, everything-is-normal fashion, "is the man to take all this"—she gestured—"to the cart? He's very late."

Locke felt his ears heat. "He isn't coming. That is, I met him along the road, and the cart is in the yard. Awaiting your pleasure." He bowed theatrically, trying to fall in with her efforts to speak and act normally.

She stared. *"You* drove that ugly old farm cart drawn by the sway-backed old nag used with it?"

"You think I could not?"

"Of course you are *able.* It is that you *would* seems odd."

"How else was I to ensure privacy for us?"

She laughed silently. "Ah! A ruse. That sounds more like! Very well, my lord cart driver. You may tote all this out and pack it so nothing will fall off, and we will go home!"

He smiled and, much to her surprise, did as she'd ordered. They were soon crossing the bridge. He drove slowly along the lane toward the Smythes' manor.

"Are you still thinking?" he asked.

"Yes. Now be quiet."

He asked the same question a day later. And again the day after that. Martin, his bags packed and piled on top of the carriage, told Locke that if his little drab ever did say him yea and they set a date for a wedding, then he'd return, but that he'd had as much as he could stand of the birds waking him each morning at some ungodly hour and then keeping him awake half the night as well.

"I don't think it will be long, Marty. Tell me where you'll be so I may write you."

Martin's eyes rolled, showing the whites. *"Home,"* he said, disgusted. "Where the birds intrude just as loudly on a man's rest!" He waved out the window of the equipage Locke had lent him for his journey.

The summer days lengthened and Brant managed to put his mind to his uncle's breeding program for long enough to give his decision about the mares.

"Is it true you rode them?" asked his uncle.

"Hmm."

"Bolton said you showed them the tack and let them watch a gelding saddled."

"Yes. Only two objected. One I never managed to saddle. One allowed the blanket but, when she saw the gelding saddled, cast a wary eye at the saddle set out for her. She let me tack her up only after I bribed her with an apple."

A slow, disbelieving smile crept across Lord Asten's face. "Bribed her?"

"When they were tacked up I let them watch the groom mount up and put the gelding through his paces. And then a gallop."

"What happened?"

"I tried my nervous mare first. She tried to bite me."

Asten's smile returned, and his eyes widened. "Bit you, did she?"

"Tried. I move very quickly when necessary."

An unpracticed chuckle rewarded that sally. "So?"

"So I told the groom to gallop again." Brant deliberately kept his features blank. "This time I didn't move fast enough." He was rewarded by a snort of laughter.

"This time she nipped you?"

"No. This time she *nudged* me."

Asten's mouth dropped open and his eyes widened. "Nudged . . . you would say she *wanted* you to mount her?"

"She's a very clever mare, Uncle. She knew I'd not let her run until I did!"

"She *nudged* you!" Asten muttered to himself, his smile growing broader. Suddenly he laughed aloud. And, everytime he thought of it later, he would chuckle softly to himself.

Locke was pleased. It was the first true laughter he'd heard from his uncle for as long as he could remember. Even from *before* the accident which had crippled the man. He concluded that, even if Tenny said him nay, he must stay and find a way of drawing a second such laugh from his uncle.

But how he hoped she would be at his side to help him do it! He had far more faith in Tenny's ability to make his uncle happy than he had in himself.

Still more days passed with Locke asking and Tenny insisting she was still thinking. One day, while Tenny taught, Locke checked the progress on the schoolhouse he'd ordered built on land provided by his uncle. He went on to the inn where he stared, with blatant hunger, at Tenny. He remembered the feel of her petal-soft skin under his hands. . . .

And suddenly he recalled there should be rumors concerning her adventure which had ended in his bed raging throughout the region. Why, he wondered, were there not? As they quickly and efficiently packed up her teaching equipment, he asked.

"Didn't you know? Your uncle promised me those in

his employ who knew about it would say nothing. He said you'd sworn I was still"—she blushed rosily—"untouched."

Brant gave her a twisted smile.

"*You* know what I mean. Anyway, he said I should not be forced by the gossips into a decision I didn't wish to make. He said I must be free to decide what was best for me."

"Blast the man! We'd be wed if he'd not interfered!"

"You sound as if you truly wished it, Locke."

"I do. As I've said on more occasions than I can count. Marry me, Tenny." He didn't touch her, but his gaze was hot and hopeful. "It would make me very happy and I think I could make you happy, too."

She sighed. "I don't know why I postpone the inevitable."

Locke stilled to stone.

"I know I want to wed you. I know I have been irrationally angry with you, and I believe it is because, as you unkindly pointed out, that I wished for perfection when I know perfection is impossible. For anyone. It is stupid of me to be feel hurt and betrayed that you are not perfect, is it not?"

She turned to him and then cocked her head to one side when she saw how he stood, so stiff and as if frozen into place. A bottle of ink was in one hand; the other held several pens from the same table.

"Locke?"

"Inevitable?" he managed. The ink hit the table with a thunk, luckily landing on its bottom. The pens dropped and skittered off in every direction. "You have known we would wed and you have allowed me to suffer all the pain of this hellish waiting? *Waiting for you to tell me nay?* You have known and—!"

Again her soft fingers pressed against his mouth, cutting off his words. He took her hand in his, kissed her fingers absently, and stared, broodingly, down into her face.

"Tenny," he said, "I didn't know you could be cruel."

She smiled. "You think it has been easy to hold back from you?" She allowed him to draw her gently against his chest, allowed his arms to close around her. "You think I have not wished to put an end to this?" Still she didn't let him speak. "If you think that, then you'd be wrong. It is that I had to be certain, Locke. Can you not see that I had to be sure?"

A trifling hint of bewilderment slipped past his guard and could be still more clearly heard when he asked, "But what has happened that you can now make a decision? Tenny," he added, before she could explain, "things have not changed. We have gone on from day to day, each day the same. Each day I've asked you to marry me, and each day you've asked for more time. So . . . what changed?"

Her smile was a bit misty when, hands flat on his chest, she stared up at him. "But don't you see, Locke? It is exactly that. *Things have not changed.* It is that you have been content to have each day the same as the last. I've concluded you will continue to feel that way. That is all."

He frowned, pursing his lips as he thought about her words. Finally he sighed. "Tenny, did I neglect to tell you that, if he'd asked me, I'd have come to live with my uncle some years ago? A man has only so many wild oats to sow. After that the life becomes mostly habit and often quite tedious. One wants to get on to the important things in life." He leaned down and pressed a fleeting kiss to her lips. "Tenny, the important things are you and any children we are lucky enough to have. *Will you wed me?*"

"Yes."

He blinked. Then he threw back his head and laughed. "I suppose I should have expected a response so lacking in verbosity. You are only wordy when you argue, are you not, my Tenny?" As he spoke, still holding her with one arm, he dug his free hand into his pocket and found the small box he carried everywhere, his uncle refusing to take it back. "And so, my love, *now* you will wear this?"

She nodded and, somehow remaining close, they managed, together, to put the Asten betrothal ring upon her finger where, much to the surprise of both, it fit.

They didn't know, and wouldn't have cared if they had, that it was part of the ring's magic that it always fit.

LOOK FOR THESE REGENCY ROMANCES

ROMANCE FROM FERN MICHAELS

DEAR EMILY   (0-8217-4952-8, $5.99)

WISH LIST   (0-8217-5228-6, $6.99)

AND IN HARDCOVER:

VEGAS RICH   (1-57566-057-1, $25.00)

YOU WON'T WANT TO READ
JUST ONE—KATHERINE STONE

ROOMMATES   (0-8217-5206-5, $6.99/$7.99)
No one could have prepared Carrie for the monumental changes she would face when she met her new circle of friends at Stanford University. Once their lives intertwined and became woven into the tapestry of the times, they would never be the same.

TWINS   (0-8217-5207-3, $6.99/$7.99)
Brook and Melanie Chandler were so different, it was hard to believe they were sisters. One was a dark, serious, ambitious New York attorney; the other, a golden, glamourous, sophisticated supermodel. But they were more than sisters—they were twins and more alike than even they knew . . .

THE CARLTON CLUB   (0-8217-5204-9, $6.99/$7.99)
It was the place to see and be seen, the only place to be. And for those who frequented the playground of the very rich, it was a way of life. Mark, Kathleen, Leslie and Janet—they worked together, played together, and loved together, all behind exclusive gates of the *Carlton Club*.

Available wherever paperbacks are sold, or order direct from the Publisher. Send cover price plus 50¢ per copy for mailing and handling to Kensington Publishing Corp., Consumer Orders, or call (toll free) 888-345-BOOK, to place your order using Mastercard or Visa. Residents of New York and Tennessee must include sales tax. DO NOT SEND CASH.